THE WAGER OF A LADY

KATHLEEN AYERS

Editing by Midnight Owl Editors

Cover by Covers and Cupcakes

PROLOGUE

L *ondon, 1836*

PREDICTABILITY, LEO MURPHY SURMISED, WAS WHAT MADE Elysium so incredibly successful.

As the owner of a gambling hell, knowing the odds of every game played on the floor and predicting the outcome was of crucial importance. He'd built an empire around the expectation that at any given time, the titled of London would enter through the front door of Elysium and proceed to lose every coin in their purse. Hazard. Piquet. Whist. Faro. There were numerous opportunities to gamble away the night, drowning your troubles in expensive scotch and brandy.

When one tired of cards, there were always the pleasures to be found on the second floor of Elysium. Each room was stocked with various items one might use to invoke pleasure or pain. The rooms and their accessories were the only things

Leo supplied his guests. One must secure their own companion for the evening. He wasn't running a bloody brothel.

He did have some morals.

Leo was the son of a duke, after all, albeit one born on the wrong side of the blanket. His father, the Duke of Averell, had been the biggest rake to strut into London in decades. Known for having the arrogance to keep his mistress and duchess under the same roof at his country estate. But that was before the tragic events at Cherry Hill which had resulted in the late duchess's death.

Leo placed his hand against his heart, conscious of the slight twist he always felt at thinking of the late duchess. Many emotions ebbed over time. Regret and guilt often did not. Finding out your husband was tupping your lady's maid beneath your nose had been bad enough, but the shock that her husband's bastard existed, a year younger than her own son, Anthony, had distressed her so much, the duchess had tripped and fallen.

Leo could still see the blood coating the base of the stairs, the smell caught forever in his nostrils. Until then, Leo hadn't known he was different. Had no idea his best friend Tony, the duke's son, was also his half-brother. Didn't know the world outside Cherry Hill would shun him for his birth or that in claiming him publicly, the duke would subject him to a life of notoriety.

"Mr. Murphy." Peckham, his man who managed the gaming floor, approached the second-floor landing where Leo often stood. A vantage point of sorts, so he could view all of Elysium.

"What is it, Peckham?" he said, relieved to have Peckham's appearance push away the horror of that day. The memory often struck him at the oddest times.

"Lord Welles has arrived. He asks you to join him below

when you're done fussing over your waistcoat." Peckham immediately put up a hand. "His words, sir, not mine."

Leo looked down at his waistcoat, a very fine concoction of purple and green swirled into what looked like sunbursts and outlined in gold thread. His brother rarely wore anything but expertly tailored suits of indigo. Society expected Leo to be a bit . . . garish due to his beginnings. He found no reason to disappoint them. He liked a bit of color. People often mistook him and Tony for one another from a distance, but not if they caught sight of his waistcoat.

"Lord Welles has terrible taste." He nodded to the gentleman below who'd just come into view, a stunning redhead clinging to his arm. "As evidenced by the fact that he's allowing Lady Dunley to assume she might one day become Lady Welles."

Peckham nodded. "Yes, sir."

Leo waved a hand. "I'll be down shortly, Peckham."

Lady Dunley, a recent widow, had once been a brief indiscretion of Leo's. Proper ladies, trapped in marriages not of their liking, were often bored with their lives. They enjoyed bedding London's most notorious bastard. Leo was always happy to comply. Lady Dunley had been very upset when Leo broke things off, as he often did after a specific length of time. No need to become too attached, after all.

She'd responded by telling Leo she'd done him a favor by lowering herself to fuck him.

The lady had an overinflated opinion of her abilities in the bedroom.

Below him, Lady Dunley let out a shrill laugh, turning her head in Leo's direction.

He chuckled to himself. Leo wasn't prone to jealousy; there were far too many desirable women in London to care overmuch about just one.

Pushing back from the railing, Leo jogged down the stairs

to greet his brother. Despite the myriad of reasons why he and Tony should detest each other, the main one being that Leo's existence had caused the death of Tony's mother, the two were closer than they'd been as children. Uniting in dislike over a man who had caused them both so much grief, one deserving of their loathing, had forged the bond between them.

Elysium belonged to both of them, but it was Leo who most enjoyed watching London's nobility swirl around a duke's bastard to curry his favor. He liked declining the requests for credit from men who, when they'd been lads, had spat on him at that fancy boarding school the duke had forced him to attend. Enjoyed fucking their wives behind their backs while they looked down their thin noses at him.

Highly amusing.

Tony's interest in Elysium, however, was purely to piss off the duke.

"Lord Welles." A gloved hand appeared on Leo's arm, along with a burst of pomade to his nostrils and the smell of brandy.

"Oh, it's you." The speaker stuttered. "Murphy." Lord Castlewaite's cheeks turned red, mustache quivering as he caught sight of Leo's waistcoat. "Pardon. I mistook you for Lord Welles."

"Did you?" Tony wouldn't be caught dead in this waistcoat. His brother had no appreciation for color, as evidenced by the constant wearing of indigo. "I can understand your confusion. The lighting is somewhat dim." Besides the waistcoat, Leo hadn't an ounce of ducal arrogance about him. That was Tony, who always looked like he'd walked out of a bloody painting in some lord's portrait gallery.

"I've never mistaken you, my lord, for anyone other than who you are," Leo said, knowing the older man would completely miss the thinly veiled insult. Snobs like Castlewaite often did. He was a marquess with nothing to recommend him but his title and his ability to make outlandish wagers which were then recorded in Elysium's Red Book. "You're very distinctive, my lord."

Castlewaite nodded. "I've often thought so."

Leo displayed an enormous amount of patience with Castlewaite, considering the relationship Leo had once had with the man's daughter. He'd meant to revoke Castlewaite's membership long ago until Leo had found out the marquess was Imogene's father.

If Castlewaite had ever suspected Leo had taken his daughter's virtue, he'd never given any indication. His opinion of Leo was formed purely on the basis of Leo's birth.

I can't possibly have you drag me down into the muck.

No, he supposed he couldn't. Leo hadn't even realized he *was* the muck. No matter; Imogene had quickly advised him of the fact after they'd taken each other's virginity. He'd been fifteen.

"Perhaps there is something I can assist you with, my lord."

"A gentleman's matter." Castlewaite refused to meet his eyes.

"Pity I can't help you then."

Castlewaite often asked Tony to witness his wagers. Not Leo, because Castlewaite didn't consider him a gentleman.

Imogene hadn't been Leo's first lesson in how society viewed him, but at barely fifteen, he'd still been coming to terms with what being a bastard meant outside of Cherry Hill. After Imogene's cruel dismissal even though she'd declared her undying love for him, Leo had decided he would give no one else the opportunity to decide his place in the world.

"I mean no disrespect, Murphy," Castlewaite muttered.

Doddering fool. "Of course not, my lord. When I see my

brother, I'll ask him to seek you out. Enjoy your evening." He bowed slightly and moved away, having no idea where his brother had wandered off to. No matter. It was early. They'd find each other eventually. In the meantime, Leo decided to check on the recently hired dealer for the faro table.

Larkin was a former pickpocket, one who'd narrowly escaped hanging when the pocket he'd picked had been Leo's. Larkin had been half-starved. Dirty. In need of a bit of kindness in the world. His mother had been a whore. He'd no idea who his father was.

Leo had brought him to Elysium. Most of the staff were strays of one kind or another.

His steps slowed as he caught sight of the faro table. Not because Larkin was nervously twitching, terrified he'd make a mistake in front of the Duke of Windmere who sat at his table. No, it was because of a slender back clad in powder-blue silk.

Gold ringlets hovered at the base of her neck. One had fallen loose, cascading down the creamy expanse of her left shoulder. Her head tilted to the right as she listened to something Larkin said. She smiled back at the dealer, answering him in a flat, nasal tone.

American.

Something stirred inside Leo, wholly unexpected at the sound of her, though it wasn't the first time he'd heard an American speak. He came up behind her, taken aback by the soft aroma of wildflowers. An entire field of them.

Arousal, sharp and swift, wound its way down his thighs. And he hadn't even gotten a look at her face. Then there was the insane urge to run his lips across her shoulder, maybe tug at that golden curl with his teeth.

Larkin looked over the woman's shoulder, catching Leo's eye. He dipped his head. "Mr. Murphy."

"Everything going well this evening, Larkin?"

The young lady seemed uncaring of his presence so close to her. She didn't turn or acknowledge him. Didn't she know who he was?

Highly unusual. Everyone in Elysium knew who he was. Leo found himself intrigued. A rare occurrence and something for which the odds were very low.

"Very well, sir." Larkin turned to Windmere.

Leo studied the delicate shape of the young lady's profile as her brow wrinkled in concentration. She was very young. Barely out of the schoolroom. And yet, she displayed not an ounce of discomfort sitting at a faro table alone at a gambling hell. A glass of wine remained untouched at her elbow as she studied the cards in her hand.

"Perhaps I can be of assistance." Leo took the seat next to her.

"I sincerely doubt that." She didn't turn in his direction; instead, her chin tilted so mulishly one might have thought she was bracing herself to take a punch to the jaw instead of being offered aid by a gentleman.

Defiant little thing. "Are you sure? I'm rather good at cards."

"Hmm. So claims every other lord in here." The neckline of her gown was almost indecent, giving Leo a glimpse of what was clearly a pair of magnificent breasts. "Gentlemen say such things," she continued, "so that under the guise of looking at my cards to assist me, they might admire my bosom." Her gaze slid to his waistcoat; she shivered with what appeared to be distaste before barely glancing at Leo's face. Her attention returned to her cards. She was completely uninterested in him.

Leo was struck speechless at her manner. A well-bred young lady wouldn't speak in such a way, and she didn't have the look of a courtesan. A courtesan would have been much more welcoming.

"You're American," he finally said.

"How astute you are, my lord."

She wasn't being coy. This girl had *no* idea who he was. Even if she were to figure it out, Leo thought she might be even *less* impressed. "I'm Leo Murphy. Not a lord. I *own* Elysium."

"How lovely for you." Her brow wrinkled between a pair of dark eyes. Such a stark contrast against her gold hair and creamy skin.

"Are you intentionally being rude? Or is this the way all Americans behave?" The odds of any female in Leo's immediate vicinity ignoring him were incredibly low. That is to say, it *never* happened.

She turned to face him with a sigh of exasperation. "Very well. I can see you wish us to become acquainted and won't leave me in peace until you accomplish your aim. I am Lady Masterson."

Leo took the small, gloved hand, giving the briefest brush of his lips against her knuckles, shocked when his cock twitched at the slight touch. Wildflowers caught in his nostrils again.

"Lady Masterson?" There was a rumor making the rounds that the elderly Lord Masterson had finally taken a wife. Mostly out of fear of impoverishment.

Her bravado faltered just slightly before she snatched back her hand. A stubborn look came over her lovely features. "Yes."

Masterson did prefer blondes, although they usually tended to be footmen or lately, barristers. He was a member at Elysium, gambling poorly and losing frequently before availing himself of the rooms on the second floor. Masterson owed Leo a great deal of money. A stack of the earl's markers sat in the safe in Leo's office. Masterson's nephew, his heir, would inherit much more than the title.

"And where is Lord Masterson this evening?" He should

8

be here with his very young bride. The decent thing to do whether or not he was interested in bedding her.

"I'm sure you already know." A tiny smirk hovered at her lips. "No need for me to tell you, Mr. Murphy."

"I can take a guess." He gave her his most charming smile. Lady Masterson was the most interesting person, man or woman, Leo had met in, well, forever. "We've established you're American—"

"Have we?"

Another bolt of arousal shot straight down between his legs. Dear God, he had the inclination to throw her over the faro table and just *inhale* her. "Where in America are you from, if I may ask, Lady Masterson?"

"You've already done so." There was just a hint of mischievousness in her dark eyes.

Flippant, sassy little thing. "Done what?"

"Asked me. I'm from New York." The clipped flattened sound of her vowels created bits of sensation across Leo's skin. There wasn't the least inflection. He could listen to her for hours.

"Are you enjoying London?"

"Not in the least." She gave him a sideways glance. "The Thames stinks, the Hudson does not."

Oh, she was quite something.

"Give it time, my lady." He assumed the Hudson to be a river in New York. He'd never paid attention much to geography outside of England. One of his worst subjects at school. He nodded to the stack of chips before her. "Are you familiar with faro, my lady? If you are not, I'm happy to provide instruction."

"Are you better at cards than you are at choosing waistcoats?" She nodded toward his chest. "Although it does appear to be finely made."

Disparaging comments about his waistcoats were a

common occurrence. He'd become immune to them. His sister Andromeda, who had a flair for clothing and fabrics, proclaimed his waistcoats an affront to the senses.

"I take it you don't care for my taste." He looked down at the swirls of purple and green splashes decorating his mid-section. "And you don't get to be the owner of a gambling hell without knowing how to play faro or cards in general. Any game, really. Will you allow me to offer you some instruction?"

"Why? You've already seen my bosom."

Dear God, she was delicious. "Because you're losing badly, my lady." His glance settled on her small stack of chips.

Leo had never once, not in all the time he'd owned Elysium, offered to teach anyone how to play one of the games offered. He surprised himself by doing so now. But he didn't wish to end his brief acquaintance with Lady Masterson. She looked in need of a friend. The fact that she also filled Leo with the most wicked, lascivious thoughts was irrelevant.

"Perhaps I should try hazard." She glanced across the gaming floor where a group of gentlemen had gathered. "I've diced before. Looks fairly simple."

Of course she had. "No, I don't think so. The odds aren't in your favor. They aren't in anyone's favor when it comes to hazard except the house."

"You probably shouldn't advise your patrons of that, Mr. Murphy."

"I don't as a rule. I'm making an exception for you."

Her cheeks pinked just slightly at his comment. Lady Masterson was really quite stunning. What a waste it was to have her wed to Masterson.

"Are you familiar with the laws of probability?" he asked.

"I don't believe so." Her dark eyes flashed at him, softening just slightly.

Well, that was progress, wasn't it?

Usually by now, Leo would have invited a lovely creature such as Lady Masterson to have a drink with him before moving to one of the rooms on the second floor where they could indulge themselves. But Lady Masterson had an air of innocence about her, so at odds with her bold manner and decadent necklines. He instinctively knew she'd refuse him.

"The law of probability states that one must look at the total number of favorable outcomes divided by the number of possibilities one has. *That* is probability. It is how odds for all games of chance can be calculated."

She nodded slowly. "I didn't realize there was a course of study prescribed for gambling hell owners." The tiniest tilt of her lips held him enthralled.

"Oh, there isn't. I merely like numbers more than most." Much more than most. Leo considered and calculated odds or strategies for nearly every possibility in his life. Except perhaps the appearance of Lady Masterson. She was rather unexpected.

"So, you know what the chance of rolling, say, a pair of sevens would be?" Intelligence gleamed from her eyes. "Or the cards I might hold in my hand if you are paying attention."

Leo wanted to drag her off her stool and take her to his private quarters. He might not even bed her immediately but spend the evening in discussion. Few people grasped the concept of probability, and if they did, their interest in such a topic was limited. Professional gamblers mostly, but rarely anyone else.

His attraction to her increased, but this time it was her mind he wanted, something nearly as appealing as her bosom. "Yes." Leo shifted, discreetly tugging at the edge of his coat to hide the erection tenting his trousers.

Lady Masterson didn't notice. She did lean closer,

however, her breasts nearly spilling from her bodice. "Explain how you do so, Mr. Murphy."

❦

GEORGINA RUTHERFORD MASTERSON, RELUCTANT WIFE OF Earl Masterson, found Elysium to be marvelous. There wasn't anything like the gambling hell in New York, at least that Georgina was aware of. Her elderly husband, Lord Masterson, after leading her to the faro table, had dropped her arm and disappeared upstairs, leaving her to face the sea of sharks on Elysium's gaming floor alone. London society hadn't been exactly welcoming to Georgina. In addition to being American, the Rutherford pedigree was a bit tattered, to say the least, which made everyone look down their patrician noses at her. Admittedly, Georgina's blunt way of speaking, laced with the bitterness of being unfairly banished to London and wed to a gentleman three times her age, didn't help matters. She supposed dressing somewhat flamboyantly didn't endear her to anyone either. That particular bit of rebellion had followed her to London from New York and was now more habit than anything.

Luckily, Georgina possessed a backbone, one forged of steel. Her adored grandmother, upon seeing her off to London, had taken Georgina's hand.

"You'll survive, Georgie," she had said. "But I doubt you'll care for London. There's a reason we fought a war or two to get them to leave us be. But you'll survive until you can come home. Your behavior forced your father's hand, though I know you didn't ruin yourself. But actions have consequences. Remember that, Georgie, and act accordingly."

Grandmother had died shortly after Georgina's wedding to Masterson. Something else Georgina blamed her father for —that she hadn't been with her grandmother at the end.

Learn to behave, Georgina, or else don't come home.

Those were the last words her father, Jacob Rutherford, had said before leaving her in England. Georgina hadn't wept. Or thrown a tantrum. She was made of sterner stuff. Accepting her marriage to the elderly earl had taken all her fortitude.

Forgiveness for her father might never come.

Not only was Masterson ancient, but he also had little interest in Georgina save her dowry. The consummation of their wedding night had been a humiliating experience, leaving both of them near tears. Masterson had barely succeeded in taking her virginity. If there hadn't been a pinch of pain and blood on the sheets, Georgina wouldn't have known anything out of the ordinary had happened. None of her curiosity about the act had been assuaged. John Winbow, the reason for her banishment, had claimed there was pleasure to be had between a man and woman.

I should have allowed him to ruin me. The result would have been the same.

Tonight, when Masterson had informed Georgina she was accompanying him to Elysium, Georgina had eagerly agreed. Entertaining callers and gossiping over tea, as most ladies were expected to do, held little interest. But she did like card games and had never been to a gambling hell. Elysium was notorious. And it was absolutely splendid. Decadent in unexpected ways. Her vision had been of a seedy, rundown building. A space much less lavish and well-appointed. Certainly not the grand, elegant mansion which had greeted her.

Elysium, all three stories, sat at the end of one of London's older but still fashionable neighborhoods. The mansion was well hidden behind a circle of oak trees and surrounded by an expanse of lawn and manicured gardens. The interior was sumptuous, done in glistening dark colors that reminded Georgina of rubies, sapphires, and emeralds.

Well-trained staff hovered only a step away, bringing refreshments to members and their guests. Delicious smells wafted out from the hall to her left where Masterson had told her members could dine. The chef was French. Chandeliers hung from the ceiling above her, bathing the gaming floor in a warm glow.

"Larkin here will take care of you, my dear," her husband had said before leaving her to struggle her way through faro. "I've other matters to attend to. Try not to lose too much."

The only card game Georgina had even the least bit of skill for was poker, a game not available at Elysium or probably anywhere except a river boat on the Mississippi.

Winbow came to mind, and she pushed him away. She should have known he'd wanted more than her virtue.

"Of course not, my lord," she had answered her husband, but Masterson had already been moving away from her, his attention taken by a tall, lanky gentleman with large blue eyes and just the scruff of a beard. Probably about the same age as Georgina. The pair disappeared up a flight of steps to the second floor.

Georgina was not unaware of her husband's habits. How could she be? The gossip greeted her at every function she'd had the misfortune to attend.

Sitting at the faro table, Georgina had tried watching the other players, hoping to grasp the strategy of the game. She had failed miserably. Perhaps she could try hazard. How hard was it to throw a pair of dice?

"Perhaps I can be of assistance." The ugliest waistcoat she'd ever seen on a gentleman flashed before her eyes as a large, male form took the seat next to her. Refusing to look in his direction, Georgina focused on her cards. Sandalwood and leather surrounded her, along with the scent of a cheroot.

Georgina did appreciate a good cheroot on occasion. Another bad habit of hers.

"I sincerely doubt that," she replied without turning to look at him. The last thing Georgina required this evening was yet another lord offering her assistance. Thus far, two earls and a viscount had offered to teach her faro, mostly so they could peer down her bodice. The only thing different about *this* lord was his incredibly poor taste in clothing.

"Are you sure? I'm rather good at cards."

"Hmm. So claims every other lord in here," she said, finally turning to look at him. "They say such things," she said, "so that under the guise of looking at my cards to assist me, they might admire my bosom."

Good Lord, he's beautiful.

Georgina struggled to force the air in and out of her lungs, struck dumb by his looks. *And those eyes.* Sapphire with bits of gold floating in the depths and a distinctive ring of deeper blue. His hair was the rich shade of old, burnished leather, a bit long, the ends curling around his ears. A wide mouth with sensual lips lifted in a half-smile at her brief perusal.

Her insides twisted in the strangest manner.

Goodness.

She was not a young lady who was easily rattled or struck speechless by a handsome face. Stubborn to the core, Georgina refused to allow this arrogant, albeit stunning, gentleman to see the effect he had on her. A man like him likely already knew what he did to women with that seductive smile and charming manner.

Always stand your ground, Georgie.

Grandmother had been full of wisdom.

She turned back to her cards, heart beating wildly in her chest, forcing herself not to stare at his hideous waistcoat. Was the pattern supposed to resemble the petals of a flower? Even with his eccentric clothing choices, Georgina decided few women were likely to dismiss him.

But she would. Perhaps it would teach him humility. Every gentleman with a title, she'd found, thought very highly of themselves. His arrogance, however, was probably deserved.

"You're American," he finally said.

"How astute you are, my lord."

His brows lifted in surprise. Had she addressed him improperly? She couldn't quite keep all the titles straight. Masterson had told her that with the exception of a duke, everyone else could be addressed as 'my lord'.

"I'm Leo Murphy. Not a lord. I *own* Elysium."

"How lovely for you." Masterson had mentioned Leo Murphy a handful of times, mainly bemoaning the fact that he owed London's most infamous gambling hell owner a large sum. Murphy was the bastard son of a duke; she knew that much. And he had terrible taste in waistcoats.

"Are you intentionally being rude? Or is this the way all Americans behave?"

Murphy wasn't the least put off by her response; in fact, he seemed amused. The man possessed a great deal of charm. Combined with his looks, she doubted he was ever lonely. She wasn't entirely sure why he'd chosen to speak to her. Georgina was well aware of her own appeal, but she was hardly the most beautiful woman floating about Elysium tonight.

When Murphy began speaking of probability and odds, all of which Georgina found fascinating, she couldn't look away from him. Mathematics had always been her favorite subject. Numbers were a sort of language to her. Georgina could calculate the profit on a shipload of goods her father imported, including the taxes which must be paid, in her head. She'd been so proud, waiting for her father to heap praise upon her.

If only you'd been a boy, Georgina. Pity the only use you'll have is in who you wed.

Her final rebellion against her father had been short-lived, backfiring in the most spectacular fashion.

Murphy seemed genuinely surprised Georgina not only found, but could also follow, what was obviously his favorite topic. Dazzling her with his presence, Murphy explained probability and how it applied to gaming while sipping a glass of scotch. He spoke to her as if she were an equal. As if she possessed some intelligence instead of treating her as if she were only capable of designing a dinner menu.

She found herself leaning into him when he spoke, the skin of her arms and chest humming with his words. Her eyes kept falling to his mouth, knowing he would taste of scotch and a great deal of sin. Georgina was already half in love with him by the time they were interrupted.

"There you are."

A gentleman stopped at the faro table, took one look at Georgina, and patiently waited for her to swoon in his presence. She did no such thing, of course, though he *was* dazzling. There was curiosity as he looked at her from a pair of eyes identical to Murphy's.

"I've been looking all over for you, Leo. And here I find you at the faro table. You don't even like faro." The man's sapphire gaze ran over her once more.

"I play at times." Leo didn't look pleased. "How is Lady Dunley?"

The other gentleman was studying Georgina as if she were of great interest. "Tedious. Looks like you're having much more fun."

"Mr. Murphy has been kind enough to instruct me on gaming."

His eyes widened just slightly at the sound of her accent. "Introduce me, Leo. I'd like to properly meet the woman you haven't bored to death with your talk of numbers." He winked at her. "She hasn't even nodded off yet."

"Lady Masterson," Leo nodded to her, "may I introduce Lord Welles." Murphy stood and waved his brother into the seat he'd vacated. "My brother."

Ah. Obviously. The two looked very much alike in addition to the eyes.

"Lady Masterson." Lord Welles took her hand. Dressed all in indigo, a perfect foil for such masculine perfection, Welles really was incredibly appealing. But he didn't cause a flutter inside her chest as Leo Murphy did.

"I had heard Masterson wed himself to a young American, and here you are."

"Yes, directly in front of you."

Leo's lips twitched.

"How interesting."

"Not really," Georgina said. "I can't imagine I'm the only one roaming about London. There's bound to be one or two more. Americans, that is. Not young ladies married to Lord Masterson. I'm the only one, as far as I know."

Welles looked at her a moment longer and then burst into laughter. "You're delicious, Lady Masterson. I'll keep you company for a bit, if you don't mind. I like faro."

Georgina had the feeling he wasn't asking her permission but Murphy's.

"Careful, Tony. She bites," Murphy said smoothly, relinquishing her to his brother's company. Taking her hand, his fingers curled protectively over hers, thumb rubbing gently over her wrist. He bowed and whispered, "It has been a great pleasure to make your acquaintance, Lady Masterson. Should you require anything, you need only ask."

You. She almost whispered. *I require you.*

Lord Welles watched the exchange between them with open interest. His mouth, just as wide as his brother's, spread into a smile.

"Good evening, Lady Masterson. I'll leave you in my brother's care."

"Mr. Murphy." She inclined her head. "I enjoyed our conversation."

He paused and took her in. "Then I'm certain we'll have another." Nodding once more, Murphy strode off, the ever-increasing crowd on the gaming floor swallowing him until she couldn't see him anymore.

1

London, two years later

"I understand you won me in a game of cards."

Leo looked up at the beautiful young woman standing outside his office, unsurprised to see her. She slammed the door behind her, hard enough to make the small painting on his wall tremble. Lady Masterson appeared as if she were about to launch herself at him. Even her fists were clenched.

Georgina had a temper. Leo had witnessed it a time or two. Lord Browden could also attest to her ability to throw a punch. To be fair to Georgina, Browden had tried to grope her in one of Elysium's many hallways. A mistake on Browden's part in more ways than one. The earl had since been informed that Lady Masterson was under the protection of the owner of Elysium and Lord Welles. If he meant to keep his membership, Browden should give her wide berth.

"I absolutely did not," Leo replied, returning to the papers on his desk. "I'm very busy, my lady. If you'll show yourself

21

out." He discreetly slid the letter opener on his desk beneath one of his ledgers. Just in case.

It wasn't an unusual occurrence for Leo to have someone in his office accusing him of all sorts of disreputable things. Such was the life of a gambling hell owner. He'd already had to explain to Lord Nivens tonight that the cards at the piquet table weren't marked, he was only a terrible player. Yesterday, it had been Lord Halifax who'd wagered, stupidly, that his grandfather, a duke, wouldn't see another winter and now wanted the wager erased from the Red Book in which it was recorded. Earlier, Lady Lowell had appeared to announce that someone had told her husband she was using one of the rooms on the second floor to service her lover.

Leo had been the lover in question. *Had.* He thought the lady more upset he'd lost interest in her so quickly. But very few women held Leo's attention for very long.

Except for the one before him.

She'd had his attention and that of his cock every day since he'd met her.

Georgina came further into his office in a whirl of wool cloak and feminine fury. "I'm rather disappointed in you, Mr. Murphy."

Wasn't everyone? "I own a gambling hell, my lady. Disappointment bleeds into the walls."

"Your sarcasm is unnecessary at the moment." She blew a puff of air at a golden curl that had fallen against her cheek. "I'm not overly fond of it to begin with."

That bloody curl. He longed to wrap the tendril around his finger. Tug on it. When he'd taught Georgina how to play whist, he'd found his attention on the curl and not the game. She'd managed to nearly win their final hand.

"You've never mentioned your dislike of my wit before." He pushed the letter opener further beneath the ledger. Best not to tempt fate, not with Georgina. Though he'd been doing so for some time. Leo would resolve to stay away from her and then find himself with his nose nearly nuzzling against the side of her neck.

This has to stop.

She looked up at the ceiling as if hoping for divine intervention. "You are so flippant. I've always found it annoying."

"Again, I've known you almost two years, yet you've never mentioned these deficits in my personality." A long, agonizing two years in which Leo had never once touched her, constantly reminding himself of all the reasons why he should not. He'd thought his obsession with her would fade with time, but now it had only grown worse. After careful consideration, Leo had decided he'd been going about Georgina completely the wrong way.

"You've a marker with my name on it, Murphy. I dare you to deny it. I can't believe you haven't returned it to me."

Blood rushed between his legs, his cock thickening as he took in the hints of her generous form, well-hidden beneath the cloak. Thankfully, he was seated, the evidence of his arousal safely hidden. As was the letter opener.

"A marker." He pretended to ponder her statement. Had he been a better man, he *would* have returned it.

She moved closer, bringing with her the scent of those damned wildflowers that seemed to hover only around her. Not roses or violets. Nothing so sedate. But a much wilder bloom.

"No answer? Is it my accent, Mr. Murphy? Perhaps you can't make out the words."

Certainly that had been the ploy used on Georgina during a gathering held at Lady Talbot's the previous year. Lady Talbot, snobbish and dismayed to be hosting a woman she felt was beneath her, had declared to hear a goose honking on the lawn each time Georgina spoke. Tony had been in attendance and had told Leo all about it.

Lady Talbot had since been denied entry to Elysium.

"I understand you perfectly well, Lady Masterson." Leo, unlike nearly everyone else in London, craved the sound of Georgina's flat American accent. Craved *her*. When Tony had noticed Leo's fascination with Georgina, Tony had warned him away from her.

"Why?" Leo had snarled. "So you can have her?"

"No." Tony had been taken aback. "Because she reminds me of Phaedra. Impetuous but easily wounded."

Well, Georgina most definitely *did not* remind Leo of his youngest sister. He wanted her. *Terribly*. If he had just bedded her that first night or on any of the dozens of nights that had followed over the last two years, Georgina would be out of his system. Abstaining, in this case, had not helped matters.

She angled her chin. Mutinous. Stubbornly defiant. Shooting daggers from her dark eyes.

"I absolutely *did not* win you in a card game," he finally said.

So hostile. He supposed he didn't blame her, given the circumstances. Leo wanted her with a desperation that terrified him.

Georgina undid the clasp at her neck, tossing her heavy cloak over a chair, exposing the swell of her magnificent bosom. The simple green wool dress she wore clung to every curve she possessed, which were considerable. There was nothing slender or willowy about Georgina. No, she possessed a form created to induce any male to sinful thoughts. Georgina reminded Leo of the statues his step-mother insisted on placing around the gardens at the Averell mansion. Greek goddesses and the like. He'd spent many an afternoon as a lad, hidden behind the hedges, staring at the abundance of breasts and thighs as he brought himself to release. He was forever out of handkerchiefs.

"Do you deny that you accepted a marker with my name

on it? Promising the bearer"—she crossed her arms, pushing up her breasts— "a night of my company?"

Jesus. His cock throbbed painfully. His fascination with Georgina had clearly gone on long enough. He couldn't concentrate when she appeared. Which was far too often.

"Do you know, Lady Masterson, I've never been able to understand why others dislike your accent. I find it makes me want to visit New York. Your descriptions are very colorful. I imagine New York to be a charming place, possibly a little rustic."

Georgina tapped her foot in annoyance.

"The ocean crossing keeps me from doing so, however. I don't care for the water." His body rejected the notion of floating on ponds, rivers, oceans, and the like. Even the sight of toy boats bobbing along the Serpentine caused an unwelcome sensation in his stomach. The dislike of water was the direct result of a fishing expedition when Leo had been a child in which he had *not* floated. "I become quite ill aboard a ship. Can't even get myself to Paris."

Georgina snorted. "A pity, to be sure. But we are not speaking of your inability to enjoy a bath."

Leo's mouth twitched. Georgina's razor-sharp wit was wasted on nearly everyone except him. "I enjoy bathing."

He imagined Georgina in a bath, rising out of the water like Aphrodite with soap bubbles sliding down her breasts. A small groan left him.

"Do not try to turn the conversation to suit you. I find it irritating and rude. You do so with regularity." One hand slapped against her hip to make her point. "I am not one of the lords downstairs whom you are determined to fleece."

"I've never fleeced anyone." Leo hid a smile behind one hand. "Are you going to curse at me?" His cock twitched again. "I hope so. I always learn a new word or turn of phrase."

"I uttered *one* curse in your presence. One."

"During faro. You played carelessly, which I counseled you against. The odds—"

She held up a hand. "I'm well aware of what they are. You've recited them to me often enough. And I read Hoyle's treatise. Or at least some." Shaking her head, she murmured, "You're doing it again."

"Doing what?" Leo gave her an innocent look.

"Distracting me." Georgina's gaze fell to Leo's waistcoat, the top of which was visible as he relaxed back against his chair. Her nose wrinkled as if smelling refuse. "Hideous. Your taste in waistcoats is nonexistent."

Yes, but my taste in women is excellent.

"I'm curious. Do all young ladies curse in America?" Leo tapped his chin with one finger.

"No, they do not. I've told you before, my grandmother was fond of foul words and taught me the value of a colorful turn of phrase. A punishment of sorts for my mother, whom my grandmother didn't care for in the least. Grandmother also enjoyed shooting squirrels out of the trees because they were eating the carrots she'd planted in the garden. Stop changing the direction of our discussion and answer my question."

"Very well. I am at your mercy." He imbued the last bit with just a bit of innuendo.

"How could a gentleman," she gave him a pointed glance, a look of defeat on her lovely features, "possibly accept a married woman—"

"I'm assuming you mean yourself," he interrupted, watching that gold curl tremble at her brow. "I am trying to make certain of the facts."

"Yes. Me. As a *wager*." Her face crumpled in disappointment. All of which was directed at him.

Leo ignored the betrayal lighting her features. "First, I am

THE WAGER OF A LADY

not a gentleman. My apologies if I led you to believe otherwise. True, my father is a duke, but as you know, I'm the product of an affair with his mistress. I run a gambling hell. I consort with all manner of disreputable people. There is little else to recommend me."

"Fair enough. Then I blame myself for *also* assuming you to be my friend."

Georgina could slice a man up with just a word. That observation, for instance, cut him to the quick. He *was* her friend. He also wanted to fuck her. Two completely different things.

"Secondly," Leo continued, "you can't imagine the sorts of things people wager. Mistresses. Expensive books of an erotic nature. A sliver of land. Houses. Wives are, regrettably, among the least interesting."

"Yes, we women are often bartered." Bitterness colored her response. "To be used at the whim of any man."

"An unfortunate truth," he murmured.

Jacob Rutherford, Georgina's father, had used her at *his* whim. Georgina had alluded to a misunderstanding with her parents that had resulted in her being wed to Masterson and banished from New York. But she had thus far refused to discuss the events in any detail. Tony speculated Rutherford had wanted a title in the family to improve his social standing. But Georgina's family had yet to visit her in London to take advantage of the connection. Nor had she gone home to New York, not even for her sister's wedding. A man was involved in Georgina's exile, of that Leo had no doubt.

Jealousy snapped against his skin, and he pushed it away.

"I suppose I am foolish. I just thought—" She looked down at her hands before straightening her shoulders again and raising her chin. "Why must *you* be one of them?"

Because he was Leo Murphy. He wanted to scream it at her. Gambling hell owner. Notorious bastard. A man who had become as much of a debaucher of women as the detested Duke of Averell. *That's* who he was. Georgina was ridiculously romantic; she refused to see him for what he was: the *muck*. Not honorable. Not a gentleman. Morals questionable.

"I'm not sure I have ever given you any indication I am honorable, my lady. I taught you how to gamble. Kept you company from time to time. Would that your husband had taken instruction from me. Lord Masterson might well have improved his odds of winning."

The curl twitched in agitation. "Are you in possession of my marker or not?"

"Very well. Lord Masterson," Leo stated coolly, "received a substantial amount of credit from me so he could finish his game of cards. He was determined to beat Lord Wentworth. Since I already own a hefty stack of your husband's markers, it did not make good business sense to allow him any additional credit without some sort of collateral."

A hint of color entered her cheeks. "You could have refused."

"Had I refused," Leo informed her, "your husband would have used the marker with your name on it, guaranteeing a night of your company, as his *wager* with Wentworth." Wentworth could have called the marker due at any time. Given Masterson's careless treatment of his bride, Georgina would have found herself in a very unfortunate situation. Wentworth wasn't known for his kind treatment of women. "I can't fathom you would have wished for that outcome."

"He could in no way make me comply."

"Masterson wouldn't even have bothered to tell you until it was far too late. He would have felt bound to honor the marker as a gentleman." Wentworth would have forced her. *Hurt* her. Which would have led to Lord Wentworth's ultimate demise because Leo would have had to dispose of him.

"Would you have found that preferable? To find yourself locked in a room with Wentworth?"

"What I would have *preferred* was not to have been bartered with as if I were a cow or a goat." A puff of outrage left her, and the curl fell back over her cheek. She brushed it away, tucking it neatly behind her ear.

"A very expensive goat," Leo drawled.

"I don't find this situation as amusing as you do."

The amount he'd given Masterson, a lord hovering on the brink of bankruptcy, had been indecent in comparison to what was offered as collateral. But Leo would have given him much more to keep hold of Georgina's marker. He'd informed Masterson rather bluntly that Georgina was not to be used in such a way again or his membership at Elysium would be revoked and his markers called in.

"Your anger would be better directed toward your husband, Lady Masterson. May I offer you a glass of bourbon whiskey?" He gave her a sideways glance, bringing out a bottle of the stuff from a drawer in his desk. Setting the bottle on the table, he produced two crystal-cut glasses. "I believe it is your favorite."

Georgina's preference for bourbon whiskey, scandalous on whichever side of the Atlantic one found themselves on, was yet another one of her intriguing habits. It mixed well with her rebellious nature, scathing tongue, and ability to curse. Of course, now he must consider she'd also been taught to shoot squirrels out of trees.

Elysium always kept several bottles of bourbon on hand for Georgina, something he'd gone to great trouble to procure.

Leo drummed his fingers on the desk, berating himself for going to such lengths just to please her.

It was only bourbon, after all. Not a poem to her eyes. Or an ode to her lips.

She jerked her chin in assent to the bourbon.

Georgina's husband, in addition to liking muscular footmen, was one of those gentlemen who became mad with lust when gambling. Always certain the very next card or the final throw of the dice would guarantee victory, but it rarely ever did. While Leo wasn't privy to Masterson's finances, the elderly earl had been desperate enough to consider marriage to a wealthy American girl barely out of the school room. It certainly wasn't to produce an heir, something Masterson had never professed any interest in. His nephew was in line to inherit.

Leo poured out two glasses of bourbon, sliding Georgina's across the desk in her direction.

She picked up the heavy crystal and took a small sip, closing her eyes in pleasure, her features blissful.

Leo thought she would look much the same way beneath him as she climaxed.

"I am not here to debate my husband's failings, numerous though they might be. I've no idea what he prefers more; gambling or visiting the rooms on Elysium's second floor with an unending parade of young, blonde gentlemen." Her eyes snapped open. Delicate hands clenched and flexed around the crystal of her glass as if she were considering whether to toss it at Leo's head. Perhaps she would even tackle him to the floor.

The image was so erotic, a sigh escaped his lips.

"Let us speak plainly." Georgina was nothing if not blunt.

"I prefer it," Leo said.

Lord Masterson, giddy at Rutherford's gold flooding his bank account, had probably thought he was wedding a weak little milksop from America. A girl who would be impressed with his title as much as Rutherford. One who would be obedient. Docile.

Instead, he got Georgina. Leo almost felt sorry for Masterson.

"That marker can't possibly be legal, not even here at Elysium where you allow all manner of lewd behavior. I should not have had to come here tonight to demand you destroy it. You should have delivered it to me."

"Because I taught you whist?" He gave a laugh. "Or is it because you wrongly assumed me to be a gentleman?"

"Both."

"My brother is the gentleman. You spend a decent amount of time with him. You should be able to tell the difference between us." His charming, very *legitimate* brother. There were times when the distinction gnawed at him.

She took another sip of the bourbon, catching a stray drop with her tongue.

Jesus, everything she did sent fire between his legs. When he'd taught her to play hazard, Georgina had leaned over the table, her breasts nearly escaping the confines of her bodice, and blown on the dice for luck, smiling at him the entire time.

He'd very nearly fainted because all the blood in his body had rushed to his cock.

"Did you really toss a copy of Debrett's Peerage into the fire? I understand it was a gift from Lady Talbot," he said. Changing the topic was a way to distract and allow some of his ardor to cool. This maddening need for Georgina threatened his control, and Leo *never* lost control of himself. Nor had he gone so long without bedding a woman. He had no interest in Lady Dunley, who still pursued him. His mistress, one he'd ceased to visit some time ago, had found another protector. Just last night, a gorgeous widow, Mrs. Brushnell, had tried to lure him upstairs to the second floor, and he'd waved her way. Her charms left him cold.

The situation was *intolerable*.

31

Georgina blinked. "How would you know I burned Lady Talbot's gift?" She waved a hand as if batting a fly. "Wait, don't answer. I imagine there's been gossip."

So much gossip.

Lady Talbot wasn't shy about expressing her opinion of Lady Masterson.

"I didn't want to read her stupid book nor do anything whatsoever which would endear myself to her," Georgina said. "She likened my speech to the sound of a wounded duck. I continue to refer to her as a baroness instead of a countess just to annoy her."

"Your husband told me about Lady Talbot's gift."

Masterson had mentioned the incident to Leo. The elderly earl often spoke of Georgina as if she were an annoying pet. A dog or a cat, perhaps. Or a parrot, given his dislike of her accent. A dislike shared by Masterson's nephew, who had been overheard disparaging his uncle's wife.

"You've deliberately steered the discussion away from the subject at hand. Once again."

It was a useful skill, distraction. Leo found it especially helpful as the owner of a gambling hell. Casual conversation often revealed another person's weakness and put them at ease, which gave Leo the advantage. The fact that Georgina was the only one to consistently draw attention to his habit was irritating.

"I want my house back," she stated plainly.

Beechwood Court, the small estate outside of London Georgina adored. A place she spent much of her time. *Not* her marker.

"Masterson had no right to offer up my property as collateral for his game of cards with Wentworth. Beechwood Court belongs to me."

There was no point in reminding Georgina that every-thing, including her person, belonged to Lord Masterson.

"Four horses, a hunting lodge in Scotland, Beechwood Court, and yourself was offered up as collateral. Signed off by the solicitor I keep on retainer. Perfectly legal," Leo said bluntly. "In poor taste, but nonetheless . . ." He let the words hover in the air.

A stubborn look clouded her features. "I want my house back," she said again.

Leo tried not to smile. "I'll be honest—"

"That must require a great deal of effort. Please don't put yourself out on my account. What would you do with Beechwood Court anyway? You live here."

"I'll sell it."

The stricken look on her face nearly made Leo take his words back.

"Lady Masterson, I run a business which is dependent, unfortunately, on the poor decisions of others. If I simply returned everything to you, I would be barraged by my other patrons to do the same for them. It would set a poor precedent." He gave a deep sigh and shrugged. "But I *will* return this to you." Leo took out the marker with her name on it and slid it across the table. "I'm making a concession because of our acquaintance and your friendship with my brother."

"But not my friendship with you?"

"I'm not the sort of man you should claim as a friend, Lady Masterson. Whether I taught you to properly gamble or not. Regrettably, this is the only item I can return to you."

"Very well." Her eyes flitted down to the piece of paper, but she didn't touch it. "Then I propose a wager."

"A wager?"

"Yes. What if I play you for Beechwood Court? Would that be acceptable?"

No one in the last ten years had challenged Leo to a game of cards. Georgina had absolutely no chance of beating him.

But she also wasn't the sort of woman who backed down easily.

"Interesting. But what do you intend to wager? Your husband is rather short on funds these days, and I'm not sure you have time to beg a stake from your father. New York is rather far away."

Her features froze at the mention of Jacob Rutherford. Her father was the last person Georgina would ever go to for assistance.

"Do you have gems sewn into the hem of your gown? A purse of gold?"

Georgina's lips tightened, her gaze never leaving his as she slid her marker back in his direction. "I have *this*."

Leo's heart thudded in his chest. "But I've only just given it back and, as you've mentioned, it can't possibly be legal."

"I swear to honor the terms." She looked him directly in the eye. "Isn't that what you wish me to say, *Leo*?"

The sound of his name on her lips made his entire body throb. "I'm not sure I know what you mean."

Georgina lifted one brow. "Isn't this how you imagined the game to proceed? Had you not predicted the likelihood of *this* outcome, you would have tossed my marker into the fire or even delivered it to me. But you didn't. You knew I would challenge you for Beechwood Court and made sure I had something to wager. Myself." She glared at him. "Am I correct so far?"

Damn, she was clever.

The night he'd first seen her, Leo had recognized her intelligence. She had stared at him so intently as he'd launched into an explanation of probability. Georgina had never once looked away from him, only listened as if Leo were the most important person in the world.

No one had ever looked at him in such a way.

Damn it. All the more reason to bed her and put her out of

34

his mind. Georgina made Leo want things he couldn't possibly have. "You are correct." He cleared his throat.

"You want to bed me."

Leo slid back in his seat. She was so bloody forthright about everything. At times it was unsettling. "I do." There was no point in denying it.

Georgina downed the rest of her drink. "Much like everything else, you fail to state your intentions outright but instead resort to subterfuge. I'd no idea that keeping me company when I came to Elysium, asking about my life in New York, laughing over my poor jokes—"

"Not all of them were terrible."

"Was only a means to an end. Very well. I suppose I'm yet another shiny bauble Leo Murphy, bastard club owner, wishes to collect." She sounded so incredibly angry. "Do you accept my challenge?" She slid her empty glass toward him.

Georgina's assumption of his character, though somewhat correct, annoyed him to no end.

Ignoring her empty glass, Leo pushed back from the desk and made his way over to her. She stiffened at his approach but didn't move away.

Spring. Leo inhaled the air around her, filling his nostrils with the scent that was unique only to Georgina. Wild things bursting forth to bloom. Lush gardens and freshly mown grass. Savage greenery. He wanted to bury himself in her.

"I accept," he said.

"Of course you do; this is the exact outcome you wanted." She tilted her chin up at him. "Because, as you've taken great pains to remind me, you are not a gentleman. Just a duke's bastard and definitely not my friend. Certainly not anything else."

Leo's mouth tightened.

"Let us set the terms for our wager. When I win—" She

pushed back another curl springing free from the messy chignon at the base of her neck.

He followed the movement, tamping down the urge to devour her. "*If* you win," he growled out.

Georgina sucked in a deep breath, forcing her breasts against the tight bodice of her dress. "*When* I win," she said more stubbornly than before, "I want everything my husband used as collateral returned."

"*If* you win," Leo replied, "I will gladly return it all to you. I'll even throw in a bloody gardener for Beechwood Court. I understand the gardens and lawn are in a terrible state of disarray."

"And I want the remainder of my husband's markers restored to me," she said boldly, surprising Leo. "The stack you keep in your safe. A paltry sum for you, but for me, it represents nearly the whole of my dowry. Do you agree?"

Leo hadn't thought it possible to want her more than he already did.

"I do," he said. The amount wasn't paltry in the least. Leo would have described the sum as obscene. And Masterson had gambled it all away over the last two years.

"I insist on an honest dealer and a fresh deck of cards. Not the marked deck you probably have hiding in the drawer of your desk."

How the bloody hell did Georgina know he had marked cards in his desk? To his knowledge, she'd never been in here before. Leo would certainly have remembered. His brother must have told her.

"Agreed."

Georgina kept her eyes on him, fingers curled into her skirts. "Is this really how you want me, Leo?" she said quietly.

Intolerable. Why must she look at him with such disappointment?

"Yes."

eorgina perched on the overly tufted, extra-wide settee of Leo's office, shocked at how she'd come to be here.

She ran her fingers over the lush velvet of the settee's cushions, marveling at the seductive feel and the crimson color, so stark against her pale hands. Would he take her later on this settee if she lost, or seduce her upstairs? Which was more tawdry?

The settee it is.

Georgina had spent the last two years romanticizing Leo Murphy and her unyielding attraction to him. It had been easy to fall into a casual friendship with him. Leo reminded Georgina quite a bit of her cousin Ben back in New York. Full of secrets and determined to be worse than he really was. Leo considered himself to be a cruder, coarser version of his brother, Lord Welles, because of the circumstances of his birth. But that wasn't how Georgina saw Leo at all.

His blatant manipulation of the current circumstances notwithstanding.

She looked out the window behind the desk in Leo's

office. The panels of glass took up most of one wall, giving a glimpse out to the street in front of Elysium. Carriages moved up the wide gravel drive in a steady flow, stopping only to deposit their richly garbed occupants. She'd visited Elysium many times since the night she'd met Leo and never failed to be impressed by the extravagant gaming palace he'd created. She gently toed the lavish rug beneath her feet, as expensive as anything gracing her parents' home in Lafayette Square back in New York. The contents of the office spoke of understated wealth—a great deal of it.

Leo Murphy, without a doubt, had to be the most overindulged, privileged bastard in all of London.

Her fingers stroked the decadent cushions beneath her. The settee's appearance struck Georgina as overly sexual and belonged in a damned brothel. She was sure it was no accident Leo had this piece of furniture in his office.

Something stirred softly inside her. Naked skin. Mouths. Tongues.

Georgina jerked back her hand.

Masterson had returned home from Elysium a week ago with yet another of his young gentlemen, a barrister. Georgina barely paid her husband or his guests any notice. She had grown accustomed to Masterson and his propensity for blonde men barely older than herself. Her only hope was that the pair would be quiet.

But as her husband had made his way to the stairs, drunk on lust and scotch, Masterson had paused to inform Georgina that *someone* might be coming by in the next few days for the deed to his hunting lodge in Scotland. Did she have any idea where he'd put the piece of paper? The drawing room, perhaps? Possibly in the desk she favored for her correspondence? Oh, and the horses he'd recently purchased from Tattersalls would likely no longer be part of his stables. Would Georgina be a dear and alert one of the grooms?

Masterson's subtle way of telling her he'd lost.

Georgina had watched her husband stumble up the stairs, arm in arm with the blushing young man, wishing Masterson would simply take a tumble and free her from this hellish existence. Two long years she'd been in London, hating every moment of her marriage.

Once Masterson disappeared, Georgina had walked into his study, a room she did not usually enter without good reason. Her husband rarely used the room as intended, and she'd accidentally witnessed things she would rather she hadn't. Secretaries were not hired for their qualifications or skills with numbers, but whether or not they were open to being tupped by their employer.

Seven secretaries alone had quit this year.

Nonetheless, Georgina set out to do as Masterson had asked and find the deed to the property in Scotland. After rifling through her husband's desk and finding no deeds, only a collection of unpaid bills, Georgina decided the best course would be to confront Masterson at breakfast. The following morning as she sat across the table from him, munching on a bit of toast, Georgina had pointedly asked how much had been lost at Elysium. Masterson had calmly sipped his morning tea and informed Georgina her beloved Beechwood Court, the hunting lodge, four horses recently purchased at Tattersall's and, as he dabbed at his lips, Georgina herself, had been used to secure a line of credit at Elysium.

"Unfortunate, my dear, that I lost."

Georgina had dropped the fork in her hand. She should have stabbed him with it.

Humiliation wasn't something one should endure over breakfast. Georgina didn't care for the way it made her eggs taste. Granted, she and Masterson didn't have a real marriage, but at the very least, she'd hoped he wouldn't go around offering the use of her body as one would a ripe peach. After stating she wouldn't honor such a ridiculous request, no matter the damage to Masterson's honor, her husband had only laughed.

"Murphy took your marker for a reason, you silly chit. And it wasn't because he enjoys teaching you faro. Let him bed you, and we'll get everything back."

Then the vile cur had patted Georgina's head as if she were twelve and left the table.

She had sat in the breakfast room until her tea went cold, replaying the conversation with Masterson. She was sure he was mistaken.

A week went by. No one came to claim the horses, Beechwood Court, or the hunting lodge. Nor was her marker returned. So now, she found herself at Elysium. And just as Masterson had predicted, Leo wanted to bed her. He'd plainly admitted as much. But that wasn't why she was angry with him.

"Larkin will serve as dealer. Smith has gone to fetch him," Leo informed her as he shut the door of his office. He'd conferred with Elysium's large doorman for several minutes while she sat on the settee, contemplating her fate.

"Larkin is acceptable," she answered, thinking of the young faro dealer she was friendly with. Still toying with her glass, Georgina's eyes flicked to the marker with her name on it.

A different young lady, one who would never wager herself, would have taken the marker and thrown it into the fire when it had been offered and fled back to her husband. But Georgina had a propensity to do reckless things.

"Good." Leo's eyes, sapphire blue with a distinct ring of indigo, fell on her. His gaze trailed over the modest neckline of her dress before settling on her lips. Long, elegant fingers clasped the bourbon bottle as he poured another splash into her glass.

Georgina sucked in a shaky breath. Leo rarely wore gloves, and his bare hands were as beautiful as the rest of him. Well-shaped and graceful. There were small callouses on his palm as if he'd been doing something more strenuous than noting wagers in Elysium's Red Book. She'd often watched in fascination as he gestured with his hands while speaking, wondering how those fingers would feel trailing along her skin.

"Something wrong, Lady Masterson?"

"No, nothing whatsoever." She picked up her bourbon, cradling it in her hands.

Leo filled his own glass, easing back into his chair with a friendly smile. Perhaps he meant to discuss the theater or the weather before playing a game of cards in which Georgina had wagered herself. How civilized.

A half-smile crossed his wide mouth, and the small dimple in his cheek appeared. A wave of leather-brown hair fell over his forehead, which he didn't bother to push away. The muscles of his thighs, apparent through the fabric of his trousers, bunched as he crossed his legs.

"Beechwood Court must mean quite a bit if you're willing to wager your honor."

She shot him an annoyed glance. "You know that it does. I've mentioned Beechwood Court to you often enough. While you were teaching me cards and pretending to be my friend. Why didn't you just bed me then?"

His smile faltered just a bit. "I should have."

Georgina looked away. She didn't understand him. He hadn't so much as flirted with her in all this time. If lifting her skirts was all he wanted, why hadn't he just done so? "You should have, and we could have avoided this chain of events for which I might never forgive you."

A scowl crossed his beautiful mouth. "You're very dramatic, Georgina. I've often thought so."

A knock on the door sounded.

"Come," Leo said, his eyes never leaving hers. There was heat in the blue depths, but something undefinable as well. "Good evening, Larkin."

The young man entered. "Sir." He nodded to Georgina. "My lady."

If Larkin was curious to find Georgina in Leo Murphy's office, he gave no indication. For all she knew, Leo held card games with his paramours every night of the week.

Dear God, I will not be one of those women.

"Here will be fine." Murphy pointed to the table between him and Georgina. "Unless you object, my lady."

"Not at all." Georgina tossed back the remainder of her bourbon.

Leo tracked her movements, his gaze caressing the line of her neck with a sort of savage hunger. Apparently, he was no longer bothering to hide his desire.

Good. Maybe it will make him careless. Men often became witless at the sight of her bosom. Leo was probably no different. Though he'd never paid it much attention until tonight.

"Another bourbon, if you please." She slid her glass across the table.

"I don't want you to become lightheaded, Georgina."

"I won't be." She shot him a defiant glance. "I've a high tolerance for a great manner of things."

"I'll allow you to choose the game." Leo waved one of those graceful hands in her direction.

"How kind, considering. I choose poker," Georgina stated without hesitation, knowing the game wasn't played in London or anywhere in England. At least as far as she knew. Certainly, it wasn't offered as a choice at Elysium. Playing a game Leo wasn't overly familiar with might be the only real advantage she had to best him. His unerring ability to recall every card played made winning against him incredibly difficult.

"I'm not familiar with the game, Lady Masterson." Her detested title rolled out of him. "As you likely know."

"It's fairly simple. I could teach you." She gave him a look. "You'll pick it up in no time. Brilliant man such as yourself."

"Larkin is not familiar either." Leo's tone grew bland. "I suggest vingt-un. Fairly simple and to the point. Though I must admit," he leaned over the table until she caught sandalwood and leather in her nostrils, "I admire your strategy. Were I in your situation, I would have done the same."

Damn. "Fine."

"Unless you'd prefer whist?"

He'd taught her the technique of how to keep track of her cards and those of the other players. She barely had a chance at vingt-un. "No. Thank you."

"We'll each start with ten chips as our stake. We play for one hour. Whoever has the most chips at the end of the game will be declared the winner. Does that suit you?"

"Yes." It wasn't as if she had a choice.

Larkin dealt the cards quickly and efficiently, setting a small stack of chips in front of each of them.

"When did you learn to play poker, if I may ask, Lady Masterson? Seems something the well-bred ladies of New York wouldn't learn along with embroidery and dancing."

"At about the same time I learned to enjoy bourbon whiskey," she replied without looking up. "Every young lady should have a hobby, don't you think?"

Bourbon and poker often brought to mind John Winbow and everything that had come after. What started as a small rebellion, a mild flirtation with a riverboat gambler she'd met at a gathering, had eventually led to her banishment. Her father had been making noises about marrying her off, largely to rein in Georgina's behavior. Mother had been busy watching the young men swarm about Lilian, Georgina's older sister. Too preoccupied to pay any heed to her younger daughter. It seemed the perfect time for Georgina to make the acquaintance of a gentleman from Savannah who made his living by playing poker on the riverboats sailing up and down the Mississippi. Winbow had taught Georgina how to kiss properly, play poker, and enjoy the caramel flavor of a good bourbon whiskey from Kentucky, and he'd have taught her more had she let him. She'd stopped far short of giving Winbow her virtue. He'd responded by threatening her reputation.

Odd. Bourbon and her virtue were still being wagered. "My poor behavior has not been limited to my time in London, Mr. Murphy."

"Leo." The rich, buttery sound of his amusement flowed over her shoulders. "I expected nothing less."

He had such resonance to him. A vibration she felt in the floor and up through her toes. The sound had certain parts of her person aching for something she could only guess at.

"Ladies first," Leo murmured.

Georgina lifted the corner of her cards, careful to school her expression and give nothing away. Leo's presence brushed against her, and her insides fluttered in response. She wished he'd sit on the other side of the room.

The trembling in her fingers was not due to fear.

3

A short time later, barely more than an hour, Georgina was still trembling. But this time with frustration and a decent amount of anger.

She'd lost.

"Close the door behind you, Larkin. Please inform Smith I'm not to be disturbed under any circumstances."

"Not even for Lord Welles, sir?"

"Especially not for Lord Welles. You can leave the cards and chips here and collect them tomorrow."

Larkin nodded, bowed sharply, and left Leo's office, his footsteps barely making a sound on the thick rug as he exited.

Georgina sat perfectly still on the obscene settee, hands clasped tightly in her lap. She often prided herself on being a good loser, but she had to bite her lip to keep from spewing out a string of curses.

I've lost Beechwood Court. And a great deal of my pride.

There was an actual physical pain at losing her tiny estate. She was far more concerned about Beechwood Court than she was about Leo bedding her. If her experience with

Masterson was any indication, she need only lie still and wait for it to end.

She glanced at Leo as a small ball of heat built inside her.

John Winbow, excellent kisser and terrible human being, had touched Georgina in a great many places. Her underthings had become damp while the rest of her had yearned for something Georgina couldn't put a name to. But Winbow's desire for her had been *nothing* compared to his greed for her father's money.

Leo Murphy was an entirely different matter.

He'd dragged out their game, intentionally letting Georgina win the first few hands until his stack of chips grew short, putting her at ease. Giving her hope. Then he'd pounced, a great cat who had merely been playing with his food before he devoured it. Leo had probably known the cards she held in her hands before she had.

Georgina hated him a little for that. "You've won."

"I have."

Murphy plopped down on the settee beside her, close enough so that the cushions dipped beneath his weight and her own body tilted toward his. He leaned back against one plump pillow with its frivolous display of tassels. "You're angry."

"I am," she responded.

"You were never going to win; surely you knew that when you made the wager."

"Surely you knew I had no hope of winning when you gave me back my marker and induced me to wager for Beechwood Court."

Firelight gilded one side of his face, turning the edges of his sculpted cheekbones to gold and throwing shadows across his shoulders. His wide mouth held the ghost of a half-smile as he regarded her, every inch a gentleman of wealth and privilege, except for the bit of darkness lurking beneath the fine clothes. A crudeness, perhaps, she might have called it. The sense that Leo could walk into a ballroom and then into a dark alley and be at home in either place. He'd had to learn to become a gentleman, had refinement forced upon him.

She expected the journey had been rife with all sorts of bumps in the road.

"Induce?"

"You knew I would come for Beechwood Court. My marker was only pickled herring."

A soft chuckle came from his broad chest. "Red herring is what I believe you mean."

"Regardless. You are deceptive."

The line of his jaw tensed. "Deceptive?"

"Such pretense, Leo. There wasn't any need to teach me card tricks and such, though I expect you found it amusing. I do hope I presented you with an adequate challenge. After all, you went to so much trouble to bring me here. I wonder if you *suggested* to my husband that he use me as a marker."

"I did not," he said quietly. "And I don't make a habit of buying up the markers of married women. You're the first."

If she didn't know better, Georgina would have thought there was regret lingering in the sapphire of his eyes. "I don't believe you. I think you run several games at once. Sparkly baubles are much to your liking. I hope I shine brightly enough. The light isn't very good in here."

His lips had drawn into a thin line; she'd made him angry.

"Very well, let us get on with things." Georgina stood, waving her hand around the room. "No need to prolong you receiving your spoils."

"I've always admired how incredibly straightforward you are." Leo set down the glass of bourbon and approached her, leaning so close her breasts nearly brushed against his hideous waistcoat. God, what was it, mustard and red with splotches of gold thread?

The warmth of his breath sifted through the fine hairs at the base of her neck, though he made no move to touch her. "You smell marvelous, by the way. Like spring."

"Spring? I didn't think you capable of such drivel. What you smell is the soap I use to bathe. Common enough. You can buy it at Hartman's at the corner of Broadway Street. My sister sends it to me." She kept her chin lifted, eyes fixed on a pair of candlesticks near the fireplace in an attempt to ignore the delicious warmth radiating across her neck. "Toss up my skirts and be done with it. You've won. Take your prize. I'll hold still."

Leo put his hands to his lips. A sound erupted behind them.

He was giggling. At her.

"Toss up your skirts? Be *done* with it? Are you serious, Georgina?"

"Stop mocking me." She tapped her foot impatiently, ignoring the dozens of butterflies which had impossibly taken up residence in her mid-section. "Hurry things along. Take your prize."

"I'm to"—Leo tugged gently on her skirts—"toss these over your head. Listen as you nearly suffocate under several layers of cotton and wool. Then when I feel you're sufficiently muddled and barely breathing, I'm to settle myself between your legs?"

"Yes," she said in a much huskier tone than she'd intended.

"I'm to slake my lust." His voice lowered a fraction until it was only a dark hum. "On you?"

"Yes," she said again. "Slake your lust. Spend yourself. Spill your seed. You've won."

"Good lord, you have an interesting way of speaking, Georgina. You make this all sound"—his voice lowered to a seductive purr—"so tawdry."

48

THE WAGER OF A LADY

"It *is* tawdry. You've made sure of it."

The barest touch of his lips against the curve of her ear had her arching ever so slightly. "Don't you want me to touch you?"

"No." Even she could hear the lie in her words. "Get on with it."

"Stroke the wetness seeping between your thighs?" he murmured, running his hand over her hip. "Does your quim ache for my touch? I think it does."

"You're crude. Vulgar." *Terribly arousing.*

"You've no idea the things I mean to do to you, Georgina." He breathed against her neck, sending tendrils of pleasure down her back.

A finger ran down her arm, a whisper against her skin beneath the green wool.

Georgina closed her eyes, not trusting herself to look at him. Her fingers crawled into her skirts, clutching at the fabric for deliverance. "If you think giving me pleasure will assuage your guilt—"

"Guilt? A wasted emotion. I won't feel the least guilty about fucking you, Georgina. I plan to do so repeatedly. Right on the settee. Then possibly the floor. Maybe bent over my desk. The possibilities are endless, and I haven't yet decided."

Georgina sucked in a breath. The place between her thighs, the spot John Winbow had touched but not satisfied, pulsed at his words. Leo was circling her like a hungry wolf scenting his prey, intent on drawing her out when she should seek safety.

He dragged the pads of his fingers along the base of her neck before tugging at the buttons lining her back. Insistent, but slow. Savoring the release of every button as it popped.

"I've wanted you for a very long time," he murmured against the slope of her shoulder as another button came free.

49

"Odd." She tried to stanch the quaking making its way up her body. "You've known me less than two years."

"I adore your sharp edges." An open-mouthed kiss fell on her neck as the dress fell from her shoulders. Teeth grazed. Nipped. The dress slid further down, trapping her arms at her sides. "What is it about your Beechwood Court that you would risk so much for it?"

It shouldn't have surprised her Leo had come back to the subject of her little house. He was distracting her from the work of his hands, which would soon strip her bare. "It isn't mine any longer."

"Answer the question." He nipped her again, hands sliding beneath the gaping wool of her dress.

Georgina arched in his direction without meaning to. "I told you before. When I thought you were listening to me and not looking at my bosom."

"I was doing both."

"It reminds me of the house my grandparents built. I spent quite a bit of time there until—until I came here. I was close to my grandmother. She died shortly after I married." Another brush of his wide mouth over her shoulder. "Beechwood Court for some reason reminds me of her. I don't know why."

"Is that why you planted tulips?"

Georgina stilled, wondering how he knew about her attempts at gardening. "She loved tulips." An entire field of tulips had surrounded Grandmother's house in a cascade of color. Georgina had run through them when she'd been a child. "But along with painting and embroidery, I find I'm not very good at gardening."

"You have your own talents, Georgina." His forefinger traced the delicate line of her collarbone. "Lord Talbot has mentioned to me in the past that he wished he'd bought Beechwood Court when it was offered to him years ago."

"Now he will have his opportunity." First, his wife sends Georgina a copy of the book dictating everyone's lineage in London. Now, he and Lady Talbot would enjoy her house. "As you probably have guessed, I don't care for Lady Talbot nor her husband. I find Lord Talbot to be vile and free with his hands.

"Vile?" Leo's big, calloused palms cupped her breasts. "No corset, Georgina?"

She trembled, instructing her legs to stop shaking. "I was in a bit of a rush. The dress doesn't require it."

"Ah." He gently teased at the tips of her nipples.

Georgina had to bite her lip to keep from moaning out loud. She hadn't imagined having him touch her like this would be so pleasurable. Certainly, Masterson had never touched her so. Oddly, Winbow hadn't been overly interested in her bosom.

"Has he made advances on you?" There was a dark edge to the casually spoken words.

"What does it matter?" She gasped as one hand left her breast to skim down her stomach and gently cup her mound through the thin cotton of her chemise. "You aren't much better, in my estimation. Please get on with it."

"Georgina, the marker states I have your company for the night. I will take as long as I wish worshipping your magnificent breasts." He pinched one of her nipples. "I can't wait to have these little peaks between my lips."

Her knees wobbled as his fingers gently traced her slit through the chemise.

"Georgie." His tongue traced the outline of her ear while his fingers moved against her.

She exhaled softly at the sound of her name, shortened into an endearment. A tiny sob left her at the feel of her body melting, like warm wax, to meld to his larger form. Must he defeat her so soundly? Make her want him so much?

"Don't be angry with me," he whispered into her hair. "Not for this." His palm stretched possessively over her stomach, while the other reached into her hair, dislodging the pins and allowing the heavy mass of her curls to fall down around her.

"I'm merely fulfilling my obligation," she whispered. "I wagered and lost. It isn't necessary for you to seduce me. Had you truly wanted to, Leo, you could have accomplished it some time ago."

"This isn't about a bloody wager, Georgie." His hands moved to grasp the edge of her dress. One sharp tug and she was left standing in only her chemise and petticoats, the wool falling to crumple around her knees.

He tugged at her waist, plucking at the strings of her petticoats until those too fell to the floor. Pausing, he nuzzled the side of her neck, his hands trailing up and down her arms.

"Step out." The words were rough.

She lifted her foot over the pile of her clothing clad only in chemise, stockings, and a pair of slippers.

His hands brushed across the back of her shoulders to her chemise, fingers grazing along the thin material as he pulled it from her body. Big hands stretched over her stomach, the callouses on his palm rasping against her skin before returning again to her breasts. His thumbs brushed with agonizing slowness over each nipple, teasing with a light touch until the peaks were aching and sensitive. Her breath caught as he rolled and squeezed one nipple between his thumb and forefinger.

"I think you're wet, Georgie. Ready to take me. Because of how *tawdry* this entire seduction is."

Her knees buckled, struck by the snapping of his words against her ear.

One hand continued to toy with her breast as the other— dear god the other—moved lower, those graceful fingers tangling in the nest of curls between her thighs. One finger eased along her slit, exploring her folds lazily, purposefully avoiding the one place craving his touch. Georgina tried to push away, but he wouldn't allow it.

"Do you ever make yourself climax, Georgie? I confess I'm curious, given you're married to Masterson. Alone in bed at night, after a trying day spent walking in the park or shopping. I expect you no longer bother to pay calls." His finger circled her entrance before finding its way back through her folds.

She had. After Winbow, after some of the things he'd made her feel. After he'd caressed her through her underthings, making her want something more. Georgina had tried to recreate the sensation herself but had failed.

"I hate you for this." A small sound escaped from between her lips.

His grip on her tightened. "No, you don't." He kissed her cheek. "Tawdry though it may be."

Despite forcing the issue, Leo Murphy didn't care to be described as tawdry. And he was also correct in assuming she didn't hate him. She *did* want to kiss his wide mouth. Feel his naked skin against hers. She'd thought of him so often, teasing her own nipples into peaks as her fingers wandered between her thighs. What harm was there in admitting it to him?

"Yes."

"Yes what?" He came around her, leaning over to take one of her breasts into his mouth, sucking and laving the nipple until her hands threaded into his hair.

"I have touched myself." The words hiccupped out of her. "But nothing happened."

The reward for her honesty was for him to get on his knees before her, one big hand stretching across her hip, holding her firmly in place. The other toyed with the ribbon of her garter, but he made no effort to discard her hose. Fingers traversed the length of one leg, drawing circles on the inside of her thigh while Georgina forced herself to stay still. The briefest of touches, like the stroke of a small brush, came closer to the spot aching for his touch.

"Like this, Georgina?" His thumb stroked around the swollen nub. "Does that feel right?"

Her hand fell on top of his, their fingers lacing together as he held her hip. "Yes."

"Is it tawdry enough for you?" he whispered, pressing a kiss to one plump thigh.

"It was an unfortunate choice of words, Leo. I meant to say sordid."

A soft sound came from him as his finger slid up into her folds. "I can smell your arousal, Georgina. Taste it in the air. I want it on my tongue."

Oh God. Please.

He stood abruptly and took her chin in his big hands, kissing her slow and deep as she sagged helplessly against him.

Georgina was in a dream, her poor mind firing in so many different directions, conscious only of pleasure, shut down, entirely intoxicated with the feel of his mouth on hers. He pushed her back to the settee where she landed awkwardly, her legs splayed open.

Without any preamble, he kneeled before her, hooking her legs over his broad shoulders. She was completely exposed, her legs trembling. Her slippers were still on her feet. Should she kick them off?

"Your waistcoat is ghastly," she murmured, falling back against the cushion.

"You aren't afraid." Leo's mouth tilted into a half-smile, showing his dimple.

"No. I'm . . . curious," she said honestly, jerking as he

stroked gently along her slit once more with his thumb. The feather-light touch had her tightening her legs, pulling him closer to her. Her entire body, sensitive to the slightest pressure, twisted as the slow burn of pleasure traveled up her limbs. She remembered this feeling, this jagged run up a hill, but there had been nothing once she reached the top, only a vague sensation that something lingered over the horizon. And a great deal of frustration. No resolution to the building pleasure. No—

A soft gasp of surprise left her as his tongue replaced his thumb, circling and sucking, while Georgina could do nothing more but whimper and push her hips more firmly against his mouth. She'd heard about this act but never—

"Oh." Her breathing grew ragged as the pulse of her body built up to a sharp edge, waiting only for Leo to force her over. He paused, his mouth moving to nibble the inside of her thighs while she thumped the cushions, frustrated that he continued to hold something wonderful just out of her reach. Over and over, he teased her until Georgina became wild with need, her hips thrusting shamelessly in his direction.

"Beg," he breathed against her sensitive flesh.

"What?" Her fingers pulled at his hair. She bit her lip. Shook her head. She wouldn't do it. Wouldn't beg. It was unfair. Cruel. "Damn you." Georgina twisted her hips, trying to put herself back in his mouth.

"Tawdry and damned I might be, but right now, I daresay I'm the most important person in the room."

In desperation, she tried to reach down between her legs, and he grabbed ahold of her wrists. "Please," she gave in with a sob. "Leo. Please."

Georgina, much to her everlasting shame, screamed out his name as the most amazing, exquisite bliss flooded her body. Pleasure rolled over her in waves. She was sure everyone in Elysium heard her. At the very least, whoever was stationed outside Leo's office door had to have heard unless they were deaf. Her heels dug into Leo's back, body straining upward until the last tremor left her. Finally, panting and sated, she lay back against the settee upon one of those silly cushions, a tassel tickling her ribs.

"So that's what all the fuss is about. I'm glad I didn't know before, else I would have cheerfully ruined myself," she whispered.

"Georgie, my beauty." His big body slid up the naked length of hers. She felt terribly vulnerable with the buttons of his waistcoat cold and catching at her skin. He cupped her face tenderly, thumb brushing at the corner of her mouth. His lips parted, as if he would speak, but instead, he only kissed her.

Oh, how he kissed her.

As if she were precious. Adored. Worshipped. She could live the rest of her days on this kiss. On his touch. The heat of his body felt so good against hers. Right in a way she hadn't expected. What was the point in continuing to salvage her pride?

Georgina fell into Leo, giving up any pretense she didn't want him. Later, she would hate herself and him. But not now, not when she could taste herself on his lips. Her arms wrapped around his neck, fingers sliding into the silky threads of his hair. There was no fight left in her. Not an ounce of pride. His mouth slanted over hers, hard and greedy, claiming her as his.

Oh God. I suppose I am. At least for tonight.

Leo Murphy collected opera singers and actresses. There was always a merry widow or two who trailed behind him at Elysium. The ladies of the *ton* may not care for his pedigree, but it didn't stop them from jumping into his bed when the opportunity presented itself. There was even a rumor that one unhappy young wife had threatened to drown herself in the fountain of her husband's estate when Murphy had ended their affair.

I'm not even an affair. I'm, at most, an indiscretion.

Georgina adamantly refused to be one of those women, waiting for Leo to turn his attention in her direction again. She had no interest in being one of his paramours. The mere thought wounded her.

He ran his knuckles gently along the line of her jaw before standing to loom over her naked form. She started to draw her legs together, aware of how exposed she was but Leo shook his head.

"No. Don't move." He shrugged out of his coat, a deep blue superfine that didn't deserve to be tossed so carelessly into one of the empty chairs. The waistcoat came next, a garish rendition of bright colors which made Georgina somewhat dizzy if she stared too long at the pattern.

"I don't understand why you wear anything so hideous."

"So you've said." The husky whisper scratched against her breasts as he tore off his cravat and unbuttoned his shirt. "Keeps me from being confused for a lord."

"I doubt anyone makes such a mistake."

There was far too much ruthless ambition humming beneath Leo's skin, something that was absent from many of the titled gentlemen Georgina had met in London. He was different from the lords downstairs, but not in the way he imagined.

The shirt was violently flung atop the waistcoat. He sat on the opposite end of the crimson settee and removed his boots.

Georgina couldn't help but stare at the ripple of muscles in his arms. Leo was broad across the chest. Solid. A dusting of dark hair covered his torso before thinning into a tight line and disappearing beneath the waistband of his trousers. The desire to touch all that skin, wind her fingers through the crisp hair, had Georgina's fingers twitching. There was nothing fine-boned about Leo. Not an ounce of refinement. His body was all rough edges, bone and sinew carved and cut beneath the flesh. Powerfully physical. Strong. Without the expensively tailored clothes, Leo's appearance of being a gentleman disappeared completely.

Leo ran a hand up his thigh, drawing attention to the heavy muscles and the thick length tenting his trousers.

"I assume Masterson has bedded you."

Georgina lifted her gaze to his. "Twice. Neither was . . . memorable."

His thumbs hooked into the top of his trousers. "And who before that, Georgina? Masterson certainly didn't teach you how to kiss. You don't behave as a woman who has never been touched."

She swallowed, not wanting to think about John Winbow with Leo standing over her nearly naked. "It isn't relevant."

"I see." He shucked off his trousers to stand naked before her. His cock jutted out from a thick nest of dark hair. "Everything where it should be?" He leaned over and brushed his lips against her mouth.

"I believe so." She reached out, fingers hovering, the heat of him wafting across the tips. Gently, she trailed a finger over his length. Velvet. Deceptively soft but hard. Masterson had kept the room dark, so she hadn't seen him completely. There were naked statues, of course. A crude drawing one of her parents' maids had drawn and Georgina had found. Ben, her cousin and dearest friend growing up, had many names for the male appendage and wasn't shy about sharing the knowledge with Georgina. Cock was the term Ben had often used. If her mother had ever found out, she would have sent her cousin back onto the streets from whence he'd come.

"Like this?"

He'd asked her the same question earlier. She wanted to know how to pleasure him as he'd done to her.

"*Jesus*. Yes." A ragged breath escaped him.

She brushed her fingers down the length, feeling the velvet heat warming her hand, the way his big body trembled at her touch. It was a heady sensation. Powerful.

He reached for her shoulders, flipping her deftly onto her stomach. One arm wrapped around her waist, lifting her. "On your knees, sweetheart."

Georgina nodded as he took hold of her neck and pushed her forward, forcing her knees apart with his leg. He nibbled down the length of her spine, holding her firmly, his hand wrapped gently around her throat. The fingers of his other hand delved between her legs, gliding over her, teasing at her flesh until she gasped and moaned. Wetness slid between her thighs. She felt faint from the anticipation of pleasure. Wanted it desperately. A needy sound escaped her.

The hand holding her down tightened ever so slowly as he positioned himself at her entrance, thrusting deep inside her with one stroke, knocking the breath from her lungs. Her body struggled to take him, and she gasped at the stretch. He was much larger than Masterson. He pulled out and thrust again, this time deeper than before.

A low moan left her as he hit a sensitive spot. "Oh, God. Leo."

"Georgie." He breathed her name. His fingers were on her throat, tangled in her hair, taking her with hard, even strokes. The pleasure was so intense, Georgina wept, screaming out her release into the cushions. She may have bitten one of the tassels off a pillow. Her hips bucked wildly, her inner muscles clutching his cock before he withdrew with a groan, spilling himself over her buttocks and thighs.

Panting, breath ragged, Leo's mouth pressed a gentle kiss

to her shoulder. His hand stroked her hair. The side of her cheek. "Don't move, love."

Georgina couldn't have even if she'd had the inclination to. She hadn't thought physical relations would be so . . . *intense*. So incredibly pleasurable, one's mind went blank. She heard him pad to the other side of the room and wrap his knuckles against the wall. Out of the corner of her eye, she watched a door swing open to reveal a small washroom. Water splashed as he cleaned himself.

She shut her eyes, enjoying the ache of her body.

A moment later, a warm rag was pressed between her thighs, her buttocks. He cleaned her as carefully as if she were a child, pushing aside her hands. When he was finished, he lay down on the settee beside her, pulling Georgina against him.

"So, you were taught to kiss and little else." He kissed her temple. "You should have told me it had only been Masterson instead of leading me to believe you were more experienced. I could've hurt you."

"You could tell?"

"Yes. An almost-virgin is what you were."

"Hmm." Her heart tugged ferociously in Leo's direction no matter how she tried to pull it back. She didn't want to grow used to being here, encircled in his warmth. She would long for the sensation later, and Georgina didn't want to. "I should go."

"No, you should not." His arms tightened. "You are mine for the whole night whether I'm fucking you or not."

"You don't need to be vulgar to make your point." A pleasant warmth crossed her chest at his pronouncement.

"I'm not bloody finished." His cock thickened against her thigh. "Georgie," he whispered, pressing a kiss to the corner of her mouth before tipping up her mouth to his. She had no idea what he was thinking or if Leo felt anything for her at all. The length of his *cock*, she thought, remembering how she'd giggled when her cousin had taught her the word, rubbed sensuously against her still sensitive flesh.

"Why did you create Elysium?" she finally asked. "There were any number of things you could have done successfully besides establish a gaming hell and pleasure palace."

His fingers paused for a moment. "There aren't as many opportunities for a bastard as you might imagine."

Georgina thought that a great exaggeration. He could have done anything. Something less notorious that didn't require taking the purses of half the *ton*. But no, Leo liked the power it gave him, having those lords curry his favor. Of course he did.

"Besides, I won this mansion in a game of cards. I had to do something with it. The gardens were going to rot. Windows were broken. Urchins were living on the second floor."

Georgina suspected that wasn't the entire truth. "Urchins?"

"Grubby little things, urchins. Full of dirt and vermin."

"Not overly fond of children, are you?" Georgina's hand slid down his hip, liking the sounds he made.

"I have four younger sisters, as I'm sure you know. Well, three half-sisters and Amanda's ward."

"Amanda?"

"Marcus Barrington's wife. The duchess." The mention of his father iced the words. "Lovely woman. At any rate, the girls were always sticky. Olivia especially adored honey and it got all over me. Ruined one of my waistcoats."

"I like Olivia already."

He gave her a look of reproach. "They smelled bad, my sisters. I suppose they've improved but not by much."

"I'm sure you're exaggerating."

"I'm not. Amanda decided all of the girls must play a

61

musical instrument except Theodosia. She paints and thus was exempted from the tuneful torture."

"The tuneful torture?"

His lips quirked. "My brother is the only one in the family with any musical talent. Brilliant on the piano. I'm not sure how he listens to Andromeda banging on the keys without losing his mind."

"I'd no idea Welles plays the piano."

"Don't mention it to him. He's a bit sensitive on the subject. Olivia, Amanda's ward, is decent on a flute. But Phaedra." Leo rolled his eyes as if praying for divine intervention. "Her violin playing is akin to the screeching of cats mating. We all have to pretend we enjoy her on the violin so as not to discourage her musical talent. Which she does not possess."

Georgina stroked the line of his ribs, wondering at the unexpected glimpse into Leo's life. He'd mentioned his sisters only a handful of times. The duchess once or twice. But never Marcus Barrington, the Duke of Averell. He was estranged from his father; everyone in London knew the gossip about the duke and his two sons. Georgina knew what it was like to have a less than friendly relationship with one's father, though Leo and his brother's loathing of the duke seemed more . . . permanent.

Leo was intelligent. Utterly charming with the sort of magnetism that drew both men and especially women to him. A brilliant conversationalist with the ability to put his audience at ease with a few casually spoken words—a skill he often used to manipulate his listener. She'd seen him do it any number of times. He wore his illegitimacy like a badge of honor, forcing others to notice it, announcing it if they did not. Georgina had yet to see him truly angry. He would never lose control of his emotions because it would leave him vulnerable. Open.

Leo never told her any of those things, but she *knew* him. Far better than he thought she did.

"Are we friends, Leo?"

"Why is that so important to you, Georgie?"

Because she wanted to matter to him. To not be just another female he'd wanted to bed. And because he meant quite a lot to her. Leo was the anchor she'd clung to since coming to London. As safe to her as Beechwood Court.

"Because it is," she whispered.

His hand folded over her cheek, bringing their foreheads together. "You shouldn't be friends with a gambling hell owner." Leo's mouth grazed hers. "Do you want to be escorted out of London?"

"I see you very differently, Leo."

The sapphire of his eyes deepened. "Don't." His mouth fell on hers, sufficiently ending their conversation. The kiss was deep and possessive. Intimate. A slow gentle burn which dug deep into her bones, searing her soul. An eternity passed; their lips melded together, long enough for Georgina's mind to lose sight of anything else but Leo. The movement of his hands over her skin left her heart racing, his beautiful fingers adoring every inch of her. His mouth and tongue followed, blazing a trail across her body, worshipping Georgina until she moaned beneath him.

Exquisite was too dull a word for the experience.

When finally he settled between her thighs, whispering beautiful, sensual nonsense into her neck and hair, Leo entered her carefully, never once looking away. Lacing their fingers together above her head, the hard lines of his body sank into the cushion of hers, hips rocking in a dance more beautiful than any Georgina had ever experienced. A lazy roll of pleasure rippled up her body as she climaxed beneath him, sobbing out his name, her heart stopping. Leo groaned before withdrawing once more, spilling himself across her skin.

If she were given to swooning, now would have been the time. There had been so much more than the physical pleasure in that joining. Georgina's eyes fluttered closed, afraid Leo would see the truth of her feelings. "That was . . . lovely."

"Hmm." His lips moved against the nape of her neck, smiling as he once more rose from the settee. He returned to the door set into the wall, producing yet another damp cloth.

"Where are the warm water and endless supply of clean towels coming from, Leo?"

A tangle of dark hair fell over his forehead as he returned to her. The thick locks curled about his ears and cheek in disarray. "There's another door on the other side. One of the maids brings up warm water and fresh towels every hour or so without disturbing me."

Georgina's mood soured. The water and towels were a reminder that Leo must require such services with regularity if he entertained women in his office. "How convenient."

Tawdry is the word I believe you're looking for, Georgina.

"It is, under the circumstances." The warmth of the cloth wiped at her stomach. "I can't spend myself inside you, not if I'm trying to prevent a child. There are other methods." He frowned. "I'm usually better prepared." He gave her a sideways glance. "You knew withdrawing is—"

"Yes, of course," she interrupted, not wanting to show her ignorance. Georgina had surmised as much because it *did* make sense given the entire seed analogy. Her mother hadn't been very forthcoming with any facts about the marriage bed before Georgina wed Masterson. She assumed Georgina's brief relationship with Winbow had relieved her of such a duty. She'd tried to tell both her parents that nothing had happened with the riverboat gambler aside from a stolen kiss or two. And some touching, though she hadn't admitted to that.

It would be best if you stay in London for a time. Your father thinks it best, Georgina.

"So, if you wanted a child—" She put the pieces together in her mind.

"I don't." Ice shards flew from his mouth.

Well, that wasn't exactly what she'd been asking, her curiosity had been less personal in nature. She thought his response unwarranted. "Yes, but what if your method proved faulty? Surely under such circumstances, your child—"

"Would still be unwelcome. I have no desire to father a succession of bastards."

Her brow wrinkled as she tried to understand his vehemence. "If you were wed, the child wouldn't be a bastard."

"No children. Bastards or otherwise. Marriage is out of the question, lest you have aspirations in that direction. I'm a bloody gambling hell owner. What would I do with a wife?"

"I wasn't referring to myself, Leo," she snapped back at him, allowing that small bit of hope in her chest to wither. "I was speaking in general. I'm already married."

He turned away from her. "If something occurs after tonight, send a note to Peckham. He'll arrange for you to visit an apothecary who specializes in helping women who find themselves in unfortunate situations. There are potions a woman can take to rid herself of a child."

"I see." She wished she didn't.

His chin jerked back in her direction. "Any child of mine would carry the taint of my own birth, one made worse by Marcus Barrington, who insisted on claiming me." The sculpted lines of his face grew cold and accusatory. "You've no idea, so don't pretend to tell me I'm wrong."

"I won't." He wouldn't listen to her even if she did so. Leo's dislike of his father had many layers, she could see that. She thought he would have been just as furious, perhaps even more bitter, if the duke *hadn't* claimed him. "But you really wouldn't wish me to tell you if I became with child?"

"No. Send a note to Peckham." His mouth lowered to her breasts, tongue flicking against the taut peak of one nipple. "And I tire of this conversation, Georgina. My night with you is not yet over."

4

Leo uttered nary a word as Georgina slipped from his side and off the settee; she was instantly chilled without his body heat. The fire had long since died to embers, barely emitting any warmth. Outside the window behind Leo's desk, the night was slowly ebbing away, turning the sky a misty gray color, signaling that dawn wasn't far off. She'd fallen asleep without meaning to, comfortable in the circle of Leo's arms, secure in the warm cocoon of his office.

Time now to return to her life outside this room.

Hours would be spent, she was sure, on examining every aspect of this evening, even while Leo was likely inclined to forget her much sooner. Shiny baubles tended to lose their luster once bedded. He'd never answered her question about whether they were friends. An answer of itself, she supposed.

Naked, she walked to Leo's desk, feeling his eyes on her as she picked up the marker giving the holder possession of her body for an evening. Why couldn't he have just returned it to her? Or better, why hadn't she taken the damned thing and burned it immediately? Wagering herself had been fruitless. She'd lost far more to Leo than Beechwood Court.

"Stay, Georgie." The husky baritone floated around her.

She didn't answer. And she really needed him to not call her Georgie again.

Georgina walked across the room and tossed the marker into what was left of the fire. When it was finally no more than ash, she turned back to face Leo.

"I don't think so," she said, straightening her spine. The motion kept her steady as cracks formed across her heart. "I hate that piece of furniture." She nodded at the settee, the object of her true ruination. "You look like you're lying in a pool of blood."

He scowled back at her, clearly not caring for her tone. "Stay." This time it was more command than request.

"I'm not a dog, Mr. Murphy. I also don't answer to 'heel' or 'lay down'."

"You did last night," he snarled, not trying to hide his annoyance.

"I simply followed the dictates of the marker." She kept her response cool, somewhat surprised he'd allowed any emotion to bleed into their parting. But Georgina refused to reply in kind. Leo couldn't even admit to *liking* her. "You succeeded in bedding me. You won the wager."

Just look at him. Beautiful and naked, partially aroused. Regarding Georgina as if she were all that mattered in the world, which was so tragically far from the truth. Leo was very good at making women feel adored, Georgina could testify to that fact. Her mistake was in assuming she was different from any other woman he'd brought here or bedded. She wasn't.

"I realize other women might respond to such commands, but I'm not one of them. I hope I provided you sufficient challenge tonight."

"We wanted each other. I don't understand why you're so bloody angry with me, Georgie."

God, please stop saying my name as if I am dear to you.

"I heard no complaints earlier when you climaxed. Repeatedly."

"No complaints at all, Leo. I enjoyed myself immensely." There wasn't any reason to lie. Her legs shook as she approached the pile of her clothing. She twisted her hair, trying to put the curls into some semblance of decency with what few pins she could find.

I'm sure I look like a prostitute.

Leo stood and came to her aid, the awareness of his naked body so close to hers causing her skin to prickle. He pushed aside her fumbling efforts, helping her dress efficiently without so much as a sound, his touch as impersonal as any maid's.

"You're very good with women's clothing."

"I've had loads of practice."

Georgina stiffened at his tone, wanting out of this room before she lost what little control and dignity she still had. She moved away from him, taking her cloak from the nearby chair, struggling to put it on. She was suddenly desperate to leave.

He took the cloak from her and gently laid it over her shoulders. "If there is a problem later, you will —"

"Not bother you at all," she shot back before he could finish. "I understood your instruction perfectly well. I have taken it to heart."

He tried to kiss her, and Georgina stepped away, heading for the door.

"I want you to stay," he said again, a look of determination on his handsome features.

Leo was used to being obeyed.

Unfortunately, Georgina was inclined toward disobedience.

She paused at the door and looked back at him, standing

before the fire, every line of his naked, powerful body taut with anger. It seemed he *could* lose control. All it had taken was her.

"You're very entitled for a bastard, Mr. Murphy."

His fingers clenched at his sides. "*Leo.*"

"I don't think so." Her fingers shook and she hid them in the fabric of her cloak. "My marker has been fulfilled."

"Georgie—"

She fled out the door, nearly tripping over her skirts in her haste to be away, and pulled the knob, slamming the heavy wood behind her. Taking a breath, Georgina looked down at her slippers, trying to decide how she could leave Elysium without being seen, and ran right into a wall.

Smith.

Elysium's massive doorman was standing guard outside Leo's office. Barely older than Georgina, Smith was built like a small mountain, with massive arms and a lilt in his voice she'd never been able to place, though to her ears, everyone in London had an accent.

"My lady. Apologies. I didn't mean to startle you." He dipped his chin. "I'm to take you out the back, thru the gardens to your carriage. Discreetly. Mr. Murphy's instructions."

Georgina took in the overly large doorman, the broad shoulders and heavily muscled forearms. As an escort through Elysium, Smith was probably a good one for a woman who was bundled up in her cloak, hair falling from the hasty bun at the back of her neck. Smith probably escorted Leo's paramours from the club often. The thought made her stomach curdle. "Thank you."

She glanced back at the closed door, feeling Leo behind it. The inclination to return to him was very strong, almost overriding her common sense. But she turned back to Smith, commanding herself to move forward.

Smith led her down the carpeted hall, stopping abruptly and pushing softly with the palm of his hand against a stretch of wall. A door, cleverly hidden like the one in Leo's office, swung open enough for Smith to step through. Picking up a lamp just inside, Smith paused to light the wick and gestured for Georgina to follow him.

She took a cautious step forward. Elysium, Welles had once told her, was riddled with secret staircases, hallways, and hidden rooms. Under different circumstances, Georgina would have adored exploring.

"Watch your step, my lady."

She followed closely behind Smith, wondering if there were spiders or other vermin trapped in these walls, but she could see nothing except the circle of light around the hulking form ahead of her. Within moments, they emerged into a courtyard. Dawn was fast approaching, the misty gray of the horizon giving way to pale pink. She needed to get home. Masterson probably hadn't even noticed her absence, but Georgina was already a pariah to her neighbors, several of whom she suspected shared her whereabouts with Masterson's nephew. Harold always seemed to know when she was home or had gone out. Georgina had taken a hack to Elysium for that very reason—to remain unnoticed.

Oily unease settled in her stomach as she thought of Harold.

A carriage sat idling, not Georgina's own but a sleeker conveyance.

"Mr. Murphy's driver will take you home, my lady."

"I can take a hack if you'll find me one." Leo's carriage bore no identification; still, she didn't want to risk it. "Far more discreet."

Smith clearly didn't care for her suggestion, nonetheless, he walked around the corner, disappearing for several minutes. He returned with a nondescript carriage behind him, waving her forward.

"Thank you, Smith."

He placed her in the hack with a nod. She heard him mumble directions to her house to the driver.

Her *house*. The London town home of Lord Masterson wasn't her home. Given her husband was very close to impoverishment, she wondered if her father would welcome her back to New York. According to her sister's last letter, the scandal involving Winbow wasn't completely forgotten. Penance was a lengthy affair, it seemed. She was doomed to stay in this cold, dreary city with no friends for some time.

As the carriage rumbled through the quiet city, her thoughts were on Leo and everything that had passed between them. Part of Georgina refused to accept the most meaningful night of her life had meant nothing to him. That *she* meant nothing to him.

Pressing her face to the window, hollowness took hold within her.

Or perhaps she was merely the reckless, foolish girl she'd always been.

✿ 5 ✿

"**M**y lady," Anderson, Masterson's butler announced from the door. "There is a messenger for you. He has been told to wait for a response."

Georgina looked up from the handkerchief she was struggling to embroider. Good lord, she was terrible at needlework. Why had she even bothered?

Boredom.

She was woefully unprepared to be anyone's wife, lacking even the most basic skills, her mother had often bemoaned the fact. Masterson, however, didn't mind. What little use he had for her had long since expired. Looking down at the knotted bits of green thread decorating the edge of the handkerchief, Georgina thought they looked *somewhat* like leaves. Shaking her head, she placed the fabric aside, glad for the interruption.

"A messenger?" A snide voice drawled from across the room. "For Georgina? Don't you find that odd, Uncle?" Masterson's nephew assessed Georgina. He had the blackest

73

eyes, the pupils barely visible. Entirely unnerving but befitting the soulless creature Georgina took him to be.

"I find it odd." Clarissa, Harold's nitwit wife, parroted.

Georgina shot her a look. Clarissa rarely espoused her own thoughts, only repeated Harold's. It was doubtful she'd ever even *had* an original thought. Clarissa's spare, delicate form, the complete opposite of Georgina's, was bent over her own embroidery hoop as she calmly placed her perfect stitches upon her square of fabric. Always dressed in pale pink and muted greens, the ribbons adorning Clarissa's hair added to her child-like demeanor. But no amount of ribbon could hide the maliciousness gleaming in her pale blue eyes. Barely older than Georgina, Clarissa was as rotten as Harold. She was the daughter of a baron. Or a baronet.

Georgina could never discern the difference.

Masterson didn't bother to look up from the chess table where he sat with his nephew. "Odd? Not in the least." He waved a hand. "Georgina is having Beechwood Court's gardens redone. The beds have been left untended for many years. Probably a note from the head gardener. She's always going on about hedges and rose bushes."

"The folly is being rebuilt." Georgina hadn't even realized Masterson paid the least attention to what she did. "If you'll excuse me for a moment." She stood.

"A waste, in my estimation." Harold's dark eyes assessed her, dripping with disdain. "I'd sooner have it torn down rather than incur further costs."

Georgina wanted to smartly remind Harold of how little his opinion mattered because he didn't own Beechwood Court. Neither did she. Or Masterson.

At least, Georgina didn't think he did any longer.

The horses Masterson had used as collateral for the line of credit at Elysium still sat in the stable. The enormous stack of markers sitting in Leo's safe hadn't been called due. No solicitor had yet come to the door demanding the deeds to Beechwood Court or the hunting lodge in Scotland.

Merely a reprieve, she supposed. Georgina expected someone representing Leo to come pound at the door any day now.

A soft flutter occurred above her heart at the thought of Leo. She pressed a palm to her chest to stop the sensation.

"Don't you care, Uncle," Harold sneered, "that she spends our fortune so lavishly?"

"*Our* fortune? I'm not in the grave yet, Harold. Best you remember that."

Georgina shut the drawing room door before hearing Harold's whining response. The animosity between Masterson and his nephew was no great secret. Harold and Clarissa's weekly visits were torturous, made only so that Harold could inspect his uncle's health and the house that would one day be his. He showed little interest in Masterson's ancestral estate, probably because it was too far away from the London social whirl.

Harold's ambitions were very transparent.

As was his dislike for Georgina. If Masterson was aware of the thinly veiled insults and disrespect his nephew threw at her, he gave little indication. Harold delighted in deriding Georgina for what he considered flagrant spending. Her trips to Elysium, Harold claimed, would put them all in the poorhouse.

Well, he needn't worry about my trips to Elysium any longer. Georgina had been studiously avoiding the gambling hell.

The worst part of Harold's visits was the blatant way his coal-black eyes studied Georgina's mid-section, obsessively searching for any sign she might be with child. He lived in fear of his uncle producing an heir, though he needn't have bothered.

Georgina made her way downstairs accompanied by

Anderson. Masterson's butler was discreet, as any of Masterson's staff had to be given his proclivities. Anderson had served her husband for years and seemed a decent sort, though he'd politely rebuffed any friendly attempts by Georgina to know him better. Overfamiliarity with the staff was frowned upon.

Anderson led her past the foyer to the kitchen door, where a young boy stood with a note in his hand. He shifted on his feet, eyeing a plate of biscuits sitting just out of reach. Georgina instructed one of the kitchen maids to feed the boy and bring him some milk as she took the note.

As she expected, it was merely a note from the newly hired head gardener at Beechwood Court. Why then, was she filled with such disappointment?

"Please wait," she said to the boy. "I'll write out a reply."

The boy nodded, already stuffing his mouth full of biscuits.

Leo was not going to send her a note. Nor flowers. Or an invitation for a carriage ride. Besides such behavior being improper for a married woman, even one wed to Masterson, the very idea was absurd. The greatest lengths Leo would ever go to for her was teaching her how to play cards or bedding her on a blood-red settee in his office. After all the time they'd spent in each other's company, Georgina thought she had at least merited a damned bed.

Elysium had become a sort of refuge for her when she wasn't at Beechwood Court, because of Leo. Now—

Pain pinched at her heart.

There would be no more evenings sipping bourbon while he instructed her on whist. No more comfort to be had from the scent of cheroot and sandalwood. She had a list of insults prepared for his waistcoats which would now go unused. Georgina was terribly lonely in a way she hadn't expected.

I hadn't thought I'd miss him nearly so much.

That wasn't entirely the truth. Missing him was to be expected because Leo meant a great deal to her. Her eyes shut as she stood in the corridor, remembering the look in his eyes as he'd joined his body to hers. He hadn't been able to hide from her at that moment, no matter the horrible things he'd said later.

"Damn." Georgina pushed Leo firmly away as she opened her eyes once again and made her way up the stairs to the small parlor she often used for reading or her correspondence. A quick note to the gardener that she did not want her hedges trimmed into the shape of a dog or some other animal was warranted. She sat down at her desk and quickly wrote out her instructions.

"A message from your lover, Georgina? Need to send a prompt reply?"

Georgina's fingers stilled on the note, then picked up the paper as she turned to meet Harold's flat, dead eyes. "The gardener, Harold. He's seducing me over hedges shaped like rabbits. Care to read my reply?"

God, how she hated his eyes. Deep wells of absolute darkness.

Harold's lip curled. "I really don't care for your waspish tongue, Georgina."

"Then perhaps you should avoid speaking directly to me." She walked swiftly to the door to slide past him, careful to avoid getting too close.

"My uncle may appreciate your insolence, but I do not. Nor will I have any tolerance at all should your lover, whomever he may be, put a bastard in your belly."

Harold couldn't possibly know about Leo. No one did. Except possibly Smith who'd stood guard outside Leo's office and likely heard her screams of pleasure. Masterson hadn't even been home when she'd returned from Elysium. "How dare you threaten me with your ridiculous accusations. Step aside." Her skin crawled with revulsion as if she were sidling up next to a snake.

He grabbed her elbow. "Don't you dare try to usurp me, Georgina. *I* am the heir."

"Yes, as you often remind me." She wrenched her elbow out of his grasp. "I don't care about titles, Harold. I never have."

"Do you think I believe you?" He leaned in. "Your tattered pedigree fairly dictates you'd do anything to raise yourself out of the filthy backwater you were born to and claim one of England's oldest titles. Rest assured, if you imagine you will bring a cuckoo into *this* nest and present it to be my uncle's, be forewarned. I won't allow it."

Stand your ground, Georgie. Grandmother's words whispered in her ear.

Georgina immediately straightened her spine. "Perhaps I should relate to my husband your concerns so he can address them directly." Not that Masterson would care or even listen.

He followed her out into the hall, stepping in front of her. "I know you do not share my uncle's bed." The black pebbles of his eyes drew down the length of her. "But I'm sure you've spread yourself all over London." He towered over her. "Don't assume you will outsmart me. I'm far more intelligent than you realize."

And insane. Why hadn't she noticed the glimmer of madness in Harold before?

Georgina held herself still, determined not to waver. She glared back at him as he moved away. Pausing just outside the drawing room door, he drawled, "Aren't you going to rejoin us? Clarissa might be induced to show you how to stitch a bit of linen properly." Then he disappeared to resume his chess game with Masterson.

She took a deep breath to calm herself. A confrontation with Harold was always unsettling. He loathed her, that much was apparent. Harold coveted his uncle's title and the fortune he assumed Masterson still had. What would he say if he knew of his uncle's markers, residing in Leo Murphy's office?

She gripped the note to the gardener in her hand, wrinkling the paper and smearing her instructions into an inky mess. The letter would need to be rewritten if she didn't want to end up with a parade of shrubs cut into animals. Georgina turned on her heel, making her way back to the parlor, Harold's threats still echoing in her ears.

She had no doubt Harold meant every single one.

❧ 6 ❧

"**C**ome, my dear."

Masterson held out a shaky hand to assist her out of their carriage.

Georgina stepped down, pulling her wrap tighter around her shoulders, wishing she hadn't worn a gown that bared her shoulders and a great deal of her bosom. But defiance, as well as old habits, were difficult to put aside.

"I'm rather tired, my lord." She tried once more to get Masterson to return home. The first attempt had been after the gathering at Lord Talbot's home she'd been forced to attend.

"Pish posh, Georgina." He slid his eyes over her. "Play a hand of faro or piquet."

Georgina pulled the thin silk more firmly over her chest. She'd protested leaving the house this evening, claiming a terrible headache, but Masterson had been insistent, turning a deaf ear to her pleas.

Elysium loomed before her, immense, opulent, and enticing as ever, but she was loath to go inside. Her slippers dragged on the gravel as Masterson led her to the door. She was in no mood to face Leo or have him treat her as if she were only another of his patrons. Nor did she wish to see another woman drape herself over his broad-shouldered form. Georgina had been avoiding Elysium because *she* couldn't pretend he meant nothing to her.

There was no help for it. Georgina summoned all the steel her spine possessed, tilting her chin and pasting a careless look on her face. She could brave this out. Welles might be here, and he would play faro with her.

Jones, Elysium's one-armed doorman, and Smith nodded to Georgina as she came through the door. The sound of the gambling hell struck her first, the low hum punctuated by shouts and curses. The sea of black from the gentleman's evening wear with flashes of color from the gowns of those few ladies in attendance.

Discreetly, she snuck a look up at the second-floor landing, but there was no sign of Leo.

Taking a deep breath, Georgina dropped Masterson's arm with a nod. "I'm headed to the faro table." Tonight required bourbon. After telling Leo several months after they'd first met of her affection for bourbon whiskey, he'd surprised her by saying he happened to have some on hand. A mix-up with the merchant who kept Elysium stocked with spirits. The bourbon sat gathering dust because no one ever requested it. But now she had. A lucky coincidence.

Leo had also had bourbon in his office that night, though he preferred scotch as a rule.

He'd known she would come to him about the marker. And Beechwood Court.

Masterson didn't say a word as he went in search of his own pleasures. He must have one of his barristers or footmen meeting him on the second floor. He was hardly in a position to request another line of credit from Leo.

She settled down on a stool, smiling at Larkin, who was

tending to the faro table as usual. Georgina studied her cards as a glass of bourbon appeared next to her, along with a large, masculine form.

Her heart paused before she raised her head, thinking for a moment it was Leo.

The coat of indigo was finely made, so dark as to be nearly black. But the waistcoat was plain. The snowy white cravat neatly tied. Welles needed little adornment—a fact he was well aware of.

"Lady Masterson." He smiled down at her. "Where have you been?" He nudged the glass of bourbon in her direction. "Bourbon?"

"Thank you." Her fingers curled around the glass, nodding at him as she took a sip. "I've been busy. I'm renovating Beechwood Court. The gardens are being redrawn. The folly rebuilt. And there is a leak in the roof."

Georgina was determined to continue to bring Beechwood Court back to life. She meant to keep working on the estate until one of Leo's solicitors arrived on her doorstep and told her to stop. There was little else to do with her time.

"Very industrious of you, Georgina." Welles brushed back a dark wave of hair from his forehead. Two women over his shoulder were staring, struck dumb by his brilliance.

Georgina looked back at the green baize of the table, littered with chips. He looked very much like Leo, or rather Leo resembled him. The sight of Welles was more difficult than she'd supposed. "Are you playing tonight?"

"Always." He nudged her in familiar fashion with his shoulder. Welles flirted casually with her, but there was never any true intent in his manner. He was purported to be a rake, though he never behaved improperly with her.

"My lord, we are friends, are we not?"

"We absolutely are." He leaned closer. "But I reserve the right to admire your bosom on occasion."

"Granted." She smiled and took a sip of her bourbon. "Why have you never made advances at me?"

Welles sat back, surprised by her question. "You'd throw a punch, as you did to that lord." He snapped his fingers. "I can't recall his name. Braden? Broward?"

"Browden," she answered. "There isn't any need to worry. I'm not enamored of you as every woman in London is, I'm merely curious."

He snorted. "I should be insulted. I suppose I haven't because I don't care for fistfights. Goodness, Georgina. I just told you I meant to admire your bosom."

"Yes, but you won't admire it. In fact, I've seen you deliberately avoid looking anywhere but at my face."

"I told you, I don't care for fistfights." His eyes grew shadowed.

Welles wasn't talking about *her* throwing a punch despite his comment about Browden. "Is there another reason?" What good would come of her asking?

"There is nothing to be gained by asking something you already know the answer to." Welles drummed his fingers against the table. "He'll never marry you, Georgina," Welles said in a curt tone. "Even if Masterson were to drop dead this instant."

"I don't think that is what I asked you," she retorted.

"It is exactly what you asked." He shook his head. "I don't want to see you hurt. And with him, you will be."

"You can't be sure of that." Georgina bit her lip. "Being a bastard doesn't dictate one's life."

"It does for him. Just as being Averell's heir dictates mine." Welles stood, handsome features shuttered, emotions carefully locked away from her. So much like Leo. "I *am* your friend, Georgina. I always will be. I'll even introduce you to my family. You'd like Amanda and the girls."

"But not the duke." She said the last bit purely out of spite.

Welles narrowed his eyes at her. "Enjoy your evening, Lady Masterson." He bowed before walking stiffly away in the direction of one of the private dining rooms at the back, the ladies in attendance tonight practically swooning as he passed.

Georgina took another sip of her bourbon, allowing the liquid to sit on her tongue. Welles knew Leo far better than Georgina did. She closed her eyes, picturing Leo standing naked before the fire, demanding she stay with him. Behavior which seemed at odds with what Welles had just told her.

She could speculate all she wished.

Or Georgina could listen to her heart.

Jerking to her feet, Georgina collected her chips and wandered away from the faro table. Glancing up to the second-floor landing, she saw Leo was still absent. She wound her way around the gaming floor, meaning to climb the stairs to Leo's office and just *ask* him. She might not care for the answer Leo gave, but it was better than sitting about wondering if there was anything more between them.

"Mr. Peckham." She paused as Leo's floor manager came down the stairs. "Is Mr. Murphy about? In his office, perhaps?"

"No, my lady. I believe he went to the garden to smoke." Peckham's gaze looked up the stairs in the direction of Leo's office before returning to her. "I can take you to him."

"Thank you." She nodded, allowing Peckham to lead her down a hall to a door, which, when opened, revealed another entrance to the courtyard and gardens. The gardens weren't open to Elysium's members or their guests. Only Leo and Welles came here.

Peckham left her with a strapping young man, built much

like Smith, standing before a metal gate. "Jasper, this is Lady Masterson. She wishes to speak to Mr. Murphy."

"My lady." Jasper bowed and led her outside, directing her wordlessly toward the sound of water. There was a large fountain sitting squarely in the middle of the garden, something she hadn't taken much notice of the last time she was here. A lamp glowed in a dark corner where Georgina suspected she would find a bench and Leo.

She skirted a row of hedges, reminded by the sudden release of butterflies in her stomach of how much she'd missed Leo. Walking past the fountain, she stopped to take in the stone monstrosity. Where had Leo found such an incredibly lewd fountain? She looked up in wonder as water spilled from the open mouth of a voluptuous woman, completely naked except for a chiseled bit of fabric flowing about her hips. Her breasts were enormous. Oversized. The peaks of her nipples protruded several inches. Two cherubs frolicked below the woman, leering up at her, lust stamped on their angelic features.

"Obscene," Georgina said tartly into the night air. "If a person were so unlucky as to stumble and fall into this fountain, they could well lose an eye to a stone nipple."

A soft, amused rumble filled the air. "Hello, Georgie."

It should be a crime, the way he purred her name, filling her mind with all sorts of illicit thoughts, reminding her of how their bodies had moved together so perfectly. Her pulse beat rapidly in her throat as Georgina sat down beside Leo on the stone bench, careful to keep some distance between them.

Light moved over his face as he lifted the lamp and took note of how far away from him she sat. "I won't bite, Georgie. Even if you ask me to."

I do wish he wouldn't call me Georgie. It weakened her. Made her long to crawl into his lap and curl up like a kitten.

"Your skin is perfect for nibbling," he continued. "Do you want to know how I'd start?" His voice lowered. "*Where* I'd begin?"

Georgina wasn't sure what to make of his teasing but thought his flirtatious manner might have to do with the scotch scenting his breath. Leo rarely drank to excess in the evenings and never alone in the garden while Elysium was full to bursting with guests.

"There is a spot right where your hip joins your thigh," he said in a whisper. "Very soft. And I can smell the sweetness of your quim." He glanced up at her, handsome features stark. "What? Were you expecting a flowery compliment? Perhaps a bloody ode to your eyelashes?" The amused note vanished. "You'll have to find another gentleman for that."

"I suppose I should." Georgina tilted her chin at him.

His brow wrinkled before smoothing out again. Reaching out, he ran his forefinger along the edge of her neckline, trailing heat across her chest before pulling back.

"Do you mind?" Leo pulled a cheroot out of his pocket without waiting for a response.

He flicked his wrist, lighting the end. The fragrant smoke spiraled up into the air above their heads, disappearing into the night. They sat in companionable silence for some time, with only the sound of the fountain.

"May I?" she said, holding out her hand for the cheroot.

He gave her an odd look but handed it over, the brush of his fingers against hers sending a tingle down her arm.

Georgina hadn't indulged in a cheroot since coming to London, and before, she'd only done so to shock whatever gentleman had produced it from his pocket. Ben, ever complicit in her bad behavior, had taught her one day when she was fifteen. Maybe sixteen. It had become a small bit of rebellion to steal cheroots from her father's study.

She took a short puff, blowing out a series of perfect smoke rings.

A sound came from Leo, sifting beneath her skirts like a wisp of the cheroot smoke, winding its way up her silken clad legs, identical to the sound he'd made when his head had been between her thighs.

"Quite a trick." Taking the cheroot from her, he drew in the smoke then leaned over and caught his mouth against hers, blowing the smoke gently between her lips before breaking away.

Georgina immediately formed her mouth into an 'O' and blew another perfect ring of smoke into the night air. She turned with a wiggle of her brows to find his gaze fixed on her. "I have many talents."

Tossing the cheroot, he ground it beneath his heel and reached for her before Georgina had a chance to move away. Fingers wrapping around the back of her neck, Leo pulled her close, mouth slanting against hers with exquisite tenderness.

"I still remember," he whispered against her lips, "the first time I saw you. Powder blue silk, your dangerously low neckline edged in Belgian lace. I kept waiting for a nipple to pop out."

"I wasn't sure you even noticed I had a bosom."

"I noticed everything about you. The way the silk of your gown rustled when you moved. The sound of your accent flattening every lovely word you spoke. Your scent, like something wild growing in the forest."

"I told you." Heat wafted off his body. "It is only soap."

"I couldn't take my eyes from you. I still can't." Leo leaned back, eyes shining with something that looked very much like anguish before he jerked his head away.

"Leo—"

"But as much as I . . . enjoy you." His voice grew brittle.

"The challenge is in *gaining* the shiny bauble, not necessarily in keeping it."

Georgina's heart tightened painfully. "I see." There wasn't even so much as a tremor in her voice as he flayed her open and compared her to a damned trinket. She could be proud of that, at the very least.

"The problem is," his voice grew icy, "I find myself unable to choose only *one* bauble."

"Oh, there you are." As if on cue, a giggling feminine voice sounded from the other side of the fountain. "I confess, Leo. When you asked me to wait for you in your office, I hadn't thought you meant to be so long." The woman's red hair shone like copper as she came closer to the lantern at Leo's feet.

Lady Dunley.

A whoosh of air left Georgina's lungs. Well, she had wanted an answer.

Stand your ground, Georgie.

How she wished her grandmother was here now, preferably with some sort of firearm. As a matter of fact, Lady Dunley reminded Georgina of one of those red squirrels Grandmother had despised so much.

"Who is this?" Lady Dunley peered at Georgina. "Oh, you're that American girl, aren't you? The one married to Masterson." Another twitter. "Whatever are you doing out here?"

"Lady Masterson was asking about her husband's markers," Leo said smoothly. "I've told her that it is a matter for gentlemen to discuss."

Georgina snorted in derision even as her heart was torn apart. "Yes. Gentlemen. Because you are one."

Lady Dunley's delicate nose wrinkled at Georgina. "I would have thought after so much time, that dreadful sound would have lessened. Quaint, I suppose you would call it."

If I had a damned acorn, I'd toss it at her.

"Lady Dunley," Leo said quietly. "I need a word with Lady Masterson. If you would return inside, I'll be along directly." He shifted in Georgina's direction, the handsome lines of his face pulled tight.

"I am very quaint, my lady," Georgina said, exaggerating her speech. "My grandmother used to shoot squirrels out of trees. Oddly enough, their fur was about the same color as your hair."

Lady Dunley gasped. "You rude little cretin. No wonder Lady Talbot—"

"I care less for Lady Talbot's opinion than I do for yours." Georgina turned back to Leo. "My grandmother was an interesting woman. Full of all sorts of wisdom. And able to see a person's true nature." Georgina stood and smoothed her skirts, her eyes never leaving Leo's face. "She would have taken one look at you, Mr. Murphy, and said you can't dress up a pig."

Leo's face darkened, his wide mouth scowling at her. "Don't, Georgina."

"Because even in the *finest* clothes," she continued, waving her fingers at his expensively tailored coat, "underneath, there is *still* a pig." She smiled broadly and turned to the scandalized woman before her who looked about to have a fit of apoplexy. Perhaps Lady Dunley would be so distressed she would fall into the fountain and hit her head on one of those stupid cherubs. Or be pierced through the heart by an elongated stone nipple. "I bid you both good evening."

Georgina turned, careful to keep her back ramrod straight and her hands still by her sides as Lady Dunley sputtered in shock behind her. The taste of Leo and the cheroot still lingered on Georgina's lips.

She had her answer, only it wasn't the one she'd wanted.

She should have listened to Welles after all.

HE HAD, IN NO WAY, THOUGHT IT WOULD FEEL LIKE THIS.

Leo had been shot. Stabbed in the ribs. Fallen off a horse. Nearly drowned, no thanks to Tony. But this? Far worse.

After their night together, Leo had thought of nothing *but* her. The feel of her supple form curved to his and the scent of spring in his nostrils. All that . . . *longing* for Georgina had made him furious. His usual control had slipped. Even Tony had commented on his ill humor.

Why couldn't he have merely fucked Georgina and been done with it?

He pulled out the bottle of scotch from underneath the bench, swallowing down several mouthfuls, listening to the muted sounds of Elysium behind him. The courtyard and gardens themselves were silent except for the water spilling from the fountain. Lady Dunley had thankfully returned inside, still hissing at being compared to a squirrel, led away by the ever-efficient Peckham. Poor Peckham, blustering out apologies for having allowed Lady Dunley to escape Leo's office. Leo still didn't know what she wanted with him. Nor did he care. The note she'd sent earlier asking to speak to him had been intentionally vague.

But Georgina had assumed the worst, and Leo had allowed her to.

"Don't you dare judge me," Leo hissed to one of the stone cherubs staring in his direction from the fountain. "A few months from now, Georgina will thank me that at least one of us had the sense to put a stop to this."

Regrets were useless. It was done. In time, he'd forget her. London was full of luscious young ladies with a taste for adventure who would welcome Leo into their beds. Possibly even an American or two.

Underneath there is still a pig.

A choked sound erupted from him, and Leo quickly took a mouthful of scotch to swallow it away. The amber liquid burned into his belly but provided little relief from the cold setting in across his chest and seeping into his bones. Leo tipped the bottle to his lips once more, knowing it would do no good. There was not enough scotch in all of London to ease the hollow feeling inside him.

7

Georgina peered through the veil covering her face, wishing she were anywhere but here, sitting in the drawing room listening to the false grief of Harold and his terrible wife, Clarissa. She'd endured their presence nearly every day the last month or so as her husband lay dying. Tolerated the threats Harold had taken great pleasure in hurling toward her at every opportunity. Had she been unconvinced of the state of his mind before, she was no longer.

Even if my uncle had managed to get you with child, which, as we both know, is doubtful at best, I would insist on being made guardian, Georgina. You are unfit to be anyone's mother. Just look at you.

Harold's determination to assume the mantel of the earldom now bordered on fanatical obsession. When Masterson became ill, collapsing after a rather strenuous bout of activity with a recently hired groom, Harold and Clarissa had arrived before Georgina could even send for them. Masterson's heir had appeared with his trunks, hovering about his uncle like some greedy vulture waiting to pick clean the bones. Harold had taken to roaming the halls late at night, examining every knick-knack, vase, painting, or other objects d'art, writing carefully in a small notebook he carried. Once, Georgina had caught Harold below stairs, counting out the silver in front of Anderson, the butler.

I do hope you haven't taken a lover, Georgina. Do remember, I won't tolerate a cuckoo in the nest.

She'd had no lovers save one. She hadn't the heart for another.

Harold wanted her gone from England, and Georgina heartily agreed. There was nothing to keep her in London now that Masterson had died. No reason to linger in a city in which she'd never felt welcome.

A pair of glorious blue eyes held hers. The movement of their hips rocking together. The sheer *rightness* of having been with Leo. Looking back on their last discussion, outside in Elysium's private courtyard beside that obscene fountain, Georgina had realized not only her love for Leo but his inability to return the affection. She was forever doomed to want the attentions of men who couldn't return them; her father, Winbow, even Masterson to some extent. All of them thought her no more than a chess piece to be moved about to suit their needs.

She missed Leo but didn't want to.

There were days, as Masterson suffered, Harold threatened, and Clarissa insulted, when Georgina had to run to her rooms to weep, desperately longing for Leo. His importance in her life hadn't become apparent until she had been faced with his absence. How she had depended on, of all people, the owner of a gambling establishment.

Welles had sent her a note just prior to Masterson's death offering to take her to the park or accompany her to Elysium, but she had refused. Georgina was never sure if he knew what had transpired between her and Leo. And even though she had been miserable trapped inside this house with a man dying a slow and painful death, Georgina couldn't bring herself to spend time with Welles. He looked far too much like Leo. No sense in torturing herself further.

Georgina's stomach pitched and heaved as she watched Clarissa, now Lady Masterson, glide across the drawing room, careful to pose herself against the light coming through the windows. Harold's wife was a vain, silly creature, full of malice and ridiculous affectations of speech. She was pretty, rosy-cheeked, well-bred, and young. Still, Clarissa had yet to provide Harold with his own heir, a fact which led to heated, whispered arguments between the two of them when they thought Georgina wasn't listening.

It was Georgina's only source of amusement.

Nausea swirled in her stomach once more. Perhaps she should have avoided the bit of poached egg at breakfast. Nursing Masterson through his illness, something he hadn't deserved but Georgina had done nonetheless, had sapped a great deal of her strength. Weeks of watching him cough out his life into bloody handkerchiefs while he hallucinated had taken a toll. She hadn't felt well in some time.

A twitter came from the ladies surrounding Clarissa as they sipped their tea and gossiped, casting careful glances in Georgina's direction.

Ugh. Georgina was glad for the veil covering her face.

A steady stream of callers arrived daily at the Masterson home under the guise of offering condolences when what they really wanted to do was to gawk at Georgina. Masterson's ill-bred bride from America. Lady Martin, a close acquaintance of Clarissa's, eyed Georgina as if she were some sort of wild animal, asking in a hushed tone if it were true, that Georgina's grandfather had *actually* sailed a barge.

Yes, Georgina had answered. *My grandfather earned his wealth through hard work.*

Clarissa had glared. Lady Martin had paled before her lips curled into a sneer.

Harold, snowy white cravat perfectly knotted, coat impeccably tailored, leaned against the fireplace, acting every inch the lord of the manor. Superiority dripped from every pore. He seemed in deep conversation with Lord Sharpton, gracefully sipping from a snifter of brandy. Every so often, his eyes moved to Georgina, frigid with loathing.

Not one moment more could she sit here among these horrid people who wished her nothing but ill. The sun was out. The air crisp. Georgina stood, deciding this intolerable day would be better spent in the gardens, which were free of Harold's dreadful pomade and Clarissa's mindless chattering. No one seemed to care that Masterson had died an agonizing death, blood spewing from his eyes and mouth as he expired. A grisly sight and one which still haunted her. True, she hadn't particularly cared for Masterson, often wishing him gone so she could finally return to New York, but he hadn't deserved such a horrible end. Even his loyal valet had deserted Masterson. Certainly, none of his young paramours had visited. Harold and Clarissa, both holding handkerchiefs to their noses, had refused to enter Masterson's bedroom even to bid him farewell.

So, Georgina had nursed her husband, holding his hand, not wishing him to die alone.

She slid quietly from the drawing room, holding the heavy bombazine skirts with her hands lest they rustle loudly and draw attention. Not one head lifted in her direction, though Georgina was certain Harold watched her.

He always watched her.

The garden wasn't much of one, at least not anymore. Masterson's gardener had been let go months before, and the once carefully manicured beds were now overgrown. A lone bench, well-hidden, sat amidst a circle of rose bushes in dire need of a trim. She would be safe for a time in the garden. Perhaps any casual observer would mistake Georgina for a large crow.

Passing Anderson, now Harold's butler, on her way out the terrace door, she noted the anxious look on his face as he hurried in the direction of the drawing room.

Oh dear. Could Cook not find haddock for dinner tonight? Harold would be so disappointed.

Georgina walked out on the terrace, looking down at her skirts in disgust. Wearing nothing but black for the next year wasn't the least appealing. She tossed back her veil and took a deep breath, feeling the sun on her face. Closing her eyes, Georgina stayed still, blotting out everything but the sound of the birds and the wind whistling through the trees.

"Lady Masterson."

Georgina slowly lowered her chin and opened her eyes at the familiar baritone. Her first thought was that Welles had snuck into the gardens, then her heart leapt at the hope it might be Leo.

But neither was true.

She didn't know the outrageously handsome gentleman before her, though she had an idea of who he must be. The tiny lift at the corner of his wide mouth was identical to Leo's, though it was Welles who resembled him most strongly. Silver was sprinkled liberally in his dark hair and small lines radiated out from his beautiful blue eyes with their distinct ring of indigo.

Her mouth dropped open at the sight of him. She was staring.

A knowing look crossed his handsome features. He was well aware of how his presence affected the fairer sex. How could he not be? Women must throw themselves at him. Probably had for years.

"I am the Duke of Averell."

It was impossible to mistake him for anyone else. She'd been avoiding Welles because he looked so much like Leo, yet here she was having not left her house, faced with yet another version of the man she was trying so hard to forget.

What were the odds she would meet Leo's estranged father?

Quite high, as it turns out. Leo would know.

"Forgive me for appearing without proper introduction." The duke nodded in the direction of the house. "I saw you sneak away as I came in."

Unsure exactly what to do when a duke introduced himself, Georgina executed a perfect curtsy. "Your Grace. If you are here for Lord Masterson—"

"I'm not," he replied in a chilly tone. "I am here to speak to you, Lady Masterson."

Georgina was sure no woman in her right mind had *ever* refused this man. His sons had inherited the same innate sensuality and arrogance. A potent draw for any female. She didn't know much about the Duke of Averell other than what she'd gleaned from gossip. He was rarely in town, preferring to spend his time with his duchess in the country, though at one time, Marcus Barrington had been the most notorious rake in London.

Who could blame him? *Good Lord.*

Oddly enough, while neither Welles nor Leo had told her the reason for their shared hatred of Marcus Barrington, Clarissa had not been so silent. Upon seeing that Welles had sent Georgina a note after Masterson's death, the entire sordid tale had been revealed at the dinner table while they enjoyed Cook's excellent roast duck. Marcus Barrington, in his arrogance, had kept his wife and mistress under the same roof for years. Both had borne sons. Leo and Welles. Welles's mother had died tragically after discovering the existence of both mistress and bastard.

"Her own lady's maid was the duke's lover. Can you imagine? She went to confront Averell." Clarissa had savagely cut into a bite of duck. "She was with child and tripped down a flight of stairs. Both she and the babe died."

Georgina could clearly see, as could anyone with a brain, that Welles blamed the duke for the death of his mother. The reason behind Leo's hatred was less clear.

"You're here to speak to me?" she said to the duke. Welles wouldn't have sent him. Nor Leo. Neither of them was on speaking terms with Averell. She doubted that had changed.

"I can see you are surprised by my sudden appearance. People often are. The advantage of being a duke. Shall we stroll about?" Without waiting for a response, he tucked her hand into his elbow and started down the small, winding path in the direction of the grouping of rose bushes.

Marcus Barrington smelled wonderful. Like leather and cheroot. There was something very protective about him, as if he would volunteer to slay dragons in her defense if only Georgina would ask. Georgina thought that part of his attraction. Leo invoked the same response in her.

All well and good, but why was Averell here and asking to speak to her?

When they reached the bench behind the rose bushes, Averell paused and glanced back in the direction of the house.

Did Harold know he was here? Anderson must be relating the news of the duke's arrival even now. Harold would be apoplectic at knowing Georgina was conversing with Averell.

"This is an odd meeting, I'm aware." Long, elegant fingers drummed against one thigh. "And don't concern yourself with the newly minted Lord Masterson. I'll merely tell him I came to discuss an outstanding debt with you. He need not know the debt is mine and not his uncle's."

"A debt? My apologies, Your Grace, but I find it difficult to believe that anyone would owe my husband rather than the other way around."

The tiny bits of gold floating in his eyes sparkled back at her. "Strange, I'll grant you. But it is a debt I must repay. I don't come to London very often and only recently became aware of his death."

"My husband had not been in the best health for some time. He collapsed one day, lingering for many weeks." Many agonizing weeks. Masterson suffered greatly before he finally died.

"Death comes for all of us." The duke looked away from her for several moments before turning back to her with a smile. "I would make amends before mine, my lady. I am trying to be a better man." He gave her a pointed look. "My debt now belongs to you."

"I don't understand." Georgina's stomach pitched again. She really should have avoided the poached egg this morning. The scent of Harold's pomade, still lodged in her nostrils, wasn't helping. And the duke looked so much like Leo. *Sounded* like Leo. It was disorienting.

"Lady Masterson." Concern lit his handsome features. "You seem . . . unwell. I didn't mean to upset you. Most people would be happy to have a duke owe them a debt."

Georgina placed a gloved hand over her mouth. "My apologies, Your Grace. The last month has been demanding."

"Hmm." His gaze ran over her face and down to her mid-section.

"Oh. Dear." She placed her hand over her lips feeling her breakfast about to make a reappearance. Her hearty constitution had deserted her of late.

"Over here." Averell pulled her firmly to a large pot filled with a spray of half-dead peonies and ferns.

To her utter shame, Georgina cast up all her breakfast and possibly some of last night's dinner. Clarissa insisted a rich sauce accompany every meal. Elaborate desserts rather than fruit or cheese. Georgina's stomach didn't care for the change in the menu.

"I'm so sorry," she murmured as another wave of sickness had her grabbing the edge of the pot. This would finish off the poor peonies immediately, though the fern might yet survive.

The duke patted her back gently, murmuring consoling words in a low tone, sounding very much like Leo. Holding out a monogrammed handkerchief, he dabbed gently at her mouth while she stood horrified at having become ill. Tears pricked her eyes. Georgina had rarely, if ever, cried, until recently. But between Leo, feeling ill most of the time, and Harold's growing hatred, Georgina found herself shamefully weeping at the slightest provocation.

"Please forgive me, Your Grace," she whispered as he directed her back to the stone bench.

"Not at all, my lady." He regarded her with concern. "Perhaps you should go inside. We can continue our conversation at another time."

"No, I'm better. Please, return to what you were saying before my unfortunate accident. You are trying to be a better man. Repaying debts and the like. Very honorable." She clasped her hands. "I forgive you my husband's debt, Your Grace." Georgina gave him a weak smile.

The sea of blue took her in from head to toe with a frown. "Do you often become ill at breakfast, Lady Masterson? Or dinner?"

"Are you suggesting Harold is having me poisoned?" It was a valid question. She had been ill. And Masterson had, unbelievably, left her a large portion of what remained of his fortune, most she hadn't known he had, as well as Beechwood Court. Harold, of course, received everything else which oddly enough still included a hunting lodge in Scotland and four horses still residing in the stables. The last time she'd visited Elysium, it had been with Masterson, and he'd insisted she accompany him. Had Masterson made some sort of arrangement with Leo, perhaps pleaded with him to forgive his debts? When she'd questioned Mr. Lind, her solicitor, he'd assured her everything was in perfect order.

Georgina didn't dare think of the markers in Leo's office.

Harold hadn't been pleased, particularly about Beechwood Court, which he coveted merely because it belonged to Georgina. But she didn't think him murderous.

Not yet.

"Masterson didn't like his nephew. If you feel you are being threatened—"

Only every day.

"—then I will apprise Harold you are under my protection."

"That isn't necessary, Your Grace. Harold and I don't get on. We never have. But I don't believe he means to do me harm." Things would become that much more difficult for Georgina if Harold suspected she'd caught the attention of Averell. And if the gossips found out Averell had offered her protection? "I do not wish to cause your duchess any distress, especially when you seek only to be kind."

A soft laugh came from him. "Her Grace knows better. But I take your point." One elegant hand fluttered in the direction of her mid-section. "However, I believe *you* require my assistance at the very least."

Georgina swallowed, feeling the blood drain from her face. "I'm not sure I understand what you're implying, Your

Grace." Heart thudding dully, she closed her eyes, willing the sudden dizziness making her head swim to abate.

"Forgive my bluntness, Lady Masterson. But you are in a delicate condition, are you not? I am a father five times over. I am familiar with the signs."

Oh. No.

Averell sat back and regarded her. "Given that the new Lord Masterson is inside," he jerked his head, "and not with us in the garden," he nodded toward her mid-section, "I will assume the child is not your husband's."

Georgina swayed on the bench and Averell caught her before she toppled over. She hadn't suspected she was with child despite the obvious signs.

No, it had been easier for me to assume Harold might be poisoning me.

A short bark of laughter came from her lips, and she immediately clasped her hand over her mouth.

"Are you going to be ill again?" Averell watched her with concern, probably thinking her as mad as Harold.

"No, Your Grace." Last night she'd left the table as her stomach had pitched unmercifully after she'd eaten turbot in a frothy wine sauce. Harold had stopped her with a hand on her elbow, pulling Georgina's face down to his.

"Let us hope it is only the sauce, for if it's anything else, I will cut the cuckoo right out of its nest."

Clarissa had pretended not to hear.

"You are correct," she kept her voice steady. "The child is not my husband's. Nor would I claim it is such. Even if I were to be so foolish, I doubt anyone in London would believe me, least of all the new Lord Masterson." Her hands curled around her mid-section.

Leo's child. The one he doesn't even want to know about.

"Please, Your Grace. Your discretion in this matter would

more than fulfill any debt you feel you owe my husband. I'm sure it is much more than he did for you."

"You would be surprised. Masterson and I weren't friends. Barely acquaintances. But he did me a very great service long ago, one I have never forgotten. And as far as my discretion, you have it. I see cruelty in Masterson's nephew, which is why I grow more concerned for you. Especially given the circumstances you now find yourself in. The law would favor him in all matters. You understand?"

"I do." Georgina looked down at her hands, still holding the duke's handkerchief. "I'm well aware of what it means to be female in a world governed by men."

What was she going to do?

"The child's father—"

Is your son. A bastard for a bastard. Georgina almost giggled hysterically and had to bite her tongue to stop herself. *Oh, Leo. I would love to watch you calculate the odds of the coincidences I now endure.*

"The child's father," she interrupted, "would not be interested to know I am with child."

I'm to tell Peckham to send me to an apothecary.

"Our relationship was brief," she continued.

Only the physical aspect.

Georgina blinked back another flood of tears which threatened to stream down her cheeks.

"I see." His voice was filled with sympathy.

Her hand stretched over her stomach. A child lived beneath the press of her fingers. *Leo's* child. She wouldn't be sending a note to Peckham. The very idea was abhorrent. How badly she wished to tell Marcus Barrington she would bear his grandchild, but she could not. No one must guess. Leo might force her to get rid of this growing life she already loved. Harold would certainly do something horrible. Her parents would either declare her a whore or announce their daughter would be giving birth to a future earl.

"You are not the first lady to find herself in such a situation. The wisest course is for you to leave London. Are there friends you can visit? Perhaps here or in America?"

"No, Your Grace." Georgina pulled the steel into her spine. Her only friend was Welles, and she most certainly could not tell him. "But there is a place I can go. Far from London." Masterson's hunting lodge in Scotland. Harold had shown little interest in the property thus far, which she assumed wouldn't change, at least at present. But Harold liked hazard, and Clarissa spent lavishly. And there were those markers still sitting in Elysium's safe. The lodge was destined to be sold at some point.

Harold.

Blinding panic assailed her. Her hands trembled at the thought of Harold finding her, swollen with child. She must hide before her condition became apparent. Careful arrangements must be made. "My husband owned a hunting lodge in Scotland."

"I have a better destination for you," the duke said. "One Lord Masterson won't be inclined to visit as he might the hunting lodge. You must allow me to handle the arrangements. Far easier for me to accomplish such a thing without suspicion than you."

"Why would you help me, Your Grace? You don't even know me." Georgina was not ungrateful for the offer of assistance; it was only that the duke's kindness was so unexpected.

"I told you, I'm trying to be a better man than I once was. Haven't you been listening?" He quirked a brow at her. "And you are in desperate need of a friend, I think. I'll consider you penance for my past sins. At the very least, I can get you out of London and help you hide. My duchess would never forgive me if I didn't offer assistance. Were she aware of your situation, she would insist I do so." He gave her a reassuring look. "But I won't tell her. You have my word."

"Thank you." Georgina looked up into the Duke of Averell's beautiful face, so like Leo's, and promptly fell into a weeping fit the likes of which she hadn't done since she was a child. His arms, solid and full of protectiveness, held her while she sobbed.

There would be no forgetting Leo Murphy now.

8

Georgina stood facing the mirror, clad only in her chemise, and pulled down the cotton over the tiny rise of her stomach. It was no more noticeable than when she'd been unexpectedly visited by a duke. She was generously curved. Rounded. Had she been reed-thin, her condition might be more readily apparent.

She had sat alone in the garden for a long time after the Duke of Averell had left her, mulling over his generous offer of assistance, which she had accepted because she wasn't sure what else to do. Harold would be told only that the duke and his uncle had been old friends and because of that friendship, Averell had extended an invitation for Georgina to stay at one of his remote estates so that she might grieve in private. Georgina didn't wish to stay in London with so many memories nor at Beechwood Court. She craved a change of scenery and absolute solitude after Masterson's horrible death. Harold would never protest nor contradict the Duke of Averell as he might if Georgina simply requested the use of the hunting lodge.

Harold had been shocked after the duke had asked to speak to him. Suspicious.

I didn't realize my uncle's death affected you so, Georgina.

But Averell, bless him, had made it clear Georgina was under his care until she returned to London. He would take it much amiss, he told Harold, if she was disturbed while grieving.

Harold had no choice but to acquiesce. One didn't deny a duke.

How she wished she could tell Averell the truth. But there were too many tangled threads. Leo. Harold. Her family. Her future as a pariah for bearing a child out of wedlock. She didn't dare tell anyone.

Her hand caressed the small bump of her belly. She would do whatever necessary to protect the life growing within her. From the entire world, if necessary. Georgina had been sent help in the form of Averell before she'd even known she needed it. So she pushed down the guilt over not telling the duke the truth and focused on the future ahead of her. Averell was providing her safe haven, but Georgina still had to get her child out of England, as far away from Harold as she could.

She refused to think of Leo. He assuredly wasn't thinking of her. He was far too busy collecting shiny baubles to be bothered with a child he didn't want. Or her.

Georgina's hand pressed against her chest. She thought in time the pain might fade. Hoped it would.

As she'd sat in the far corner of the drawing room yesterday, pretending to read, one of Clarissa's callers had mentioned Welles and referred to Leo as *that handsome mongrel.* Georgina had immediately gone still, keeping her breathing even as she turned the page of her book.

Welles and Leo, it seemed, were competing over the affections of an opera singer. In a rare departure, it seems the opera singer wasn't Italian, but French. Stunning. Sophisticated.

Georgina had nearly torn the page, she'd turned it so ferociously.

"My lady."

Her stout Irish maid, Stella, interrupted her thoughts, slipping into the room. Stella, close-mouthed and loyal to a fault, had been Georgina's maid for only a short time when her marriage to Masterson was announced. The maid had nodded in her no-nonsense way upon being informed her mistress was bound for England and had assured Georgina she had no intention of seeking other employment. She didn't want to return to her parents' house in the Bowery. Stella had ten siblings and things were a mite crowded at home. And she'd always wanted to go on an adventure.

"I overheard Ingrid speaking to Lady Masterson," Stella said, keeping her voice low. "She's poking about in your business again. Asking all sorts of questions."

Ingrid was Clarissa's maid. Nosey and as superior as her mistress. She'd taken a keen interest in Georgina's health of late. Fortunately, Georgina and Stella had hidden the worst symptoms of Georgina's pregnancy. The maid had found a tea that helped with the nausea. Georgina stayed away from eggs and claiming her grief along with the need for solitude, took most of her evening meals upstairs.

Whenever Clarissa or Harold questioned why she mourned so deeply for a man she hadn't even liked, Georgina launched into a detailed recitation of Masterson's final moments, complete with blood and excrement. Georgina didn't have to pretend to be horrified.

Clarissa had eventually stopped asking. Harold had merely watched with his pebble dark eyes and said he hoped seeing such a thing hadn't permanently harmed Georgina's mind.

A trickle of fear slid down her spine. She couldn't wait to leave this house.

"Your courses. That's what Ingrid was wanting to know. Whether you've had them or not. Even asked me if you'd had relations with your husband before he died and how often."

"The very idea is offensive."

"Says her mistress is just wanting be certain of your welfare due to the tragedy you've suffered so that she can properly care for you. *Concerned*." Stella gave a wiggle of her brows. "That's what she is."

Georgina snorted. "I'm sure she is, especially given her own state." Clarissa, it appeared, might be barren.

"Don't worry. I have the situation well in hand." Stella gave her a determined look. "Pig's blood. Took a small bottle from the butcher when he was busy flirting and boasting about how fine his shop was. I'll make sure Ingrid sees me launder your underthings. Might ruin something." She frowned.

"I'm more concerned you flirted with Mr. Simon so you could steal pig's blood," Georgina whispered. "His wife is known to be jealous."

"Mrs. Simon was right around the corner and didn't seem the least concerned. I think she'd appreciate it if I took him off her hands for a bit."

Under no circumstances could Clarissa or Harold suspect what Georgina was about to do. The pretense she still had her courses was one that must continue until she left for the country. In a few days, Georgina and Stella would be leaving for a small, very remote estate in Cumberland belonging to the Duke of Averell. A forgotten piece of property that he assured her no one had been to in years. He only ever remembered he owned Green Glen when his solicitor reminded him of the property's existence.

"Do you think he'll try to find you? His lordship?" Stella asked.

"No. The duke is a master of diplomacy. He assured Harold, confidentially of course, that it is best for Clarissa to have me gone for some time so she can firmly establish herself as Lady Masterson. Harold plans to invite Averell to a dinner party."

"The duke is very wise, my lady. I've taken to speaking quite freely down below. How terrible it was for you to nurse your husband. How gruesome his death. You just need to put all of it from your mind." Stella bit her lip. "Are you *sure* we can't return home, my lady? I've heard Charleston is lovely. No one knows you there."

Georgina shook her head. "The way to ensure my child's future is to make sure Harold never knows a child exists. If I run off to America and don't return, Harold might seek me out." Not for her own sake, but for Beechwood Court and the sum Masterson had left her. It would be disastrous if he found her alone with an infant. "The only reason he hasn't questioned my leaving London is because he wants to further his connection with a duke."

Once her child was safely in New York with her sister, Lilian, Georgina would return to London. Not forever. Six months at most. Only long enough to put any lingering suspicions Harold had to rest. She didn't want to spend the rest of her life looking over her shoulder, waiting for him to appear.

Just the other night, Harold had sat by the fire, brandy in his hand, staring at Georgina, the dark, flat gaze moving to her mid-section, then her breasts. Calculating her worth. He'd become even more dangerous if Masterson's debts were called due by Elysium. The existence of the markers was just the sort of information her husband would have kept from his detested nephew and heir.

"Will you write to Mr. Cooke again when we're settled?"

"Yes." She'd only written to Ben and Lilian once, entrusting the letters to the Duke of Averell. Another service he'd done Georgina because she didn't trust that Harold wouldn't read her correspondence. Once settled at the duke's estate, she would write both her cousin and sister with detailed instructions. At least one of them would come to her aid. Hopefully both. Ben had been her best friend since she was a child, and she trusted him completely.

"Your plan is a good one, my lady." Stella gave her an encouraging smile. "A tad complicated, mind you, but sound, for all of that. But are you certain you must go to such great lengths?"

"I am. Harold *is* mad, Stella."

"Then I'm grateful we are under the duke's protection. What about *him*, my lady?"

Georgina looked away, pretending to study the view of the maple tree outside her bedroom window. Most days, she was successful in not thinking of Leo, at least for the most part. Now that her anger had abated to a dull wounded hum, Georgina could examine their conversation in the garden in a more objective light. Stella's question brought with it a small prick of guilt, especially when she remembered that flicker of pain in Leo's eyes. But not enough to change her mind about what she must do.

There was someone else to consider now.

"He isn't important, Stella."

Stella nodded. "Why don't you have a rest, my lady, from all this planning? All will be well. I'm sure of it. I'll have tea brought up in a bit."

"What would I do without you?" Georgina impulsively hugged the maid, feeling the other woman's surprise before she returned the embrace. "I truly do not know. I would be so alone. You have been a true friend to me. Not just my maid."

"I'll not leave you, my lady," Stella said in a fierce tone.

"Nor let any harm come to you. Now rest." The maid gently pushed her in the direction of one of the chairs before the fire. "I'll be back."

Georgina nodded as Stella shut the door firmly behind her. She slumped into a chair, curling up until her knees nearly touched her chin.

Stand your ground, Georgie.

She was trying. Honestly, she was. But she'd never felt more afraid or alone in her life.

A tear fell down her cheek before she even realized she was crying. A thin wail left her. Then a sob. She started shaking. Grabbing the pillow beneath her arm, Georgina pressed it to her mouth to quiet the sound.

❦ 9 ❦

London, 1839

Georgina looked at her cards, then at Larkin standing behind the faro table, and lastly at her small stack of chips. She hadn't been very lucky at faro tonight, which was a pity because she could do with a bit of luck. Taking a sip of her bourbon, she saw how her fingers trembled. But she smiled brilliantly and placed her wager, trying to focus on her enjoyment of the game.

Difficult in light of nearly having been murdered that morning.

The lavish garden party she'd thrown at Beechwood Court meant to prove Georgina was nothing more than a merry, *childless* widow who would soon leave England and put to bed any of Harold's lingering suspicions had, in retrospect, been a grave error.

Don't think to place a cuckoo in the Masterson nest, you trollop.

Well, she *hadn't*. Harold *was* Lord Masterson. He would *stay* Lord Masterson. There wouldn't be another claim to the title, at least not from Georgina. But in the time since her return to London, Harold had become increasingly desperate. *Unhinged.*

Earlier this month, Harold had demanded, with spittle forming at the corners of his mouth, that Georgina return Beechwood Court to him as well as whatever sum his uncle had left her. Both rightfully belonged to him. He'd stomped into her drawing room at Beechwood Court, stopping in his rant only to examine the rug beneath his feet. She'd *done* something to his uncle, he'd screeched, to make him bestow such wealth on her.

Georgina had calmly explained that he was free to take up the matter with Mr. Lind, her solicitor.

She was to stop spending *his* money, he insisted, on lavish entertainments like her garden party. Stop draining *his* account. Stop wasting gold on remodeling the estate he meant to sell.

A small, painful laugh bubbled up inside her.

It was *impossible* to drain her account. Even after the large sum she'd spent on Beechwood Court's renovations and furnishings, the amount in that particular account had *never* changed.

Of course, after a rather difficult and pointed discussion with Mr. Lind, Georgina now knew why the sum in her account never altered. She wasn't sure how she felt about it. Or the fact that she didn't actually own Beechwood Court. Nor did Masterson.

Today had been incredibly awful, even by Georgina's standards. Full of unwelcome visitors trying to kill her and disturbing discoveries about a man who she'd assumed cared nothing for her.

She raised the glass of the fine bourbon whiskey to her lips. Delicious. Hard to find so far from home, except at Elysium.

Presumptuous bastard.

Generally, on the occasions she still visited Elysium, Georgina kept the company of Welles or his bride, Maggie. She would laugh and drink wine, refusing to ask for bourbon. Play endless rounds of faro. Sometimes whist. Hazard only to prove a point. Generally, Georgina behaved as if she were the happiest widow in London. She deliberately dressed in hues other than black, pewter, or lavender, because she had decided after a little over a year that her mourning period was over.

More than enough time to grieve a man she hadn't even liked very much.

Every one of her gowns possessed a scandalous neckline guaranteed to have every male in Elysium salivating over her. Punishment for the one gentleman roaming the second-floor landing like a king overseeing castle walls before invaders attack.

Yes, it was childish, and precisely the sort of behavior that had gotten Georgina in trouble repeatedly throughout her life.

When Leo noticed her, as he often did, the brilliant blue of his eyes remained unreadable. Cool, like the surface of a frost-covered pond.

Georgina glared back before dismissing him with a flick of her chin.

If he came near her while Georgina sat with Welles or Maggie, she turned away. Avoidance was a terrible game, one she and Leo had been engaged in for some time. Neither would ever win. Sometimes, Georgina wanted to climb atop one of the faro tables and scream at Leo for tossing her aside for the likes of Lady Dunley. Or whatever opera singer was currently his mistress. Or even the slender widow Georgina had seen circling Leo one night, like a lion about to take down a gazelle.

Turning her lips up in a smile, Georgina set down another

chip, not caring whether she won or not. A fool and his money were soon parted, an apt description of herself. She adjusted the neckline of her gown, a shimmering burgundy edged in black jet beads. Eye-catching. Definitely not mournful. Standing out at Elysium would protect her.

At least she was hopeful it would.

The couple seated across the faro table from Georgina, Lord Pompous and his equally forgettable wife, Lady Scornful, eyed her with distaste. Usually, when faced with such censure, Georgina made an outlandish comment, thickening the nasal quality of her voice until even she barely tolerated it. Or she leaned over to deliberately draw the gentleman's eye to the dip of her neckline. An amusement she allowed herself to distract her from the fact that Ben and Lilian had carried away a part of her heart. The rest of her soul, though she hated to admit it, was on the second-floor landing of Elysium.

Tell him.

She took a shaky breath and brought the glass of bourbon back to her lips, waiting for the feeling to pass. Georgina had managed to keep that voice silent all during her time away from London, then during the months since her return. Always, she'd told herself it wouldn't matter. He didn't want her. Definitely not their child.

But after today, now that certain things had come to light, she'd found herself hiding at Elysium and reconsidering the choice she'd made.

"Another, please." Georgina held up her empty glass and nodded at Larkin, who in turn whispered instructions to a passing member of Elysium's staff. The drink helped settle her. Somewhat. Being attacked this morning had shaken her, though thanks to the steel she'd inherited from her grandmother, Georgina kept herself outwardly calm.

Grandmother would have shot the intruder as she had any

squirrel brave enough to venture into her garden. She'd be terribly disappointed to know Georgina didn't go about armed. Or even have a pistol next to her bed. After all, London was full of creatures more vicious than any red squirrel determined to eat the carrots.

Meaty hands tearing at her skirts. Ripping at her underthings. Squeezing her throat.

If Georgina could be grateful, it was for the fact that Harold had hired an assassin who decided it would be preferable to rape Georgina *before* fulfilling his duty and killing her. The moment she'd walked into her suite of rooms at Beechwood Court, she'd stopped, halted by the nauseating smell of onions and garlic. Gowns were piled outside her wardrobe. Her jewelry box was open, the contents strewn across the floor. Her new maid, a thin-nosed girl with a churlish attitude, was nowhere in sight.

The brute came out of her dressing room, tall and wiry, dressed in dark clothing. He rushed at Georgina before she could even open her mouth to scream.

Fortunately, like most of his species, even those intent on murder, lust had made her assailant careless. He'd grabbed Georgina, placing one hand across her mouth to silence her while tossing her on the bed. His hand, smelling of filth and onions, had moved down to wrap around her throat, choking the air from her lungs. His other hand had groped at her breast, frustrated by her corset, before he'd started to rip at her skirts.

Georgina, terrified, had gone limp. She'd closed her eyes, pretending to faint, which in turn made him more careless. When he'd paused to breathe over her neck, nearly gagging her with his foul breath, she'd stretched out her fingers, grabbing the heavy ormolu clock on the bedside table. She swung the clock, the marble making a satisfying thud as it made contact with her assailant's temple.

She'd screamed then and pushed away his body with her feet. His trousers were undone, his now limp appendage pale and disgusting. Gagging, she'd screamed again.

Her footmen had taken their time in coming to her aid. The maid she'd taken on to replace Stella, whom she'd sent back to New York, was curiously absent. Her butler had seemed unable to tell Georgina how the man had gotten into the house and found her chambers. After Georgina instructed the staff to call the constable, she then had the man hauled away to be locked in a room downstairs.

Precarious, was how Georgina would have described her situation at that moment. Almost murdered. Surrounded by untrustworthy staff, all likely in the employ of Harold.

"Georgina." Her name drawled out in a hideous, over-exaggeration of her accent. "There you are. I wondered where you'd gotten off to."

If Harold were going to insult her, she wished he'd do so properly. "Harold. What a surprise. By the way, your imitation of my speech could use more work," she said, focusing on keeping her hands still and her features expressionless. "Flatten and draw out your vowels just a bit more." His appearance didn't shock Georgina. She'd known, hadn't she, Harold would look for her?

He made an ugly sound.

"And I didn't realize my whereabouts were any of your concern," she stated without looking in his direction. He couldn't touch her. Not at Elysium.

Harold fluffed out his expensively tailored coat, bottle-green and perfectly fitted. Folding his lean, angular form, he took the seat beside Georgina, sticking out his pointed chin at her. Everything about Harold was thin and sharp. His elbows could cut her to the quick with one swipe.

"I rode out to Beechwood Court today only to be told you'd gone to London." One finger toyed with the end of his mustache. "The staff told me you were in a rush to come to town."

"A rush?" She gave a small laugh, congratulating herself for having the sense to flee her estate for London. "Beechwood Court, though I adore the property, can become tedious at times. I felt a change was in order." Someplace she was less likely to be attacked, perhaps. "I sometimes miss the delights town has to offer."

His gaze bored into her. "You should have sent word. Clarissa would have prepared a guest room for you."

"I'd hate to trouble you." Georgina swished the bourbon in her mouth, the sting helping to fortify her.

"No trouble at all. We are family, after all. Foolish for you to take on the expense of renting a house for the rare times you visit." Beady eyes regarded her, full of false solicitousness. A broad smile crossed his lips, showing uneven teeth. Any observer would assume their relationship to be warm. Friendly, even. No one would believe he'd sent someone to murder her this morning.

"Except, you aren't staying at your rented house either, are you? I was so concerned when I arrived at Beechwood Court and was told you'd left in a flurry of trunks. I grew concerned. Your mind hasn't been the same since my uncle's death. Poor lamb."

Ah. There it was. Of course. In *plain sight.* If Harold failed to murder her, he was just as likely to have her committed to gain access to what he thought Masterson had left her. Her wonderful plan to allay Harold's suspicions by returning to London for a short time hadn't accounted for murder or being taken to an asylum.

"My mind?" Georgina nodded to Larkin as she placed another chip. "I'm not the one counting the silver at night."

Never show a mad dog your fear or the mongrel will bite.

More wise words from her grandmother, though at the

time, Grandmother had been speaking of Georgina's father, Jacob Rutherford.

"You should return home with me tonight where your family can care for you. I grow ever more concerned with your erratic behavior." He said the words loud enough for the entire faro table to hear. "Look at you." He leaned in. "Dressed like a trollop instead of the proper widow you should be." His gaze flicked to her bosom. "You aren't even out of mourning. Another sign, I think."

"I abhor gray. Burgundy suits me better." If he thought she would follow him blindly out the doors of Elysium, Harold wasn't only mad, he was stupid. She said a silent prayer of thanks for whatever small voice had whispered to her earlier not to open the small house she kept in town for the night.

"Pity my uncle was never interested in such things," he continued, nodding to her breasts. "Only your money. Or rather, *my* money. I think we can both agree on that."

Dread pooled in her stomach. Georgina had to stomp out the fear threatening to overwhelm her. But the staff all knew her at Elysium. Harold couldn't drag her out of here. She was under the protection of Lord Welles.

No. Not Welles.

The bourbon soured a bit in her stomach. Or maybe it was the presence of Harold, which was certainly enough to make anyone ill. Possibly it was the guilt leeching through her system mixing with her fear.

"My money, Georgina. Which you insist on keeping from me. I've found a buyer for Beechwood Court. You'll be happy to know that the renovations gained me a better price." He smoothed his mustache again. "I was wrong about that."

Wouldn't Harold be surprised when he realized she didn't own Beechwood Court. Pity she wouldn't be around to see the humiliation sure to crumple his sharp features.

"I'll admit, you were gone for so long after my uncle's death, had I not known how devoted the Duke of Averell is to his duchess, I would have assumed you'd become his whore." He whispered the ugly words into her ear before he leaned back. "Because I'm certain you do have a lover, Georgina."

"My personal affairs are none of your concern. Why don't you visit the hazard table? Faro isn't really your game, I understand. Though neither is hazard, given the sums you lose."

His upper lip trembled; he was likely struggling not to sneer at her and ruin the calm image he wanted to present. "You know, I heard the most interesting story from Lord Wentworth the other day." He cast her a sideways glance from his disturbingly flat, expressionless eyes. "Very interesting."

Georgina looked back at her cards. "Who?"

Harold snickered. "*Fascinating* story. The tale of a wager my uncle once made. I relayed all the details to Clarissa. You know what else I find strange?" He tapped his forefinger against his thin, almost non-existent lips.

"I've no idea. Is there a point to this conversation, Harold? I went away to grieve my husband. I stayed away longer than expected because I was enjoying myself. I wrote you and Clarissa frequently." She had, mostly to keep their suspicions at bay, though it appeared to have done little good.

"You sent your maid back to America. Clarissa and I found that so odd. Stella. Wasn't that her name?"

The only way Harold could know Stella was no longer in her employ and had been sent back to America was if one of the servants at Beechwood Court had told him. Which confirmed her suspicions that at least one member of her staff, if not all of them, were reporting back to Harold. She'd sent Stella back with Lilian and Ben to guard over the person more precious to Georgina than any other. Her son's safety was all that mattered. And Georgina had been afraid Harold might . . . harm Stella.

"She wished to return to America, and I released her from my service. England didn't agree with her."

"A shame she's gone. You were so close. Overly familiar, Clarissa often said. I'm sure your maid knew all your secrets." His voice hardened ever so slightly, one lip twitching at the corner. Madness gleamed at the edges of the dark, polished stones of his eyes.

"Is there anything else?" Georgina said casually. "I've enjoyed our conversation, Harold, but I have a game of faro to return to."

"One small minor thing." Harold's lips brushed her ear as his fingers curled around her wrist, bruising her flesh. "I want what's due to me, Georgina," he hissed. "Every farthing."

Larkin paused in dealing out the next round, clearly preparing to intervene.

"You *have* your inheritance." Georgina tugged at her wrist, but he held firm. "You received everything due to you. It isn't my fault if you toss it away on the hazard table."

"Bitch," he said so softly she barely heard him. "I'm not sure how you convinced my uncle to leave you *anything*—but Beechwood Court rightfully belongs to me." Madness flared in his eyes. "As does the sum my uncle left you."

"I am his widow. He merely provided for me."

"It should be mine." His fingers dug into her skin. "It *will* be mine. No overdressed harlot is going to keep me from it." Pitch black eyes grew wild, like some rabid beast. "You aren't nearly as clever as you think you are, Georgina."

"Go away, Harold," she murmured. "Or I'll find something to brain you with as I did your man earlier today."

Harold stepped back, the smile once more on his lips. "I won't go far." His voice raised so that the other players at the table could hear him. "I don't mean to upset you." He sent an apologetic look toward the others surrounding the faro table. "I'll return later to escort you home."

Georgina forced her gaze back to the queen of spades in her hand as Harold walked away. It was late but still too soon to make her way to the docks.

She had visited Mr. Lind earlier this afternoon. Hand the estate over to Harold, she'd instructed him. Beechwood Court wasn't worth her life. Besides, she was leaving England. *Forever.*

Mr. Lind had flushed. And stammered. Unfortunately, what she'd asked was impossible. She didn't actually own the estate, though the solicitor declined to say exactly who did. His instructions were to ensure that Beechwood Court was to be used and maintained for her exclusive use. Further questioning of the solicitor eventually revealed Masterson had never set up an account for Georgina.

Was it her father who had done so? She demanded to know, even as she acknowledged that Jacob Rutherford had likely forgotten about her the moment he'd left her behind in England. Her cousin Benjamin Cooke? Lord Welles? The Duke of Averell? As she spoke each name, Georgina knew, *just knew.*

Shock filled her as she'd looked down at her lap. She remembered the pain in Leo's eyes the last time she'd seen him. Masterson's markers had never been called due. The hunting lodge had never been taken. Even the damned horses had remained. Because the only thing he'd truly wanted had been her.

"Leo Murphy." She'd whispered his name and watched Mr. Lind turn the color of a beet.

The solicitor had neither confirmed nor denied her statement. He didn't have to. There was no one else who would have done such a thing for her. She couldn't believe Leo had.

Mr. Lind had fetched her a sherry, which she drank in one swallow before asking for another. Afterward, she'd instructed Mr. Lind to make arrangements to send the entire sum still sitting in her account to Harold. It was her money, after all, no matter how it had gotten into that blasted account. The solicitor was to inform Harold, should he inquire, that she was taking up residence in France. Or Italy. It didn't matter. Once Harold had the money, he wouldn't look for her.

She did hope Mr. Lind would follow her instructions.

Her passage on the ship *Betty Sue*, bound for Boston, was the very first bit of business Georgina settled upon after leaving Beechwood Court. She'd hoped to get out of London without Harold finding her first, but now that wouldn't be the case. Her carriage would need to be abandoned, along with her things. When she arrived on board the *Betty Sue* in the wee hours of the morning without any baggage, Georgina would pretend upset—

I will hardly have to pretend.

—and inform the captain she'd been robbed on the way to the docks; she would seek his protection and that of her cabin.

"Another hand, Lady Masterson?"

Georgina smiled up at Larkin, whose features softened on her. He really was a lovely man, for all that he'd once been a pickpocket. "I believe so, Larkin. Thank you."

She would stay for another quarter of an hour and then slip away. Georgina knew Elysium fairly well. Leo had explained to her that the merchant who'd once owned the mansion had built multiple exits. There were dozens of hidden rooms, staircases, halls.

Georgina pressed a hand to her lips, trying to still the rising panic Harold's little visit had brought.

Leo.

His efforts to see to her care didn't change anything. Couldn't. Not now when she was leaving England. He had been very clear at not wanting to father a child, especially a bastard. He *did* bear her some affection. She supposed that should make her happy. But instead, the knowledge of what he'd done for her filled Georgina with a raw, gnawing guilt. Sorrow at what might have been.

It's too late.

Georgina set off in the opposite direction of the main doors toward a thick velvet curtain trimmed in gold fringe. Behind the velvet was a short hall leading to the room set aside for Elysium's female patrons. There was even an attendant to help with clothing mishaps or to repin a lady's hair after a visit to the second floor. Nettie was the attendant's name. A hook-nosed, scarred, older woman who had grown up in St. Giles. Another stray Leo and Welles had collected for Elysium. Like the one-armed Jones who sat at the door with Smith. Or Smith himself, who Georgina was certain had more secrets than she did. But Nettie, for all her vicious looks and brusque manner, was a surprisingly sweet woman. She was also good with a knife and handled a pistol competently, according to Welles.

Most importantly, there was another exit to the room Nettie guarded. Should any female patron seek to avoid the attentions of a gentleman, she need only slip thru the hidden door which led to yet another hallway and eventually a very private exit out of Elysium. The exit was always guarded by one of Leo's employees. Whoever stood just outside would summon Georgina a hack. She would be aboard the *Betty Sue* within the hour. Harold had undoubtedly watched her flee down this hall, but Nettie wouldn't let him past her.

Georgina weighed the risk of going to Leo and asking for his protection. He might save her from Harold, but what then? Leo didn't want a child. He'd made that abundantly clear. Georgina even understood, *somewhat*, why he didn't. His reasoning was flawed, tangled up as it was in the death of Welles's mother and the dislike Leo had for his father. But even beyond his aversion to children, bastard or otherwise, Leo had quite adamantly stated he would never marry.

Where would that leave Georgina, even if Leo wanted her to stay?

As a mistress. Without her son. Living far away from her beloved New York.

She stopped for a moment, her fingers trailing along the wall. The very idea was unfathomable, no matter her feeling for the proprietor of Elysium.

This was a game Georgina couldn't hope to win.

10

L eo studied Georgina as she played faro for the better part of the evening, careful to stay out of her line of sight. His eyes lingered over the generous curves he longed to touch. The cascade of curls springing about her temples like bits of spun gold. She would smell of spring. Wildflowers. The burgundy gown she wore tonight suited her much more than black widow's weeds, or any of the other dull colors society dictated she wear. The *ton* was still gossiping about the gown she'd chosen for that silly garden party Georgina had hosted at Beechwood Court.

The only part of tonight's ensemble Leo *didn't* approve of was the near spill of her breasts over the edge of her bodice. The neckline dipped so low, Leo imagined any male close to her could see Georgina's nipples.

Punishment. Meant to remind Leo with every glance in Georgina's direction of what he'd so carelessly tossed aside. He gripped the banister, jealousy biting at his skin. It wasn't the least bit amusing to have every gentleman at Elysium ogle what belonged to Leo.

A snarl left him. Pushing her away all those months ago

had done little to banish Georgina from his thoughts. Leo no longer thought himself remotely noble for having "saved" her from him. He despised himself for wounding her. The terrible ache her absence caused had started as a hole that widened to a gaping maw within his chest.

Some mornings, Leo woke up with the scent of spring in his nostrils, hoping that when he opened his eyes, Georgina would be beside him, only to find himself alone. His fingers would stretch across the sheets, searching for her warmth.

Such a dream would put Leo in an incredibly foul mood for the remainder of the day.

Jesus, just go to her.

Words roared at him by his brother, who had inexplicably allowed himself to fall in love. Tony had nearly lost Maggie and the child she carried because of his refusal to let go of the past. It had been Leo who insisted his brother was a bloody idiot if he didn't go after his wife. What was to be gained by allowing your past to dictate your future?

Take your own bloody advice, Leo.

Leo looked back out over the gaming floor, watching the light catch on Georgina's hair.

When Georgina had fled London to spend her mourning period in the country, Leo had rejoiced. The temptation of her would be gone. He needed only to immerse himself in Elysium and the arms of the scores of available women in London. The series of brief affairs Leo engaged in, with any blonde, bold, voluptuous female he could find, hadn't lasted. None of the women spoke with a flat American accent or dared to insult his waistcoats. His cock knew the difference. He hadn't even bothered to bed the last woman.

Months had gone by. An agonizing amount of time. Leo had calculated down to the last second how long Georgina had been gone. Ten months, six days, three hours, and thirty-six minutes.

When she'd finally returned, Georgina had avoided Leo as if he were a beggar covered in pox sores. Whenever Leo approached her at Elysium under the guise of speaking to his brother or one of his staff, *because he bloody well couldn't stay away from her*, Georgina lifted her chin in that stubborn manner he adored before strolling away in the opposite direction. If absolutely forced to, she would permit him to greet her politely. But nothing more. Very few words had thus far been exchanged.

He'd spent quite a lot of time convincing himself he was relieved Georgina kept her distance.

One event, Leo knew, could change a person's life forever. The death of Tony's mother, for instance, had altered the course of Leo's existence.

But he hadn't thought fucking one slightly improper American girl would affect him so much that he would no longer find any other woman appealing. Leo's gaze was always drawn to Georgina, the shiny bauble he wanted above all others. In the last few weeks, especially after hearing about that ridiculous garden party, Leo had considered storming into Beechwood Court, which was *his* bloody house by the way, and just dragging her into bed.

After that, Leo wasn't completely sure what would happen.

His eyes traced the delicate line of Georgina's stubborn jaw as she studied her hand of cards. Her head tilted, and she smiled up at Larkin.

Leo gritted his teeth. Now he was jealous of a bloody pickpocket.

Her chin dipped as a wash of sadness crossed her lovely features. The emotion hovered about her slender shoulders and coffee-colored eyes, as it had since her return. Outwardly, Georgina appeared unchanged by her sojourn in the country, but Leo knew better. He wondered if he was the cause of her sorrow or if it was something else. Surely, she didn't grieve Masterson.

A gentleman dressed in bottle green crossed the busy floor below, caught sight of Georgina at the faro table, and changed direction, heading toward the empty seat next to her.

Masterson's nephew.

Harold strutted through Elysium as if he were royalty instead of merely an earl of little importance. He continued to swill expensive brandy and play hazard poorly, more like his dead uncle than anyone would have thought. The idiot had no idea how close he was to impoverishment. How soon, he wouldn't be able to afford an expensive coat. Possibly not even a valet.

Leo still held the previous Lord Masterson's markers. Not out of respect for Masterson. Or his bloody nephew.

But for *her*. Georgina.

There would be no duns beating at Georgina's door demanding payment.

The only reason Leo had kept Beechwood Court was so Georgina would *always* have a place of her own. She might never speak to him again, but Leo had still given her an obscene sum, deposited into her account monthly and to be managed by her solicitor. Mr. Lind was paid very well not to disclose the source of Georgina's wealth or the true owner-ship of Beechwood Court but to allow Georgina to believe Masterson had given her both. Leo told no one what he'd done. Not even Tony.

His eyes flicked to Harold, who took a seat next to Georgina.

Larkin, manning the faro table, looked toward the second-floor landing and, when he didn't see Leo, nodded to Peck-ham, who was wandering about the floor.

Peckham turned his attention to the faro table and nodded back at Larkin.

His entire staff knew to have a care for Lady Masterson. No one questioned Leo regarding why he insisted Georgina be protected so fiercely, her comfort seen to before all others. He suspected they knew.

On the floor below, Harold leered in Georgina's direction, coming far too close.

She paled as he spoke to her but otherwise showed no outward signs of distress. But Leo noticed the slight purse of her lips and the way her shoulders braced as if about to take a blow. He knew Georgina and Harold didn't get on well. Harold liked to insult Georgina.

Leo made a mental note to revoke Harold's membership.

Finally, Harold straightened and sauntered away, threading through the crowd.

Georgina returned to her game, laughing as she collected her chips. Leo's eyes lingered over her; brazen, wild spring, savage and sharp. How defiantly Georgina had faced Leo, declaring she didn't care for being bartered as if she were a goat. That she'd dug out the rows herself to plant tulips at Beechwood Court for a grandmother who had shot squirrels out of trees and taught her to curse.

Leo missed Georgina so *fiercely*.

Years ago, he'd asked his stepmother, Amanda, how she could tolerate the *arrogant prick* known as Marcus Barrington. Leo, bitter illegitimate lad that he was, had done everything in his power to make Amanda despise him.

Because she *should* have despised her husband's bastard.

He'd said Andromeda, his recently born half-sister, resembled more a shriveled mushroom than a baby. When Amanda had gifted him with a puppy, he'd told her he didn't want the dog. Leo diced with the footmen. Stole the tarts out of the kitchen meant for dessert and sold them on the street. Pretended he didn't have proper table manners.

Nothing worked.

That day, he'd deliberately used crude language to describe his father, hoping to shock her and perhaps make her call for the smelling salts. Instead, Amanda coolly took a sip of her tea, clearly unimpressed with his attempts to annoy her. She slid the plate of biscuits they had been sharing across the table in his direction.

"The ancient Greeks believed in soulmates, Leo," she'd said calmly.

Leo had rolled his eyes, looking up at the ceiling, rudely dismissing her. Amanda was always going on about someone named Homer and offering him her copy of the Iliad. She adored those bloody Greeks. Frankly, Leo didn't see what all the fuss was about. The only thing he'd liked were the statues of half-naked ladies Amanda kept putting in the garden.

"Why should I care?" he'd said, crunching loudly on a biscuit.

"Well, because we all have one. One day, your soulmate will appear."

Slurping his tea—loudly—he'd answered, "Not bloody likely, Your Grace. Bastards don't have soulmates, whatever they are. Can't imagine we're worth the trouble." What else must he do? Stick a finger in his nose? Have a rude sound come from his arse? What would it take to give Amanda a fit of the vapors?

Leo had burped, not bothering to cover his mouth.

She had only smiled. "You are so very determined to set yourself apart from us. You weren't to blame, Leo."

He'd stilled when she said the words, then grinned to hide the fact that inside, he was screaming. "I am not like you, Your Grace."

"We are more alike than you know. But we'll discuss that

at a later time. The Greeks, you see, believed everyone had their special person."

Leo had taken another biscuit from the plate, relieved she'd changed the subject from the topic of the previous Duchess of Averell's death and back to the Greeks. "I don't," he'd said with a scoff.

"You do, Leo. You aren't meant to be alone. Apart. A soulmate is your heart's dearest companion. A person perfect only for you."

"I don't understand why you think I care, Amanda."

A wry smile crossed her lips. "Because for me, that one perfect person is the arrogant prick known as Marcus Barrington."

Leo's fingers bit into the fine mahogany of the second-floor railing. The conversation, long forgotten, had recently come to mind, about the same time Georgina had returned to London. He no longer annoyed his stepmother, at least not on purpose. Andromeda was now a beautiful young woman, not mushroom-like at all. And Leo *adored* Amanda, though he rarely told her so. His own mother, Molly, had died only a few years after leaving Cherry Hill. It was Amanda who'd demanded Leo allow her to care for him. Be a Barrington.

He'd been thinking quite a lot about that lately. Who he was.

Leo dropped his hands, smoothing his fingers over the swirling gold, crimson, and purple pattern of his waistcoat. Particularly ghastly. Georgina would take one look and make a horrible, disparaging remark. At least he hoped she would.

Because he meant to end this estrangement between them.

Tonight.

11

"Lady Masterson." A warm hand took Georgina's elbow, startling her as she hurried toward Nettie and the room she presided over. Sandalwood and cheroot filled her nostrils along with a scent that remained solely his.

Leo.

Her heart squeezed painfully. Why would he seek her out tonight, of all nights? Her decision had already been made. She was leaving England tonight, and nothing, not even Leo, would change her mind.

Her eyes fluttered closed at his touch, allowing herself a moment of sheer pleasure as his presence enveloped her. She wanted nothing more than to sink into his warmth.

"Good evening, Mr. Murphy." She opened her eyes as a bubbly feeling filled her stomach, like she'd taken a large swallow of champagne. *Move.* She commanded her feet, but her burgundy damask slippers seemed stuck to the floor. "I was just on my way out." She tried to pull her elbow free. "If you'll excuse me." Her traitorous body leaned in his direction, toward all the wonderful heat that was Leo.

"I should like to speak with you," he ground out.

"Why?" She looked down, trying not to stare at his thighs so close to her skirts. "The last time we spoke wasn't at all pleasurable."

"Aren't you tired of avoiding me, Georgina? I've grown weary of watching your efforts." His finger slid along the edge of her bodice. "This gown, for instance, is especially tempting. Did you wear it for me?"

She pushed his hand away, her skin tingling. "Stop looking then. And I rarely think of you at all, let alone dress purposefully to attract your attention."

He raised a brow. "Yet you come to the one place I am known to be."

A fair point. She had always found comfort in the knowledge he was near, whether avoiding him or not.

A thick curl fell against his cheek and Georgina stared at the bit of dark hair, wanting so much to rub the strand between her fingers, to bask in the remembered feel of all those silken locks between her thighs. "Perhaps I find the odds better at Elysium than other gambling hells. There is also the advantage of the rooms on the second floor. Now, if you will step aside."

"No." His arm shot out, palm flat against the wall, trapping her against the flocked wallpaper, which frankly was quite lovely.

"I'll scream."

"Bloody hell, Georgina. Go ahead. Do you really think anyone at Elysium will save you from *me*?"

No, she didn't suppose they would. She glanced down the hall but saw no sign of Harold.

"I'm grateful for the dim lighting else your waistcoat might make me dizzy," she said. "It's hideous. Your sister designs clothing, for God's sake. Allow her to create something that doesn't strain the eyes and roil the stomach."

A tiny half-smile crossed the wide mouth. "No one is supposed to know about Andromeda's hobby. *You* shouldn't know."

"Welles introduced me to your sisters." And the Duchess of Averell. Georgina's entire return to London seemed filled with nothing but Barringtons. Except for the occasional murderous assailant. The duke, thankfully, had been tending to his estate in the country, so she'd never had to pretend she didn't know him. How awkward that would have been.

"Welles thought it would be nice if I had some friends." He'd mistakenly assumed Georgina wanted to stay in this dreadful city even though she'd told him often enough she meant to return to New York. "Andromeda showed me an entire portfolio of her work."

"Andromeda draws sheet after sheet of gowns and adornments. When she was young, she created an entire trousseau for her favorite doll, Miss Tipplewort. I bought her the doll, thinking she'd force me to sit through one of her tea parties, but instead, she took poor Miss Tipplewort and cut the dress from her body. *Green isn't her color,* Romy informed me. She must have been all of nine. Always has feathers or bits of ribbon stuck to her. And—"

"Stop it," she said softly, looking up at him, holding back the tears threatening to fall at his blatant attempt to distract her from the seriousness of their conversation. "You didn't stop me to discuss Andromeda's hobby."

The blue of his eyes sparkled in the muted light of the hallway. "No, but isn't it better than avoiding each other, or making uncomfortable polite platitudes when we do meet?" He leaned over her shoulder and . . . *inhaled* her.

Georgina shivered in pleasure at the way his breath floated over her skin. "I would prefer you get to the point."

His hand reached out, tugging at a bit of her skirts. "We haven't talked since before Masterson died, Georgina."

"Yes. As I mentioned before, a wholly unpleasant experience. Didn't you tell me I was merely a trinket? A piece of tin used to scare away birds?"

"I said nothing of the kind." The tip of his nose glanced off her temple, his eyes fluttering closed, his dark lashes falling to brush his cheeks. A sound left him, one that sent a wave of heat curling around her mid-section. "Your anger toward me is justified. Deserved. I was intentionally cruel."

"Yes, you were." Her body arched toward him, and Georgina had to force herself to straighten and take a step back. She'd forgotten how it felt to be so close to Leo. How intoxicating it was to be near his warmth. If she pressed her ear to his chest, Georgina would hear his heartbeat, more soothing to her than any lullaby.

"I have thought a thousand times about storming Beechwood Court." His fingers twisted in the folds of her skirts, pulling gently to bring her near him once more.

"No need to storm. It belongs to you, after all."

His eyes widened a fraction at the knowledge she knew what he'd done. "As do you, don't you?" Leo brushed the pad of his thumb gently over her bottom lip, the touch as light as a butterfly's.

The sensation had her heart fluttering madly within her chest. She pressed her forehead to his chest with a little sob. She *did* belong to him. That was why this was so hard.

"I would wager myself this time." His lips brushed hers. "Do anything to ensure your happiness."

Georgina forced herself to remain true to the course already set. "So you would wed me?" She looked up at him, sorrow constricting her heart at the look on his face. "Make me your wife?"

"Georgina—" His hand dropped from her skirts.

"No?" The words scraped horribly against her throat.

"You'd keep me as your mistress? Unofficially, of course. As your father did to your mother."

Leo paled. "I haven't—"

"Will I live upstairs in your rooms? No, wait. I'll live at Beechwood Court, won't I? You'll visit when you can, I'm sure. Unless another bauble catches your eye." Every word tumbling from her lips pierced her heart.

"I would not stray from you." The line of his jaw had grown taut. Hard. *Furious.*

"Unless I grew round with child. Which would happen eventually. What will you do then?"

Sadly, nothing *had* changed except now she knew Leo cared for her. But the knowledge brought her no joy, only another wash of pain.

"Stop," he hissed.

"Will I be sent to the apothecary, Leo? Or possibly you'll find a husband for me. I'm sure you wouldn't wish me to be a pariah."

Leo opened his mouth to speak, but a discreet clearing of a throat filled the hall before he could answer.

"Mr. Murphy."

Leo turned to face Peckham, who stood a few paces away. "What is it, Peckham?"

Georgina took a step forward, but Leo's hand reached out to take hers, lacing their fingers together, holding her in place. Her eyes moved over his profile as he waited for Peckham to speak, struck, as she often was, by how beautiful she found him. She tried to memorize the curve of his mouth, the small lines around his eyes, the way he smelled, because Georgina doubted after tonight, she would ever see Leo again.

But I will always have a part of him.

It was better Leo never knew. This discussion, brief as it

was, only assured Georgina she'd done the right thing. The only thing.

"Lady Masterson." Peckham gave her a short bow before returning his attention back to Leo. "I apologize for the interruption, sir. But there is an urgent message from Cherry Hill."

"A moment, Peckham."

"I'm sorry, Mr. Murphy. But even now, the messenger waits for your reply. It is *very* urgent. He's waiting in your office."

Leo released her fingers, but not without reluctance, intentionally dragging his thumb across her palm.

"Don't you dare leave, Georgina. I need to talk to you." Then his voice lowered to barely a whisper. "Please."

Georgina looked away. She couldn't wait for his return. Didn't dare to. She pressed back against the wall and stayed silent until his broad shoulders disappeared into the crowd on the gaming floor.

"Goodbye, Leo," she whispered to the empty hall. A tear rolled down one cheek and she hastily brushed the drop away, cursing Harold, Masterson, Leo, and even that brash girl who'd met a notorious gambling hell owner and lost her heart.

All actions have consequences.

Grandmother and Georgina's own past foolish behavior had taught her that simple truth. She'd been forced to make decisions. Leaving England had been the easiest, but even that was colored by the fact that Leo was here. But there was someone else now. Her son. He needed her far more than Leo ever would.

Georgina took a deep breath. She glanced in the direction of the gaming floor. Harold's bottle-green coat caught her eye near the faro table. He was looking for her. If he turned, he'd see her.

She swallowed down her panic.

Quickly, she made her way a little farther down, careful to stay close to the wall. Georgina paused to greet Nettie who stood in her usual spot. "Good evening, Nettie."

"Lady Masterson." The older woman inclined her head.

"There's a gentleman in a bottle-green coat, Nettie. He might ask if you've seen me. Please say you haven't."

"Never, my lady." The older woman nodded, flashing the gap where she was missing two teeth. "Mr. Murphy would have my head if I were to cause you any ill."

Georgina nodded, wiping at another tear as she walked through the door behind Nettie. The room was empty of other female patrons, thankfully. Moving to a small alcove, Georgina pressed gently at one side until the wall swung open, as Nettie had once shown her it would. A narrow hall was revealed, painted a pale cream and lit by a single lamp. A shadowy figure stood at the end, becoming larger as he stood and waited for her to approach.

"Good evening, Smith."

"Lady Masterson." He bowed, his eyes flashing silver as he glanced over her cheeks; he likely saw the tears she hadn't completely been able to hide. "May I offer assistance?"

Georgina nodded. "Yes. Would you summon me a hack, Smith?"

"Of course, my lady." He opened the door behind him.

Cool air rushed into the hall, finding its way up her skirts. She thought of the carefully packed trunk in her carriage, but it was too much of a risk. While she'd never had cause to distrust her driver, it would be best if he continued to believe she was still inside Elysium. Harold would be watching her carriage.

The door opened onto a narrow gravel pathway that split in two directions. To the left was the main entrance of

Elysium. The line of carriages was clearly visible, including Georgina's.

Smith's brow wrinkled in confusion. "You wish me to call you a hack, my lady? Your carriage——"

"I need a hack. As discreetly as possible, Smith. From that direction." She pointed to the right. "Please, Smith. It is a matter of some urgency." Georgina looked at the horizon. It would be dawn in a few hours. Her arrival at the *Betty Sue* wouldn't be as early as she'd thought.

"I have somewhere I need to be."

12

Some months later.

Leo pushed at the tray of untouched food at his elbow. There wasn't anything worse than a cold omelet, in his opinion. Of course, no omelet, even one seasoned with herbs and dripping with his favorite cheese, mixed well with the scotch he was drinking. He hadn't any appetite when Peckham had brought the food to him piping hot nearly an hour ago.

The decanter of scotch was nearly empty. *Again.*

Betrayal, Leo found, made a person thirsty. Though it could also be because Peckham wasn't filling the decanter properly.

His gaze bumped over the table before him. The letter, that *horrible, terrible* letter, lay open, as it had for weeks. Possibly longer. He hadn't been paying attention to the passage of time. The ink was barely visible on the pale vellum, but it didn't matter. He'd read the words dozens of times.

The coiled asp, as he imagined the letter to be, had sunk its fangs into Leo, refusing to let go. The words, destroying him from the inside out, were for him and him alone. The final communication Marcus Barrington would ever have with Leo.

A shudder ran through him, along with a great deal of grief, though not all of it was for his father. Regret nearly choked him. Anger mixed with the scotch, souring in his stomach.

No wonder he didn't have a bloody appetite. No one would after reading that fucking thing.

The news of the Duke of Averell's death had interrupted his heated discussion with Georgina that night.

Damn her.

Leo had been determined in that narrow hallway, with Georgina trapped between his body and the wall, that she *never* leave him again. He'd meant to tell her that they belonged together. But then she'd started hurling accusations at him, and Peckham had appeared.

Now she was gone.

He'd faced the news of his father's death alone, deprived of the one person whose presence he needed. Tony had left for Cherry Hill earlier in the week and the messenger was from his brother.

Another thing I'm really bloody angry over. I needed her.

Leo splashed some more scotch into his glass. Georgina was essential to him. That was the problem. He couldn't breathe without her. At least not properly. He'd been so furious to find she hadn't waited. So—

Devastated. There didn't seem to be a point in lying to himself.

There he was, *baring his soul to her—*

Leo took another swallow from his glass. At least it felt like that to him. Georgina must not have agreed because she hadn't stayed.

You'll keep me as your mistress? As your father did to your mother?

He hadn't known the answer when she'd thrown the question at him. He'd had no bloody idea what a future with Georgina would involve. The only thing he'd been considering was how much he missed her, and he couldn't bear it any longer.

Leo had immediately made arrangements to go to Cherry Hill in the morning. He hadn't even bothered to try to find her. He'd expected she'd gone to the small house she rented in town or back to Beechwood Court. It didn't matter, Leo had told himself as his coach had lurched in the direction of Cherry Hill. Peckham's interruption that night had been fortuitous.

What would he have done? Offered to marry her?

He stretched a hand across his chest. It felt as if he'd been in the worst tavern brawl of his life. Leo's entire body ached.

Deceitful Georgina.

Marcus Barrington had been dead several days when Leo had finally arrived at Cherry Hill, still smarting from Georgina's dismissal. The unexpected regret and sharp, horrible pain over his father's death had nearly choked Leo. He'd wished for her presence again. For just a scent of spring.

Amanda had been inconsolable, so stricken with grief she could barely speak. She'd glared at Leo with accusation instead of offering her customary warm welcome.

"How does your righteous indignation suit you now, Leo?" she'd said. "Why not continue to rail at him for making you a bastard? Go on. He's dead. He'll hardly protest."

Leo had fallen back at Amanda's words.

Tony had stood off to the side, his features pinched. "I received much the same greeting. Though I think mine may have been worse."

Tony was now the Duke of Averell and not happy about it. Maggie, Tony's new duchess, round with child, was devastated at his father's death, for she'd loved Marcus Barrington, as most women did. Leo's sisters and Olivia, Amanda's ward, had fluttered about hopelessly lost, like a flock of wounded doves, uncertain where to land without Marcus to direct them.

God, the paintings Theodosia had done.

Horrible, stark expressions of anguish on canvas. Painful to look at.

The staff of Cherry Hill had been prostrate with grief over his father's death. Black armbands adorned their arms. Cook had burned dinner two nights in a row. Maids had wept while they cleaned and dusted. Even the bloody horses in the stable had worn expressions of loss.

Because *everyone* had loved Marcus Barrington, it seemed, but his two sons.

"I loved him," Leo whispered, his breath rustling the paper of the letter. "Only I didn't want to." Something else he'd realized far too late.

Blame and regret were such dangerous emotions, especially when mixed with bitterness and anger. Leo had spent his whole life keeping his feelings tucked carefully away, safely hidden beneath his charming demeanor, pretending so many things didn't matter when in fact, they did.

He eyed the letter, reached to touch the pages, and just as quickly jerked his hand away.

Those pages were the last words of Marcus Barrington, Duke of Averell, to his bastard son. Amanda had tossed it at Leo, still unable to even speak civilly to him.

Tony, she wouldn't even look at.

After reading the letter, Leo had calmly folded the paper and placed it in his coat pocket. He'd stared out at his assembled family, snarling out that he must immediately return to

London. No one had seemed shocked. Tony hadn't tried to stop him.

Now he had read the letter so many times he could recite every word, trace every flourish of the shaking hand which had laid out the truth to him. A truth Leo had missed in that hallway at Elysium as Georgina had slid away from him. And all the truths that had come before.

He took a mouthful of the scotch, swishing it around in his mouth.

What about when I become with child. What then, Leo?

But there already was a child. *His* child. She'd failed to mention that very pertinent fact to Leo.

A bastard just like him.

He'd sworn never to have children. He only had to think of Tony's mother to know what havoc a bastard could cause. He'd always been so careful. Made sure his bed partners used tiny sponges soaked in vinegar. Covered his cock in those awful French letters.

What a bloody stupid name. French letter.

Except with Georgina. He'd taken no real precautions with her besides withdrawing, a method not in the least fool-proof. Part of him, Leo finally admitted, had wanted the sight of Georgina round with his child. It had taken over a month and a great deal of scotch for him to admit *that* truth.

He'd sent a note to Beechwood Court, *finally*. As furious as he was at Georgina's deception, they *would* come to some sort of understanding, he just wasn't sure what it would be yet.

The reply had come from her butler.

Lady Masterson has extended her stay in London.

Next, he went to the town home she rented in Mayfair, but the staff there insisted she'd gone to Paris.

Georgina didn't even speak French.

The longer Leo went without being able to find Georgina,

the angrier he became. She was clearly hiding from him. So, in an effort to flush her out, he called in Masterson's markers. But that only succeeded in bringing Harold to his door.

God, he detested Harold.

Harold had begged. Pleaded. Blamed his lack of funds on the American girl his uncle had had the bad fortune to marry. Interesting, considering it was Georgina's dowry that had kept Masterson's estate afloat. When *Harold* found Georgina, the earl had whined, his debt to Leo would be repaid in full. She was on the Continent, according to her solicitor, because her family wouldn't welcome her return to America. No doubt Georgina was living extravagantly. Spending the sum in her account she'd coaxed his uncle into giving her which rightfully belonged to Harold.

The fortune *Leo* had given Georgina. He'd nearly corrected Harold. Lind had been instructed some time ago to never, under any circumstances, release the sum to anyone but Georgina. Even if Harold or his twit of a wife brought an army of solicitors to Lind's door.

Leo had waved a hand at Masterson's nephew in dismissal, giving no hint of his intentions toward the markers or anything else. Harold, besides being greedy, was an idiot.

Georgina would *never* go to the Continent, no matter the trail she'd left for Harold to follow or what Lind claimed. Whether Jacob Rutherford would welcome his daughter or not, Georgina would go home. She'd longed for New York the entire time Leo had known her.

When Leo had finally confronted Lind, the solicitor admitted he'd arranged passage for his client, Lady Masterson, to Boston. He'd also added he may have led Lord Masterson to believe she was in Italy. All of which, Mr. Lind insisted, did not violate his agreement with Mr. Murphy.

Mr. Lind had been correct. It had not. Nor had Leo ever

specifically stated that Lind was to inform him of Georgina's whereabouts. An oversight on Leo's part.

He reached again for the nearly empty decanter. How much scotch, he wondered, would it take to render him unconscious? He plucked up the first page of his father's letter, forcing himself to reread the words he already knew by heart.

Dear Leo,

I love you.

You have always been my son as much as Anthony. I never saw you any differently, but I know the world has. I could have allowed another man to claim you as his, but I refused. You were my son. My child. I wanted you. I won't apologize for that though I know it has caused you hardship. I alone am to blame for the tragedy of Katherine's death. Anthony's mother did not die because of your existence, Leo. The guilt you carry isn't yours, but mine.

He'd hated Marcus for making him different. Felt, deep inside, that it was the knowledge of his existence that had led to the death of Tony's mother. Blamed Marcus every time Leo had been taunted for his birth. For every sneer thrown in his direction. For being spat on at school. *For being muck.*

True, Leo had loved his father as a child, but after Tony's mother died, after she and the rest of the world finally saw Leo for what he was, it was Tony who'd deserved his loyalty. Not Marcus. And Tony wanted to punish their father in the worst way possible. Leo had agreed.

"What a rotten human being I am," he whispered to the room.

I must ask that you take great care of your sisters and Olivia, for they will need your guidance. You are calm and decisive where your brother is not. They will need your patience. Please take great care with my duchess. Amanda loves you as if you were her own, and I fear she will be lost for a time when I am gone.

"Yes," Leo choked out as moisture gathered behind his

eyes. He slammed his palm on the table, relishing the sting of the wood. "Because *you* are her fucking person, Marcus."

Remain close to your brother. If there is any bit of good that came from the selfish man I used to be, it is that my mistakes bonded you and Anthony to each other. He will need you now that he is a duke. As will Maggie, especially if Anthony continues to behave like an idiot. Something else I am to blame for and for which I take responsibility.

Tony was a *massive* idiot at times.

Leo took up the final page of his father's letter.

I know of your feeling for Lady Masterson.

Leo scratched at the pain blooming and cresting across his torso. Yes, his *feeling*. What a bland way to describe what Georgina was to him. He both hated and longed for her.

You will find this somewhat amusing, Leo, that I owed a debt to Lord Masterson. You will wonder what it is, but I will only say he did me a great service many years ago. We were not friends. Barely more than acquaintances. But I promised Amanda I would be a better man, so I resolved to repay Masterson the debt which I owed him. I thought it would involve helping him avoid impoverishment, but before I could offer him my assistance, Masterson died. Which is how I came to offer my aid to his widow, should she require it.

The statement never failed to surprise Leo no matter how many times he read the letter. He couldn't fathom any circumstance in which Masterson could have helped the Duke of Averell. He meant to ask Amanda one day. When she was speaking to him again.

Lady Masterson dismissed my honorable intentions. Then she promptly turned and cast up her accounts into a pot of peonies. Women do not lose their breakfast at the sight of me, Leo.

Arrogant to the last, that was Marcus.

The room tilted slightly, blurring at the edges. Leo gripped the table to keep from toppling over. He really should eat something, but the omelet wasn't the least bit appetizing. He ought to send Peckham for something more edible.

Lady Masterson was with child. One she refused to claim as Masterson's either in London or in America, for various reasons.

He hated the next paragraph. Detested the words. His fingers shook as he poured from the decanter, spilling some of the scotch across the table.

The child was the result of a brief indiscretion with a gentleman who no longer had any interest in her and would not welcome a child. She was adamant on that fact. Under the guise of friendship to her late husband, I invited her to visit one of my remote estates to grieve. I gently told her there was an orphanage nearby should she require their services. Her response was to ask me to post a letter to her cousin in New York. I know she returned to London because Amanda told me of Lady Masterson's garden party, but there was no talk of a child. A child I now suspect is yours.

His entire family teased Leo about his liking for Lady Masterson. It wasn't a secret. Amanda had probably mentioned it to Marcus when she returned to Cherry Hill after Marcus's health took a turn for the worst. He must have made the connection shortly before he died.

Leo had told no one what the letter contained. Not even Tony. The news of Georgina's deception had shaken him to the very core of his being. He'd been so bloody incensed by what she'd done, keeping the news of a child from him if he'd come across her immediately after, Leo might well have strangled her.

Instead, he'd thrown himself into running Elysium. Then when he'd finally sought her out, she'd been gone. And Leo had slowly started to unravel.

He'd tried, unsuccessfully, to forget her and the grief over his father in every bottle of scotch he could find. Invited women to his rooms but found little desire to bed any of them and always ended up sending them away. He drank alone in the garden. He hadn't even gone to Cherry Hill when his nephew had been born.

She must have known I was your father, but she never once confided the truth to me. It pains me to tell you I have no idea what happened to your child.

Marcus's own grandchild.

Such deceit, Georgina.

Leo pressed his forehead into the desk and sucked in a breath, smelling the scotch soaked into his skin. His father could have stayed silent on the matter of Georgina. Leo would never have known. Certainly, her behavior when she returned to London gave no indication of what she'd done. Having a bloody garden party. Floating about Elysium to play cards with Tony and Maggie. Calling on Amanda and the girls, *his family*, sipping tea and eating biscuits. Avoiding Leo. Yes, he'd told her he didn't want a bastard. And yes, he'd also mentioned the apothecary. But now this child, this part of Leo, was alive in the world. She had no right to keep such a thing from him.

He'd been locked away in his rooms for weeks, it seemed, his only companions a continuous stream of scotch and trays of food which he sometimes picked at, allowing the hollowness inside him to grow until it filled his entire chest. Now it broke apart. Shattered. Taking Leo with it.

"I want my child." It was the first time Leo had uttered those words out loud.

Christ, I'll have to cross the fucking ocean.

Georgina wasn't stupid. She wouldn't go marching into Manhattan with a child on her hip, not after going to such lengths to hide its existence. Remarriage was really the only option if she meant to adopt her own child. She was very clever. Much more intelligent than anyone but Leo had ever given her credit for.

Another man might, even now, be touching that magnificent bosom. Or telling her she smelled like spring.

A snarl came from him.

If she thought for one bloody instant Leo would allow *his* child to be raised by another man, Georgina was very much mistaken.

Marcus hadn't allowed it. Leo wouldn't either.

His nose wrinkled as he caught another whiff of his clothing, the darkness edging into his vision again. A bath might be needed. Along with a tray of food. Which he would eat. It had been hard-fought, his decision. Change was difficult. The scotch hadn't helped as much as he thought it would. The thought of crossing a large expanse of water made his stomach heave and his fingers tremble.

"I want my child," he said again to the empty room.

At any rate, Tony was bound to show up at Elysium sooner rather than later. Someone, probably Peckham, that worthless cur, had written Tony that Leo hadn't been himself in months, not since the duke's death. Elysium was suffering. The staff was growing disgruntled. And as of late, Mr. Murphy barely left his rooms, leaving the running of the gambling hell to Peckam and Smith.

Tony had enclosed Peckham's letter in the note he'd sent, informing Leo he would return to London within a fortnight. And he wasn't pleased to be leaving his duchess and his newly born heir.

Yes, well, I'm not pleased my child is a bloody ocean away.

Leo pushed himself up, ignoring the alarming way the room spun; the fireplace seemed miles from him. He stumbled to the door, bumping his knee and tripping over a pile of books. Opening the door a crack, he saw Jones standing guard at the top of the steps. Motioning Jones over, Leo ignored the one-armed man's wince at catching a whiff of him.

"I think we can both agree I need a bath, Jones. No need

to be so blatant in your opinion. And send up some food. Something to drink other than scotch."

"Tea?" Jones asked. "Perhaps I should send for a physician."

"Tea is fine. No physician." Leo shut the door in the man's face then opened it again. "Food first."

His stomach pitched in an unpleasant fashion again as he shut the door once more. It was probably the scotch and the lack of food, but Leo thought it the knowledge he'd have to be on a ship. On the water.

One more reason to be furious at Georgina. Having to chase her across the ocean. He hated the ocean. She *knew* that.

"I want my child," he whispered. Leo had never thought he would say those words.

Marcus Barrington expected Leo to be a better man. Demanded it, else he wouldn't have bothered uttering a word about Georgina. Leo would tell Tony only that he was exploring business opportunities in America and might be gone for some time.

His brother wouldn't believe him, but Leo didn't care.

eorgina smiled up into the late afternoon sunshine
as she trailed after the tiny boy crawling along the
grass at the edge of the blanket. He pushed
himself up, struggling to stand, then fell back on his bottom.
With a grunt, he flung out his arms, pulling the lower half of
his body behind him.

"Oh, my little wiggly worm, come here."

He scooted away from her, chubby legs and thighs
pumping furiously as he set out across the lawn. Pausing, his
little hand dug in the dirt. He sat up again, a stone clutched
in one hand. Waving his treasure about, he gave her a half-
grin. Blue eyes, with a distinct ring of indigo, sparkled back
at her.

Her heart skipped a beat.

Sunlight streamed through the trees above their heads,
dappling the deep brown curls adorning her son's head. There
was very little of Georgina in Daniel. Certainly not in his
coloring or the shape of his mouth. He'd been born with a full
head of dark hair, and while many children's eyes were blue at
birth, Daniel's had changed only to become a darker, more

vibrant shade of sapphire. He would look very much like Leo one day.

She tried to coax him over to her, but Daniel shrugged away from her, grabbing at her sister, Lilian's skirts. Bracing himself, he pulled himself up using her knee for balance.

"Ma ma ma." Tiny fingers held on tightly to her skirts as he shoved the rock he held beneath her nose.

"Glorious, Daniel." Lilian took the rock from him, pretending to admire it. "A very fine specimen. But let us put this aside lest you try to chew on it." She handed him a small, stuffed horse. "Perhaps this would be best."

Daniel immediately began to gnaw on the fabric of the horse.

Georgina reached for him again and he pulled away, laying his head in Lilian's lap.

"Ma ma ma."

She sat back, deflated, her heart aching. Looking up into the nearly bare branches of the maple tree above them, she blinked back tears at her son's rejection. Ridiculous to feel this way. Lilian was all he'd known for most of his short life. Still, his preference for her sister cut Georgina to the quick.

"Georgina," Lilian whispered, fingers stroking Daniel's curls. "It will take some time for him to grow accustomed to you. He was barely five months old when I brought him home."

Lilian, in the company of their cousin, Benjamin Cooke, had come to England just before Georgina delivered Daniel. Their trip had been fairly easy to arrange. Ben told Lilian's husband, William, he was taking her to visit Georgina, who was in mourning for her husband. They'd stayed in Cumberland at the duke's remote estate until Daniel was deemed able to travel. It had broken Georgina's already frayed heart to let her child go. But she had.

"You're right, of course." Georgina nodded, wiping away a

tear falling down her cheek. "How could he possibly remember me? I was nothing more than a pair of bosoms when I handed him to you." She gave a weak laugh. "I doubt Daniel knew the difference between myself or the wet nurse Ben found."

"I don't think that is entirely true." Lilian took her hand and gave her fingers a gentle squeeze. "Daniel felt your love for him."

"How can you be so sure?"

"Because *I* did," Lilian said.

"I should have come back with you." Georgina looked away into the thick woods surrounding her sister's home on the outskirts of Brooklyn Heights. As much as she loved the bustle of Manhattan, there was something to be said for the peace one could find so close to nature. Eventually, she would like to live in such a place outside the city. The home her grandmother had once inhabited in Garrison on the Hudson River still stood vacant.

"But I was so worried about Harold." She turned back to her sister. "I—couldn't let Harold know about Daniel. He would have taken him from me. Or hurt him. I think Harold's plan was to lock me away since he failed in having me killed." She'd told Lilian and Ben everything when they'd balked at returning to New York without her. Stella had begged to stay with her. "Harold would have used him, I think. I still worry—"

"Even if Harold knows about Daniel, which he doesn't, you are safe here. He would be a fool to chase you across the ocean, and for what? You told me yourself you instructed your solicitor to give him the sum in the account Masterson left you. You fled with the clothes on your back. You didn't even take your jewelry."

There was Beechwood Court. The estate, though small,

was worth a great deal of money. Only it wasn't hers to give to Harold.

"Not even Father knows about Daniel. Only me, you, and Ben."

"And William." Georgina mentioned Lilian's husband. "He knows." It had been necessary to tell William some of the truth, but not all. To society, Daniel was introduced as the son of one of William's distant relations, a couple who had died while making their way out west. William's parents were dead, and his only brother, of whom he rarely spoke, lived in New Orleans. There wasn't anyone to contradict the story.

"William isn't going to say a word. He's happy to help you. Once you're remarried, you'll have the protection of your husband and can adopt Daniel." She reached out to wipe a tear from Georgina's cheek. "In the meantime, rest assured that Ben would never allow anything to happen to Daniel. Nor would I."

"Did I tell you that while I was in England, before I left for Cumberland, I fell asleep before the fire in the drawing room? I awoke to find Harold standing over me. Just staring with those soulless eyes of his. I was terrified. He's quite mad. I'm sure of it. And you can't reason with the mad."

"Grandmother often said that, didn't she?"

"Among a great many other things." Georgina had always been their grandmother's favorite, while Lilian had been doted on by their parents.

And why wouldn't they dote on her? Georgina reasoned. *Lilian is perfect.*

Lilian smoothed a curl from Daniel's cheek. He was busy gnawing on his fist, oblivious to them both, his eyes fixated on the stark branches above them. His head rested on the small mound of Lilian's stomach. Finally, after nearly three years of marriage and several failed attempts, Lilian was with child.

"Curses, mostly." Lilian laughed softly. "I'm sure she only taught you such words to annoy Mother. She succeeded. That's why Mother finally gave up and allowed you to spend a great deal of time in Garrison while I was stuck in the city, learning how to walk properly with a book on my head."

Georgina snorted. "Not walking, *floating*, Lilian. She did try with me, but the book kept falling off and hitting the floor. When the spine finally broke, so did Mother."

Lilian laughed again. "Yes, well, she liked to claim one of the ways a gentleman chose his wife was based on the way she walked into a room."

"I'm not even sure Masterson noticed when I entered a room. Or paid very much attention to me at all. Just my money."

"I know you blame Father for your marriage—"

"Is there someone else I should take to task for wedding me to an elderly man who preferred bedding his grooms to me? Or for banishing me all the way to England because of a silly mistake? I don't even know how Father met Masterson."

"Your reputation was in tatters, Georgina," Lilian said quietly. "There was little else they could do. Masterson and Father had a mutual acquaintance, I believe. Lord Penny-broke. Don't you remember when Father went to London on business one year? I think he met Masterson through Penny-broke then. At least that's what Ben told me after your marriage."

"They wouldn't even allow me to come home and see you wed, Lilian."

"The gossip was very bad." Her sister patted Daniel on the back as he chewed on the stuffed horse. "Not even Ben could sway Father. You're still talked about, though a bit more quietly."

Georgina knew her cousin had tried to dissuade her father. But there was no moving Jacob Rutherford once he'd made up his mind. "Father wanted a title, and I suppose he thought Masterson would do. Just as he wished for a lawyer in the family."

Lilian's calm expression faltered. "That isn't fair. William and I were enamored of each other before Father encouraged the match."

Georgina wasn't sure that was the case, but Lilian loved William Harrison and seemed oblivious to whatever machinations their father had been part of to ensure he had a lawyer and budding politician in the family. Jacob Rutherford rarely did anything without a reason.

"I'm sorry." Georgina touched her sister's arm. "I know of the affection you and William have for each other. The proof," she smiled at the bump of Lilian's stomach where Daniel's head rested, "is before me." Her sister had gone through the agony of two miscarriages before finally conceiving and carrying the child long enough that the fear of loss had finally diminished. Her physician, one of the best in Manhattan, deemed Lilian and the child both healthy. "Perhaps I am only jealous. My marriage was hardly a love match."

An image of Leo flashed before her eyes, and Georgina bit her lip. She didn't want to miss him as much as she did. Some nights, she wondered what would have happened if she'd told him about Harold. Or Daniel. What more might he have said?

It would have changed nothing.

"Speaking of marriage, how is Mr. Fletcher?" Lilian said.

"Handsome enough, I suppose. But not the sort of gentleman whose attentions I wish to engage. I find him to be boring and tedious. Always droning on about laws and dropping the names of prominent people, hoping I'll be impressed."

"He's a congressman, Georgina. Wealthy and well-connected. Related to the Biddles of Philadelphia. Fletcher is completely besotted by you."

"According to Mother." Lustful would be a better term for Fletcher's affections. Were they to wed, Georgina expected she would need to tolerate an entire array of mistresses when Fletcher tired of her. "She mistakes his desire to bed me with something else."

"Georgina." Lilian's cheeks pinked. "I'm sure that isn't the case."

Lilian was a bit of a prude. She wasn't even sure anyone else had ever kissed her sister except for William. Whereas Georgina had deliberately allowed a kiss to be stolen by her beau. They were nothing alike, she and Lilian. Georgina always flouted convention while Lilian embraced the gilded cage most women found themselves in.

"And Fletcher speaks to me as if I can't understand the simplest subjects. As if his political maneuvering were beyond my female comprehension." Had he approached Georgina more as an equal and less an ornament—

A shiny bauble.

Georgina looked away across the expanse of her sister's lawn edged by rolling hills covered with thick trees that stretched as far as the eye could see. Her sister's home was somewhat isolated now, but Georgina thought in time, as more prominent merchants, lawyers, doctors and the like moved here, the landscape would become less untamed. "I'll find someone soon, Lilian. I promise. It just won't be Fletcher. I don't want my problems to become yours. Nor Daniel to become a burden."

"He isn't. Nor are you. I took him gladly," she emphasized. "Good practice for me, don't you think?" She patted her mid-section. "I would do anything for you, Georgina. And Daniel. You know that."

"I do."

Lilian, her beautiful older sister. So full of light, it practically radiated from her very pores. Unlike Georgina, Lilian was slender. Willowy. The perfection of her features, the porcelain skin and striking white-blond hair, gave her the appearance of a fairy princess. Lilian had always been the very embodiment of the perfectly well-bred young lady. She was soft-spoken and docile where Georgina was determined to disobey. Ben taught Georgina how to swordfight and climb trees while Lilian practiced her embroidery and took ladylike walks in the park.

"You would have made a much better countess than I did," Georgina blurted out. "I was disliked the moment I set foot in London."

"And did nothing to change anyone's opinion, did you?" Lilian gave her a sideways glance. "I would guess you went out of your way to be thought outrageous."

Georgina shrugged. "My speech was compared to that of a wounded waterfowl."

Lilian gave her a wry smile. "I don't think I would have enjoyed being a countess either, at any rate. Even in New York, our family's pedigree doesn't stretch back far enough for some. I would have been disparaged the same as you and not handled the ridicule nearly as well. You will have to speak to Father at some point, you know."

"I've spoken to him. I think he'd like to send me back to England where he can forget he has another daughter. Perhaps have me ruin myself for a duke this time so he can add another title to the family." Georgina's eyes ran over Daniel. "But I'm not going back. Ever."

"No, you are not." Lilian's eyes widened. "Oh. He's kicking."

"He?" Georgina placed her hand on the small mound, brushing her fingers against Daniel's cheek.

He smiled up at her, taking Georgina's breath away.

"William insists the child will be a boy. You know how men are. They want a son to carry on the family name."

"Then it's a pity Ben won't change his to please Father." Ben had been her father's son in everything but name from the moment he appeared on the Rutherford doorstep that cold, winter day. But Ben didn't always agree with her father and refused to be put under Jacob Rutherford's thumb. "I don't think all men want a child to carry on their name."

Leo hadn't.

Georgina had had nothing to do but think while on her way from London to Boston where the *Betty Sue* docked. She'd spent quite a lot of her time thinking of Leo and wondering at the events that had shaped him.

Leo Murphy was a highly complicated, brilliant man who brandished his illegitimacy at the world like a weapon, using it to both excuse his actions and to protect himself. Instead of remaining in the shadow of the Barringtons, Leo deliberately chose to operate a gambling hell and pleasure palace which catered to the very people who looked down their noses at him. He demanded attention with his charming manner even while his gaudy waistcoats sent a clear message. *Don't mistake me for one of you.*

The attraction between them had been immediate and mutual but instead of seducing her outright, he'd gone out of his way to make their encounter nothing more than a wager. He couldn't afford to allow their joining to have any meaning.

Because he was a bastard.

Because he thought his illegitimacy *mattered* to her.

"You're thinking of him, aren't you? Daniel's father. You get a faraway look in your eyes when he crosses your mind. Wistful. As if you're remembering a wonderful dream. I think you would feel better, Georgina, if you—"

"No," she snapped, startling Daniel who regarded her with

Leo's eyes. "I'm sorry, my love." She patted her son's back before ruffling his hair. "Mommy's sorry."

Georgina had never told Ben or Lilian about Leo, thinking that the fewer people who knew the truth, the better off she and Daniel would be. Ben probably knew. He'd taken a trip to London after he arrived with Lilian. Exploring opportunities, he'd said. But Georgina knew her cousin.

"Ma." Daniel patted her knee with one small hand. "Ma."

The most perfect bloom of love opened up in her chest. "Yes. Mommy."

"You love him. Daniel's father." Lilian's casual statement hung in the air between them.

Yes, she did, even after everything that had happened. She also hated Leo for caring more about his illegitimacy than her. Or Daniel. She'd screamed for Leo as she brought Daniel into the world. Wanting him so badly she'd nearly had Stella send for him.

"I did the right thing. He didn't want a child, especially a bastard."

"But he cares for you. You've admitted that much to me. I think he would want to know, Georgina."

"It's far too late for that now. Telling him would serve no purpose other than to alleviate my own guilt. Because if it *did* matter to him, the fact that I hid Daniel and fled to America without telling him would make him hate me, don't you think?" Georgina didn't think she could bear that. Leo's hatred.

Lilian gave her a worried look. "Possibly. But—"

"What's done is done, Lilian."

Lilian finally gave a delicate roll of her shoulders and looked in the direction of the house. "William will be home soon if he isn't already prowling about. Will you stay for supper?"

"No, I don't think so." William wasn't overly fond of

Georgina, nor she of him. She'd met him briefly during the social season some years ago. The scandal between her and John Winbow had been months away and William hadn't yet decided to court Lilian or caught Jacob Rutherford's calculating eye. At their introduction, William had been polite, but disdain had fairly dripped from him as he took her hand.

Winbow, as Lilian had reminded her, wasn't Georgina's first venture into improper behavior, and William was rather staid and upstanding. He'd probably cheered from the docks when she was sent to England.

"I know William isn't happy with the situation, especially lying to our parents."

"He's fine," Lilian said with a firm press of her lips. "He understands. Ben explained everything to William. As you know, our cousin can be very persuasive. My husband is happy to help."

Persuasive was a kind way of saying Ben either promised William a very large favor or he'd threatened him. Probably the latter. No favor would have been big enough for William to fabricate a long-lost relative no one had ever heard of whose child he'd suddenly inherited. Lilian loved her husband, so Georgina didn't speculate out loud. But William had always struck Georgina as secretive and not nearly as accommodating as he pretended to be.

Ben had likely found William's weakness and exploited it.

Her cousin was also not as nice as he liked others to believe.

"I could never repay you or William for all you've done." She looked down at Daniel, who struggled to keep his eyes open, the rock still clutched in one hand. If Georgina had ignored her instincts and foolishly tried to pass off Daniel as Masterson's, all of London would have known the truth just by looking at her son.

Irrational panic flooded her. She pressed a hand to her heart.

Daniel is safe. I'm safe.

"You can repay us by finding a wonderful gentleman worthy of your hand. I want you and Daniel to be happy. Protected. Safe. But there isn't any rush. Besides, now that William has hired a nanny to help me with both Daniel and this little one," she looked down happily at her stomach, "there isn't any reason why my nephew can't stay here indefinitely. If Fletcher doesn't suit, someone else will."

Georgina wasn't so sure.

A small hand thrust up before Georgina, palm open, offering her his rock. "Ma."

"Thank you, my love." She reached up and brushed a wave of dark hair from his face. She blinked, willing the tears away from her eyes once more, refusing to allow her son to see her weep. Daniel might start to think of her as only some perpetually sad woman, covered in tears, who brought him presents.

The love she had for her son, this one tiny person, eclipsed everything else in her life. She would do *anything* to protect him. Had done *everything*. The worst day of her life had been giving Daniel to Lilian for the journey back to America. She'd fallen to the ground into a sobbing heap, Stella refusing to leave her until Ben had forced her maid into the waiting coach. Georgina had been inconsolable for weeks. Once she'd returned to London, she had to wander about pretending Daniel didn't exist. It had very nearly destroyed her.

"Ma," Daniel said, this time patting Georgina's knee with his empty hand. "Ma." He looked again at Lilian.

"I told you he would start to figure it out," Lilian whispered. "When he truly begins to speak, it will be you he calls Mama, not I. I'll just be Aunt Lil, and he won't remember any of this. Does he look like him?"

"Yes. The spitting image." She hesitated, thinking of Leo. "He's a very handsome man. Beautiful, most would say." Georgina picked up Daniel and placed him against her hip, ignoring the pinch in her chest at the thought of Leo.

Lilian nodded but thankfully didn't ask anything more.

They strolled leisurely across the lawn toward the house, Daniel clasped firmly in Georgina's arms. When they stepped inside, she nodded to Lilian. "I'll take him upstairs."

"William doesn't appear to be home yet. I think I'll have some tea." Her sister pressed a kiss to Daniel's temple before wandering off in the direction of her parlor, where she would probably doze off until William arrived home.

Georgina climbed the steps, her nose buried in Daniel's hair as she went up to the nursery.

"Ah, there's Master Daniel." The nanny, Mrs. Gibbons, looked up from where she'd been folding a blanket and stepped forward, her arms outstretched. Clean linen and lemons, with the hint of some spice, filled the air around Mrs. Gibbons. Cinnamon, maybe. She was tall for a woman. Pretty. Young for a nanny, but then Georgina was quite young to be a widow.

"I think I'd like to rock Daniel for a bit. Mrs. Gibbons. Why don't you enjoy a cup of tea in the kitchens? I'll put him down for his nap."

"Very good, ma'am," she said. "A cup of tea is always welcome. And I've an errand to run at any rate." Smiling, she shut the door of the nursery behind her.

Georgina relaxed into a nearby chair where she rocked her son to sleep, humming softly as Daniel's little hand pressed against her heart. "I love you," she whispered into his head of curls. "More than anything. And we are home now. Mommy will keep you safe."

When Georgina had caught sight of New York after first arriving in Boston, she'd wept, clinging to the railing with sheer joy. She'd sent word to Ben immediately upon disembarking, since her father's offices were fairly close, then waited patiently for him to retrieve her. It was to his home she'd gone first before facing her parents. He'd been worried that she'd arrived far sooner than he'd expected, cursing Harold and even Georgina's father for sending her to England in the first place.

On the carriage ride to Ben's home, after Georgina had been assured Daniel was well and Ben would bring her to him the following day, she'd relaxed against the cushions, staring out the window at a city that had changed dramatically since she'd wed Masterson. There had been a terrible fire the year before her marriage, destroying entire city blocks. The wood buildings had gone up in an inferno that couldn't be put out because there wasn't enough water to keep the flames at bay. Now those wooden buildings had been replaced with stone and granite, larger and far more elaborate than their predecessors. Manhattan had become unrecognizable in the years since she'd been gone, the city surging northwest and creating new neighborhoods. Immigrants flooded the streets, their accents and languages melding in a loud cacophony when she walked to the park a short distance from her home. The harbor was busier than ever, the wharves teeming with ships and crates. The other day, she had stood on Broadway Street and simply looked around in awe.

A small snore met her ears and Georgina looked down at her son, now sound asleep in her arms. She continued to rock, staring at his sweet face. She would never give Daniel up again. Not for anyone. If she didn't remarry, and Georgina wasn't sure she would, she would find another way to keep him with her.

After a time, the sun began to dip low in the sky, a signal it was time for Georgina to leave. The last ferry to Manhattan was rarely late, and she had an event to attend this evening. Her mother's pet project had finally come to fruition. The Rutherford opera house was opening tonight.

Her mother disliked the Italian Opera house on Church and Leonard, finding the building antiquated and not nearly luxurious enough. Determined to be responsible for bringing more culture to Manhattan, and to tweak the nose of Jacob Astor who was determined to do the same, Cordelia Rutherford had struck first. *Her* opera house, into which she'd poured enormous amounts of her husband's money, was to be dedicated to both opera, preferably Italian, *and* theater. A concession Mother made because opera, even performed in Italian, wasn't nearly as popular as one would think. A theater also had the advantage of attracting the lower classes to performances, which meant greater profitability overall.

Mother had learned a few things from Jacob Rutherford.

Georgina hadn't attended many events since returning to New York—a select number of gatherings at the homes of people she'd once been acquainted with and a dinner party or two her mother had hosted. While she adored being back in Manhattan, she was less enthusiastic about returning to society, though it was necessary for her to do so if she meant to find a husband. And Mother was adamant that she find one.

I'm to be trotted out like a prize mare. Or a sow.

Making her way down to the foyer after kissing Daniel once more, Georgina's steps faltered as she caught sight of William at the bottom of the stairs. While she and her brother-in-law kept their mutual dislike for each other well-hidden from Lilian, there was no reason to be in each other's company more than necessary. William was a lawyer, his specialty contracts, legal writs, wills, property, and the like. Perfect for her father, who always needed to find a loophole or a way out of a contract he'd since found not to his liking. William also had the advantage of being related to the Beekmans, one of the city's older, monied families, which was probably why Father had looked so favorably on his courtship of Lilian. He was handsome enough, Georgina supposed, with his sandy hair, pale blue eyes, and athletic build. More importantly, William adored Lilian.

"Georgina, you'll have to hurry to make the last ferry." He nodded at her, white teeth flashing a brief, polite smile. "Unless you're staying?"

"No, though whatever your cook is making smells marvelous. I promised my mother I would attend her grand party tonight."

Part of her wanted to ask William exactly what Ben had used to get him to agree to take in Daniel. She couldn't imagine it was anything nefarious. William's reputation was impeccable. He was highly respected. Well-liked. So much so, he was already being groomed for political office. First, alderman, she thought. Then with her father's backing, possibly mayor one day.

A maid hurried forward with Georgina's cloak, and William placed the wool over her shoulders.

"Lilian—"

"Is sound asleep in the parlor," William said, "embroidery perched on her lap. Your visit wore her out, I'm afraid. I'll tell her you got off all right. I hate to wake her."

"No, please don't. Let her sleep." Lilian was often very tired. But Georgina had been as well when she'd carried Daniel.

"The air has grown brisk. I smell snow in the air," he said.

"Let's hope your nose is wrong." She tugged on her gloves, pulling the cloak's hood over her head. "How is it you and Lilian aren't forced into attendance this evening, yet I must go?"

Georgina's father was out of town on business yet again. Mother was livid he wouldn't be present for her big evening.

"Lilian's condition is a fine excuse to not enjoy the opera.

Your mother wants nothing to happen to her first grandchild."

Georgina paused as she secured her cloak. William didn't mean anything by it. Her mother didn't *know* Daniel was her grandson. To Georgina's knowledge, she'd never even seen him.

"I'm sure you'll enjoy the event, though." A hint of whiskey scented his breath. "I'll have Warner see you safely to the ferry. Enjoy the opera."

"I shall certainly try." She slipped out the door to see Warner, one of Lilian's staff, waiting patiently by the carriage. She turned to wave back at her brother-in-law, but he had already closed the door behind her.

❧ 14 ❧

"**M**a'am." Her maid walked into Georgina's bedroom, her cheeks a lovely shade of pink, fingers twisting in her skirts. "Mr. Cooke is waiting downstairs for you and begs me to tell you to hurry along. His exact words."

Georgina resolved to take a few more minutes just to annoy her cousin. "My word, Stella. Are you blushing?"

"Not in the least," the maid replied tartly. "It's a bit warm in here is all, and I ran up the steps. Emily has put Mr. Cooke in the front parlor."

Georgina tried not to smile at her maid's obvious attempts to hide her adoration of Mr. Benjamin Cooke. He always sent her female servants into near swoons whenever he appeared.

"Very good, Stella." She smoothed down her velvet skirts. "What do you think?" Georgina turned before the oval mirror and picked up her fan, taking in the yards of crimson velvet curling around her body.

Scandalous.

Bits of jet dangled across the neckline, which wasn't

modest in the least. The waist was tight, hugging the outline of her curves. She tried to take a deep breath and failed.

"Laced you tight, I did," Stella said from the door. "Only way to get the dress on."

"I hope I don't faint." Georgina snapped the fan, thinking of the face her mother would make if she did so.

"You look like a sweet on Christmas Day." Stella took in the rise of Georgina's bosom above the velvet. "Mrs. Rutherford is unlikely to approve of the gown."

"Splendid," Georgina answered. "That is exactly what I'm hoping for."

Georgina was still working out her anger toward her parents after what they'd sent her to endure. Of course, they couldn't have predicted Harold being mad as a hatter, but still, banishing her to England had been extreme. Her relationship with her mother was strained, though it always had been. Cordelia Rutherford dictated. Georgina rebelled. At least they were on speaking terms, which was more than Georgina could say of her relationship with her father.

Her parents wanted her to remarry. The quicker the better. Preferably to a man her father would choose for her. Fletcher had been deemed suitable by Father, which had quickly sealed the politician's fate. Georgina would never wed him.

She made her way to the front parlor, a cozy room Georgina had decorated in pale greens and golds. Ben had gone with her to order the furniture from Phyfe and Sons. Standing in the doorway, she took a moment to admire the clean lines and gentle curves of Phyfe's sofa and tables, custom-made for this room. A painting of the Hudson filled with vibrant fall colors hung on the wall. Sometimes, as she settled in with the coffee she liked each morning, Georgina would stare at the brushstrokes depicting the water and trees, longing for the home her grandmother had once inhabited.

The gentleman prowling around the parlor sent her a mischievous grin as she entered, making him appear carelessly boyish when he was nothing of the sort. Overly tall, with a lean, athletic build clothed to perfection in his expensively tailored evening clothes, Benjamin Cooke was the very picture of a well-heeled gentleman. Hard to believe Ben hadn't been born to wealth and privilege. He'd had to earn his place at her father's side, becoming a younger, slightly kinder version of Jacob Rutherford. But the ruthless ambition, something he had in common with Leo, hadn't been learned. Ben's nature in that regard had been apparent even when they were children.

She often wondered where her cousin had spent the first ten years of his life.

"There you are, George." Ben turned to her, lifting a glass filled with amber liquid. "Helped myself. Didn't suppose you would mind. Very fine whiskey you keep in your home. But I don't see any sherry. And here I'd thought you'd become a lady after all that time in London."

"Perish the thought."

A vision of a shivering ten-year-old boy superimposed itself over the brutally handsome man before her. He'd stood on the steps of the Rutherford mansion, clothing so threadbare she'd been able to see his skin beneath. The flecks of green in his hazel eyes had glowed with resolve and determination. He'd been dirty. Starving.

Ben was still hungry, just not for food any longer.

He was a mystery, her cousin, though she deemed him her dearest friend. They'd been close their whole lives, since Georgina had found him at the door, begging to be let inside, pointing at the note pinned to his chest. The note declared him to be the son of Alice Rutherford, her father's younger sister who'd run off and married a sea captain years ago and hadn't been seen or heard from since.

"You aren't supposed to call me George." She strolled into the room. "Don't dare do so in front of Mother. You don't want to give her fits on her big night."

Ben looked down on her from his much larger height, a shock of brandy-colored hair falling over his brow. He wore it longer than he should intentionally. The length annoyed her mother along with Ben's very existence.

"Cordelia already doesn't like me. I doubt calling you George will alter her impression of me in any way. I am always thankful your mother didn't find me on the step that day. She would have shooed me away with a broom."

"My mother has never lifted a broom in her life. The most she manages to lift is a hairbrush. Occasionally, she strains herself by fluffing a pillow."

"I think I saw her lift a rose to her nose once, but she struggled. Her maid had to step in."

"You are awful." Georgina laughed.

Mother tolerated Ben much the same way she had once accepted Father's drooling hound, Cannonball. Cordelia had tried to send Ben to an orphanage, using every ounce of flirtatious charm she possessed to convince Father, but he'd flatly refused. Mother had finally given up when she was reminded that her husband wanted a son, which she had failed to provide. His nephew, Benjamin Cooke, would do very nicely.

Alice, Ben's mother, never appeared in New York. Ben claimed he had no idea where she was; he only knew she'd brought him to the city, written the note, and pushed him in the direction of his uncle's mansion on Lafayette Square.

Jacob Rutherford *finally* had a son to shape into his image.

Mother's displeasure had been shown in her refusal to leave her rooms and her instruction to Cook to serve fish at dinner for the remainder of the week.

Father detested fish.

Ben whistled as his eyes trailed over her attire. "Quite a

gown, George." His eyes were tilted up at the corners like a cat's, turning more green or brown depending on his mood. The unusual hazel color must have been inherited from his father, the unknown Mr. Cooke, for no one in Georgina's family possessed eyes like Ben's. "Red is definitely your color, George."

"Crimson," she informed him. "A shade darker than scarlet."

"I stand corrected. Cordelia is bound to faint at the sight of so much of her widowed daughter . . . exposed." He tipped his chin in the direction of her plunging neckline.

"Mother swoons. She does *not* faint. In any case, I'm sure she'll have smelling salts tucked away somewhere on her person. Or Bradt will carry them. I'm sure he'll serve as her escort tonight since Father is out of town once more."

"Business, George," Ben said in a mild tone.

"Luckily, Bradt is always available to fill in for Father." Mr. Piers Bradt was the scion of one of the city's oldest founding families. The gentleman her mother *should* have married. But Jacob Rutherford had pushed Bradt aside with his enormous wealth and determination to marry Cordelia. Bradt hadn't stood a chance against her father. "Do you think they're lovers?"

"George." Ben gave her an exaggerated, scandalized look. "Cordelia would *never* stoop to such a thing."

Georgina's parents had what was considered to be a successful partnership. There was a mild amount of affection between them. Mutual respect. But little else. Father had a mistress in Baltimore, a widow whom he kept in fine style. Ben thought Georgina and Lilian didn't know, but it was Lilian who'd told her.

"*I* think Mother and Bradt are lovers. He's always sniffing about her. Hovering over her shoulder at events when Father is out of town or offering his escort. I'm sure his help with the opera house was only to win more of her affection."

Ben shrugged. "Even Cordelia deserves happiness. Besides, Bradt will fade into the background once she sees you in that gown. I really do hope he's carrying her smelling salts."

"My gown isn't that scandalous." It was. It really was.

Annoying her mother was something she excelled at. Just yesterday, Mother had sent a list of approved, eligible gentlemen for Georgina to peruse.

"Don't breathe too deeply. I beg you."

"I'm laced far too tight for that."

"Are you sure you haven't taken your mother's direction and are looking for a husband among Manhattan's upper tens? Because in that gown, you'll attract dozens of proposals, both proper and improper. I suppose it's fortunate I have a pistol tucked in my pocket, should I need to defend your honor."

"A pistol? Really, Ben, I've little honor to protect, as you well know. And the most danger I'll face tonight is a rogue champagne cork hitting me in the eye." She looked down at her decolletage. "Or elsewhere."

"Still, it isn't wise to go about the city unarmed." A glint of ice shone in his eyes. There was a coldness in Ben, dark and frigid, like the waters of a pond in January. Georgina only ever saw flashes, but among those who did business with Rutherford Shipping, it was well-known. Ben wasn't a man anyone wished to cross. His connections stretched across Manhattan, encompassing all of New York City. Contacts not formed by his association with her father.

"It never hurts to be prepared. The city is dangerous. You know that."

"Even an opera house?" Her smile felt strained. *Or on the ferry.*

Georgina debated mightily over relating the incident that

had occurred earlier on the ferry to Ben but decided to remain silent. She was sure it had all been an accident. And Ben had a tendency to be overprotective. He'd be sure to insist she never visit Lilian without his escort.

Still, the incident on her return trip from Brooklyn had been terrifying. She'd nearly been pushed into the East River, a fall that would surely have led to her demise. Georgina wouldn't have stood a chance in the frigid water, with a heavy cloak acting like a weight to pull her beneath the waves. An accident, she was sure.

"Especially at an opera house. The entire building will be filled with well-dressed wolves hiding among the sheep."

Georgina smiled back at Ben, her mind still on the ferry. At first, she'd been confused, even startled, to find herself suddenly dangling over the railing, staring at the black water of the East River. The stranger's hand at her back had knocked her forward. Georgina's toes had scraped against the deck as she tried to gain her footing before the man had suddenly grabbed her cloak and jerked her back, which was why she was sure it had been an accident. In her brief experience with assailants, most tried to kill you. The next thing Georgina knew, she had been sprawled on the deck near the rail with a young couple hovering over her, asking if she was well.

"What is it, George?"

She had the oddest sensation Ben knew about what had happened on the ferry and was only waiting for her to confess.

"Just envisioning my mother and Piers together. She would have been much better off married to him, I think. Happier, to be sure."

"And much poorer."

What struck Georgina as odd was that the man who'd pushed her wore torn, dirty clothing but smelled clean. Like fresh laundered linen. She hadn't really gotten a good look at his face; her only impression was that he'd worn a plaid coat with bits of hay and dirt clinging to the sleeves and a broad-brimmed hat.

It was an accident.

Harold had his money, or rather Leo's money. She'd instructed Lind to give it to him and to casually mention she said she was leaving for France. Or Italy. There was no reason for Harold to look for her in America or look for her at all.

Ben knew about Harold and the attempt on her life at Beechwood Court. He'd told her in a calm tone that a more permanent solution might be required for Lord Masterson should he have the poor sense to follow Georgina to New York.

Georgina assured Ben that Harold wasn't that stupid.

"Come, we'll be late." He set down his glass. "Cordelia will have my head if we make a grand, late entrance and draw attention from her. Which you're bound to do in that gown."

Georgina smoothed down the folds of velvet as Ben placed a wrap over her shoulders. The night was cool, but not cold. The inside of the opera house would be such a crush, she'd have no need for anything heavier.

"I know you consider Harold to be smart enough not to follow you to New York, but what about Leo Murphy?" His hands landed on her shoulders.

Georgina grew still. "Leo Murphy?"

"Yes. Daniel's father."

Her first thought was to ask her cousin how he knew the identity of Daniel's father, because she'd not mentioned Leo by name, not once. But Ben had taken a trip to London while they'd all been in England together and been gone a fortnight before returning to her and Lilian.

"I know who he is," she said quietly. "I asked you specifically to leave it alone, as I recall. I didn't tell you about him for a reason. You have a habit of poking about in other people's business. Especially mine."

"Would that I had done so before you ran outside with Winbow that night while the rest of us were dancing."

"You weren't dancing. You were stealing a kiss from Miss Cortland."

"True." His lips twitched. "Lovely bit of baggage was Miss Cortland. She's married now. An older gentleman from Albany, I've heard. But you are right, Murphy is nothing like Harold. Bastard son of a duke. Impressive from a business standpoint. Elysium accounts for the smallest part of his wealth. Were you aware?"

"I was not," she whispered. Why would Ben bring up Leo now?

"I would have thought you'd rid him of those terrible waistcoats."

"You vastly overestimate my influence on Mr. Murphy. Whatever prompted you to scratch around in the dirt, Ben, I want it to stop. That part of my life I have blessedly left behind in England. There is no need for me to revisit it."

"Don't be cross, George."

"Then cease poking about. Leo Murphy and I had a brief, pleasant affair. We were friends of a sort, as I was with his brother, Lord Welles, but nothing more. He was a way for me to pass the time while in London. Leo doesn't form attachments, him being a bastard and all." She tilted her chin, furious to even be having such a discussion, especially when she had to spend the evening sparring with her mother. "He lost interest in me some time ago. Well before Daniel was born." The lie came smoothly off her tongue. "If he knew I'd had a child, I assure you, he wouldn't care."

Why must Leo haunt her thoughts? He had nearly all day. First, at Lilian's, and then now, in what should be the safety of her own parlor.

"Or be furious at you for hiding a child from him. Which I think you're more concerned about."

Georgina looked away. "You don't know him."

"True. I don't. Not personally. I made sure to stay out of his line of vision when I visited Elysium."

Damn Ben.

"But I think a gentleman who went to *all* the expense and subterfuge to ensure you had Beechwood Court and an income isn't the same sort of *bastard* who would casually toss you aside. Or a child. *That* sort of man will want his son, George. I'm not sure what happened between you and Leo Murphy, nor do I need the details."

"Good. I've no intention of recounting them to you. He won't come to New York. Besides having no reason to—"

Ben raised a brow.

"—Leo is deathly afraid of water. He won't even cross the Channel to France. He's hardly apt to board a ship to New York."

"Very well, George. I concede. No more talk of Leo Murphy. You are correct that it is only women who are known for changing their minds." He stuck out his elbow. "Shall we?"

❧ 15 ❧

Leo slid his gaze around the party goers swilling champagne as if it were water. They were all expensively dressed, their clothing as fine as anything Leo had seen society wear in London. He'd heard some female patrons of Elysium decry the fashions and poor taste of their cousins in America, but Leo found no evidence of that here. The entire room fairly reeked of wealth and riches. Nothing, it seemed, could put a damper on Manhattan society's gaiety; not a fire which had destroyed parts of the city the year before Georgina had wed Masterson, nor the near-catastrophic financial collapse that had followed.

Leo appreciated resilience. And overindulgence. He did own a gambling hell and pleasure palace, after all.

New York City, particularly Manhattan, had little in common with London other than the massive amounts of people clogging the streets. The crowds were familiar. The smell of so many bodies being pushed into much too small a space. A plethora of languages met his ears, most he didn't recognize, but he was familiar with the lilt of the Irish because his mother had possessed the same sound to her speech.

The island of Manhattan wasn't large, but there was still plenty of room for streets and buildings as the city expanded north. Everything about New York was raw. New. No centuries of breeding. No tedious customs in place for hundreds of years. No titles. Many of the wealthiest gentlemen in the city were self-made, of lackluster origin, and armed with only raw ambition and a work ethic. That wasn't to say there wasn't an upper class firmly in place. The evidence of their existence crowded the marble floor around him. Old Dutch and English families mingled with the dreaded newly monied citizens, like the Rutherfords, Georgina's family.

The future, as Leo often told Tony, wasn't in tenants and the rent they paid to titled landowners. Or in the landowners themselves. It was in gentlemen like Georgina's father, Jacob Rutherford. In factories. Railways. Textile mills. Gambling hells and pleasure palaces were incredibly amusing and vastly profitable, but Leo didn't see himself standing on Elysium's second-floor landing into his dotage.

Particularly not given recent events.

Leo had spent the last month since his arrival studying and noting everyone and everything in New York. Georgina loved this place, and he wanted to understand why. He didn't intentionally hide his presence in Manhattan, but neither did he announce it. Tonight would change all that.

His attendance at the grand opening of the Rutherford opera house wasn't because Leo was enamored of opera, though he did enjoy a good Italian soprano. His first mistress, Lucia, had been an opera singer. Lovely woman, though she had a tendency for the dramatic. Tried to stab him when he ended things.

Nor was he here to gasp in awe at the ornate building

done in gray stone, replete with marble and gold fixtures. The sweeping, majestic interior, painted in soothing tones of pale cream and adorned with expensive landscapes, perfectly complimented the glass dome stretching above his head with its view of the night sky, complete with dozens of sparkling stars.

Magnificent. Truly.

The champagne was nicely chilled. The oysters delicious.

Still, not enough reason to attend an event which would start with dancing and culminate in a performance of Rossini's *La gazza ladra*.

Strange he'd never learned Italian.

No, Leo's only purpose in appearing tonight among Manhattan's elite was Georgina. The bloody opera house was named for her family, and Cordelia Rutherford, Georgina's mother, was the hostess and patroness.

Georgina was certain to be in attendance.

Leo had been a guest at a half-dozen or so events since he'd arrived. Dinner parties. Small gatherings in which he'd been introduced to an incredible number of lovely, young ladies. Not once did Georgina appear. Frustrated that his quarry remained elusive, Leo made very discreet inquiries. Luckily, the Rutherfords were well known, and there was no end to the whispers about them.

Jacob Rutherford was respected and often mentioned in the same breath with Mr. Astor, among others. Not necessarily a compliment, Leo soon learned. Still, connections to the Rutherfords were sought after, despite their lineage extending only as far back as the docks lining the harbor. Sadly, money and boldness could only get you so far when you were the son of a former barge owner.

Leo really did *adore* Americans.

Conveniently, it seemed Georgina had become embroiled in some sort of scandal, and Jacob Rutherford had found a way to rid himself of a troublesome daughter and garner a title in his family at the same time. Leo already didn't like Rutherford, and he had yet to meet him.

Leo spent quite a bit of time in Manhattan's finer clubs and restaurants, listening more than talking, learning who was important and who was not. Jacob Rutherford *was* important. His shipping company, the third-largest in New York, had started with one small barge, manned by Amos Rutherford, Jacob's father. Amos had sailed up and down the East and Hudson rivers loaded with goods to sell or trade. One barge became several. When the Erie Canal was built, Amos's business had expanded. The barges had turned into ships. Rivers into oceans. Warehouses bearing the Rutherford name soon lined the harbor. Amos was affluent at this point, but it wasn't until his son Jacob entered the China trade that the family reached a summit of riches previously unknown. The Rutherfords were now one of the wealthiest families in New York, possibly in America.

The story of Georgina's family riveted Leo. Her pedigree started with a barely literate barge owner, who had been her grandfather. No wonder she was so bloody defiant.

Leo peered over his glass to regard the elegant blonde across the room. Cordelia Rutherford was a slender, graceful woman with hair so blonde it gleamed white. Her fingers fluttered at the servants circling the room, who all hurried to do her bidding. Diamonds sparkled at her ears and throat. A few twinkled in her hair. She was a stunning woman, attracting the admiration of many of the gentlemen in the room. Particularly the one hovering by her elbow, who was not Jacob Rutherford.

Georgina had rarely spoken of her parents to Leo, only saying she didn't get along with them. She'd mentioned her sister, Lilian, and a cousin, Ben, both of whom she spoke of with great affection.

And no one, since he'd been in New York, had mentioned Lady Masterson having a child.

"Mr. Murphy." A pretty, dark-haired young lady approached him. "I'm so happy you took advantage of Father's invitation to join us this evening."

Miss Ann Schuller, peacock blue skirts floating about her ankles, took his arm with a flirtatious batting of her eyes. "I'm sure it can't compare to the events you've attended in London, but I do think it's a very fine party, nonetheless. Don't you agree?"

Leo gave her one of his most charming smiles, the sort he used on chattering women he wished to quiet.

A lovely shade of rose bloomed on Miss Schuller's cheeks.

"Undoubtedly." Leo kept his tone very clipped, sounding aristocratic, much like his brother. He'd found the accent worked wonders here, which was highly amusing. He planned to use the snobby, patrician tone with Jacob Rutherford when they finally met.

Miss Schuller blushed a bit more. She was a lovely girl with doe-like eyes giving her the appearance of a fawn. Miss Schuller was also a notorious gossip. Her small tidbits of information about society in Manhattan had been instrumental in helping him learn more about Georgina. Leo had claimed a brief acquaintance with Lady Masterson, whom he'd met in London at a ball. All rubbish, of course.

Miss Schuller ate up every word.

Her father, Mr. Adam Schuller, owned a bank, one of the few that hadn't collapsed during the recent financial upheaval. When Leo had deposited a large sum, he immediately drew Mr. Schuller's attention who in turn invited Leo to dine. Miss Schuller had been presented along with the roasted chicken and potatoes.

"Will you be staying for the performance tonight, Mr. Murphy? I confess I only know a few words in Italian." Miss

Schuller flirted shamelessly, turning so he could admire her bosom. "Do you speak the language?"

"Alas, no."

When Leo had asked about Georgina, casually over the second course while dining with the Schuller's, the first words Miss Schuller had spoken were *bold as brass*.

Ignoring the pointed look from her father, Miss Schuller had whispered to Leo that Georgina's hasty marriage had surprised no one in society. The only shock had been she'd somehow managed to marry a titled English lord.

His little American had been getting into trouble for years, it seemed, her rebellious streak not limited to scathing retorts and daring necklines.

"A scandal involving, of all things, a riverboat gambler," Miss Schuller had continued. "I believe from Savannah. Possibly Charleston. Somewhere south of here. At any rate, he was found dead sometime later, right after Georgina left for England, to no one's surprise. A gentleman like that doesn't last very long in New York."

The gambler had been found dead in an alley, shot right through the marked deck resting in the pocket above his heart. He'd cheated someone.

"Georgina married an earl," Miss Schuler had said. "So I don't suppose it turned out too poorly for her. Oh, I shouldn't gossip about such things, Mr. Murphy. I fear I've overstepped."

So Georgina had an affinity for gambling and drinking spirits, one she'd come by long before meeting Leo. A liking that had caused her to be careless and gotten her wed to Masterson. Leo only wondered if Jacob Rutherford had shot the gambler himself.

"I hope you'll join us in our box for the performance, Mr. Murphy."

Christ, she was so bloody hopeful. Miss Schuller's interest and that of her father would wane dramatically were they to know he was the bastard son of a duke. There were many differences between New York and London, but he was sure the taint of illegitimacy was the same at least among the people drinking champagne at Cordelia's opera house.

"Mrs. Rutherford." Miss Schuller dipped her chin in the direction of Georgina's mother. "Our hostess for this evening. All of this," she waved a small hand, "is her doing. She's a Van Matre."

Leo nodded as if the name should mean something to him.

"Barely a ship leaves the harbor without Jacob Rutherford's approval. At least, that's what my father says." Miss Schuller paused. "Importing and exporting."

"Ah, yes. The parents of Lady Masterson." Leo pretended he'd only just remembered.

"She doesn't use her title. Georgina, I mean." Miss Schuller's brow wrinkled. "Not since her return from London. She prefers to be addressed as Mrs. Masterson." She lowered her voice. "Truthfully, she probably would rather use Miss Rutherford again."

"How odd." But not surprising. Georgina wasn't impressed with titles.

"I find it rather silly, Mr. Murphy. If I were a countess, I would certainly want everyone to address me as such. But I've known Georgina since we were girls. She's always done as she pleased."

Yes, she certainly has.

His fingers twitched against his coat just thinking of seeing Georgina. He wasn't sure if he wanted to fuck her or strangle her.

"Was my father's agent helpful in your property search?"

"Indeed. I've just leased a home near Spring Street."

"How wonderful." Miss Schuller's fingers fluttered lightly

on his arm. She wasn't the least subtle. "A perfect address, Mr. Murphy. One of the newer neighborhoods. I'm very familiar with the area." She hinted for Leo to ask her to show him around, which he avoided by grabbing another glass of champagne.

"Oh, dear." Her fingers tightened on his sleeve. "Our prodigal countess is here. I wasn't sure she would come tonight. I can't believe she would wear a dress so—"

Marvelous.

That was the first word Leo thought at catching sight of Georgina in a spectacular crimson gown decorated with bits of jet. The velvet clung to her, similar in cut to the gown she'd worn the last time he'd seen her. The bits of jet edging her dangerously low neckline dangled enticingly over her breasts as she walked, drawing every male eye in the room.

Including his.

Whispers echoed against the marble floor at her entrance. Georgina hadn't been out in society very often; this was a rare appearance. Considering the stir she created, it wasn't any wonder she kept to herself.

God, she's beautiful.

The lower half of his body tightened pleasurably.

And mine.

His eyes traced every curve, and because this was Georgina, there were dozens. Leo remembered each one, all smelling of spring and something wild.

Mine.

Whether she wished to be or not.

Leo had the urge to throw his coat over her shoulders, hide that spectacular bosom, and carry her away.

She surveyed the room with a mulish tilt of her chin, a dare to anyone who might challenge her. It was a familiar gesture that filled Leo with savage longing.

Ah, Georgie. I've missed you. So much.

A gentleman, expertly tailored evening clothes hugging his tall frame, appeared at her side, his fingers curled around Georgina's elbow.

"Who's that?" Leo bit out.

"That's Mr. Cooke," Miss Schuller whispered. "He's—"

Touching her.

Leo blotted out the remainder of Miss Schuller's pretty speech as he sized up the gentleman holding Georgina's arm. Her lover? Or something more?

Above average in height, taller than either Leo or his brother, athletic. Expensive clothing. There was an emerald pin stuck in the snowy whiteness of his cravat. Still, it wasn't enough to wash away the mud of the streets Leo could practically see clinging to the hem of his coat no matter how much he tried to hide it.

Leo could always spot a fellow mongrel.

Miss Schuller's voice was nothing more than a muted hum in Leo's ear as he struggled to compose himself amidst the jealousy simmering beneath his skin. The gentleman's grip on Georgina's elbow was far too tight and spoke of familiarity. Intimacy. A low sound came from his throat.

"Mr. Murphy?" Poor Miss Schuller had removed her fingers from his arm and now regarded Leo with apprehension. "Are you well?"

No, he wasn't well. Not at all.

"Will you excuse me, Miss Schuller?" he said. With a polite nod, Leo drifted away, leaving Miss Schuller sputtering behind him. His emotions, always held tightly in check, spiraled out of control whenever Georgina was in the vicinity. Frustrated he couldn't simply march across the floor and claim her, Leo firmly pushed down his anger before it could escape. He grabbed another glass of champagne, barely tasting the fine vintage as it slid down his throat.

Angling himself against the far wall, careful to stay well

hidden in the crowd, Leo watched Georgina as she greeted her mother and the man at her mother's side. The smile on her lips was false. Pasted on. He'd seen her don the same look dozens of times.

Mrs. Rutherford didn't look pleased to see her daughter. Even from where Leo stood, he could see her scathing glance run down Georgina's form in disapproval.

Georgina tilted her chin higher, a smile teasing at her lips as she greeted her mother.

The gentleman holding her elbow hovered protectively over Georgina. Probably looking down the front of her bodice.

Feeling murderous, Leo swallowed down the rest of his champagne.

❧ 16 ❧

Georgina stared at her mother's carefully controlled horror over the crimson gown, counting silently to ten, about the length of time it would take Mother to recover.

"Dearest." Her mother's frank gaze flitted over Georgina's revealing neckline. "Is there a reason for such a reckless display this evening? We are at the opera."

"Not at all, Mother. I simply liked the gown." She smiled sweetly at the woman whose disapproval she garnered more often than anything else. Georgina had a complicated relationship with her mother.

Mother didn't understand why Georgina questioned every rule and restriction placed upon her. Couldn't fathom why her youngest daughter rejected playing an instrument or paying calls in favor of visiting her father and Ben at Rutherford Shipping. Why Georgina delighted in being outrageous, playing the flirt and speaking so boldly.

At times, Georgina wondered too. Defiance hadn't served her well. Her parents hadn't believed her when she'd told them she hadn't lost her virtue to John Winbow as he'd claimed. Father had already been suggesting to Georgina a season in London. She'd played right into his ambitions.

Lilian, on the other hand, never so much as raised her voice. Her sister would never have dared to wear such a gown, but then Lilian didn't possess Georgina's bosom.

"Yes, I'm sure you simply liked the gown. Can you not appear in society, just once, Georgina, without drawing unwelcome attention? I thought your time in London might have matured you, but here you are, at the ripe age of twenty-two, still determined to be childish."

Piers Bradt, at her mother's side, frowned, distorting his distinguished features as he nodded in agreement.

Well, Georgina didn't care what Piers Bradt thought.

"How lovely to see you, Mr. Bradt. Is your wife in attendance tonight? I should like to say hello." Georgina looked around the room as if searching for Mrs. Bradt, who she knew wasn't among the guests. "I don't believe we've spoken since my return."

The lines on Bradt's forehead deepened. "Gertrude was unable to come this evening. One of her headaches is plaguing her."

How convenient. Bradt's wife hadn't been seen in public in ages. She suffered many such headaches, but luckily, her personal physician saw to her. "A shame. Please give her my best wishes. She's so kind to allow you to escort Mother to events when my father is away on business and can't do so himself."

Mother pursed her lips in obvious annoyance.

Bradt inclined his head, the silver at his temples catching the light. "Why don't I bring you some champagne, Cordelia? I'll only be a moment." He wandered off, clearly not willing to trade barbs with Georgina tonight.

"That was unnecessary, Georgina. Piers is a kind man." Mother's eyes took in Ben with a small curl of her lip. "And an old and dear friend. As is his wife. You've made your point. Dare I hope your display this evening is meant to attract potential suitors?"

"I received your note yesterday, Mother. Would you like me to ask Mr. Bradt more about his wife's condition?"

The smallest bit of a smile crossed her mother's lips. "I was trying to be helpful. Mr. Woodstock, perhaps? I saw him earlier with that awful Mary Barclay following him about. I should speak to Mary's mother about her behavior."

"Please don't, Mother. I'm certain Mrs. Barclay wouldn't welcome your opinion of her daughter's behavior. And Mary isn't awful. She's quite lovely once you get to know her. She and Mr. Woodstock are very nearly engaged, as you well know."

"Perhaps before he reacquainted himself with you, dear. Now I fear Miss Barclay's future as Mrs. Woodstock might be in jeopardy." Mother fluttered her fan about her eyes, likely searching for Bradt. Finding him, the pair locked eyes and a look passed between them before Bradt quickly turned away.

Georgina sucked in a breath. *Bradt is in love with my mother and she with him.*

She was sure she'd looked at Leo in much the same way. And didn't Mother deserve happiness? Before she'd wed Masterson, the knowledge of her mother and Bradt would have angered her, but not now. She shouldn't have been so unkind. "I'm sorry I was rude to Mr. Bradt. I'll apologize."

Her mother waved her hand. "Piers understands. Now back to Mr. Woodstock. He seeks only a word of encouragement from you, dear." She turned back to Georgina. The Woodstocks are very well thought of. You could do worse."

"I believe I already have. Please refrain from matchmaking. I'm quite happy as I am."

Ben chuckled softly from her shoulder. "Well done, George," he murmured quietly so only she could hear.

Georgina's mother shot him a quelling look.

"Masterson was your father's idea. Never mine. And eventually, Georgina, you will have to find an escort who is not your cousin. Unless there is something more to your relationship than there appears?"

Ben coughed, his cheeks pinking, mouth gaping open like a fish at her mother's remark.

Mother nodded to him. "Cousins marry."

"*No*, Mother." Georgina's jaw tightened. Just when she'd been feeling charitable. "And Ben is more brother to me than cousin, as you well know. The very idea is abhorrent."

A tic appeared in Ben's cheek, the only sign her mother's barb had struck. He nodded to both her and her mother before whispering, "You're on your own, George. I forgot my armor tonight. Didn't think I'd need it for the opera. I'll retrieve you later."

Dammit.

Scaring Ben off was punishment for Georgina causing Piers to disappear. She should have known a sincere apology to her mother wouldn't have been enough. Mother never behaved in such a mercenary manner toward Lilian. She *cooed* over Georgina's sister, never once launching a verbal assault.

"There are dozens of suitable gentlemen who would vie for your attention if you would only allow them to do so." A thin, smug smile crossed Mother's lips as she watched Ben flee into the crowd. "Don't you *want* to remarry?"

"Not really. I find I quite like being a widow."

"Certainly, it isn't because no gentleman can replace Lord Masterson." The sarcasm in her mother's voice grated against Georgina's skin.

"Certainly not." The very idea of having to return to a life like the one where she had been tied to her late husband made her stomach hurt.

"Then what is it? You have your pick of eligible gentlemen. Fletcher has expressed quite a bit of interest in you. You'd make a wonderful politician's wife."

Fletcher wasn't Leo. *None* of them were. They were all deficient in some way. But Georgina could hardly explain that to her mother.

"Father already has his politician, or at least he will. Isn't that the plan for William? Lilian will make a much better wife for a future senator than I."

For Daniel's sake, Georgina must remarry, but she wasn't ready. Not yet.

Her mother made a sound in her throat.

"You've made yourself clear, Mother." Remarriage had been a constant topic of conversation between them since Georgina had returned. "But not Warren Woodstock. His fingers are overlong." Georgina gave a shudder. "Like the legs of a giant spider."

"Georgina." Mother shook her head, clearly exasperated, but a laugh escaped her lips. "You would be far happier if you were more like your sister."

Lilian was the good daughter. Perfect. She'd found William, whom Father had instantly approved of, and fallen in love.

Georgina, on the other hand, delighted in imperfection. She'd been caught kissing Tommy Richards when she was fourteen. Flirting with one of the grooms who kept her father's stables. George had been the groom's name, a sure sign to fifteen-year-old Georgina that they were meant to be together. She dressed to draw attention because it made Georgina feel powerful. She hadn't been thinking about the effects to her reputation. Then she'd been forced to wed Masterson.

Mother was right. Georgina's life *would* be easier if she were more like Lilian.

But Masterson ultimately led me to Leo, her heart whispered. *And gave me Daniel.*

Ben reappeared at her side with two glasses of champagne.

"Here you are, George." Ben handed one of the glasses filled with sparkling liquid to her. "Try not to be alarmed, but it appears Woodstock, despite your lack of encouragement and evident disregard for him, is making his way over to you."

"Oh, dear."

"It's a shame." Georgina felt Ben's fingers at the back of her head, tugging at her hair. "You've lost one of your clever little combs. Or maybe two." He stooped down, handing them to her with an innocent look.

"Oh, goodness." Georgina took a mouthful of champagne. "I should take care of this immediately."

"You are the most difficult girl," her mother intoned with resignation. "I am only trying to ensure your future happiness. So your father," she said under her breath, "does not."

Georgina hurried away from Ben and her mother, heading in the opposite direction from that of the approaching Mr. Woodstock. The layout of Mother's opera house was simple once you got past the grand staircase. The less expensive seats were situated down this hall next to the area where less wealthy guests would enjoy their refreshments during intermission. Upstairs were the luxurious boxes and seats for the more socially affluent. Mother had built this opera house for them, not the masses who would crowd below to enjoy a play or musicale.

Staff bustled about, trays laden with glasses of champagne. The party must be costing her father a fortune. A small price to keep Mother happy while he spent his time in Baltimore. Georgina neatly sidestepped a tray on her way across the marble floor, her heels clicking as she hurried along.

The work of numerous architects and designers, the

THE WAGER OF A LADY

Rutherford opera house was elegant, richly decorated, and slightly chilly, exactly like the woman who'd championed it.

The Rutherford.

Georgina shook her head as she passed a portrait of her mother hanging on the wall. The building was more statement than structure. Cordelia Rutherford would not be ignored or pushed aside because she'd married *new* money. While many of her contemporaries were determined to be pedigreed but less affluent, Cordelia was not. So what if her father-in-law had been a barely literate barge owner. *She* was descended from one of the finest Dutch families in New York. How dare anyone turn their nose up at her?

The Rutherford was Mother's revenge, so to speak.

Georgina looked up at the enormous marble staircase as she passed, wondering how on earth any of the ladies, after a glass or two of champagne, would keep from tripping on their skirts as they made their way up to the luxurious boxes above. There would be a performance tonight, of Rossini's *La gazza ladra*, an opera Georgina had never heard of.

Very well. I'm not overly familiar with opera.

Lilian liked the opera. She even spoke some Italian.

The guests below would, after more champagne and some dancing, make their way up the stairs to their seats. The boxes were horribly expensive and available for purchase on an annual basis only. No more passing of boxes down thru generations. Not at The Rutherford. Another snub from Cordelia. No more coveting the best seats for only the oldest families in perpetuity.

There was already a waiting list.

The small group of musicians, hidden behind a screen, struck up a tune. The dancing was about to begin and would continue for approximately an hour.

She slowed her steps. Georgina didn't care if she danced or not. It was much more important to avoid Mr. Woodstock.

Georgina's mind wandered from her mother's machinations regarding Mr. Woodstock and back to the incident on the ferry. She probably should have sat below. Most women did. But the air was colder on the water, and she preferred the chill to the stuffiness of the seats below deck. She liked to watch the shore as it approached. The wind helped dry the tears she never failed to shed at leaving Daniel. Seeing her son always brought Leo to mind. Her heart would ache for a time but for a completely different reason.

Had she been pushed? Georgina had been so absorbed in her thoughts, she'd barely been paying attention to her surroundings. Harold surely wouldn't come to America, and there wasn't anyone else who wished to do her harm.

Stop, Georgina.

All her energy, every waking thought, had been directed toward hiding Daniel's existence, getting her son to America, and then returning herself. She hadn't given much thought to her future other than acknowledging she would have to remarry to claim her child.

The only other option was to leave New York forever. William would eventually balk at keeping her secret. Mother would one day see through Ben's carefully crafted deception. Her parents might well cut all ties with her. And as problematic as their relationship often was, Georgina loved her family.

But she would never, under any circumstances, give Daniel up. Not again.

Her grandparents' home still stood empty. The property was isolated. She could settle there and raise Daniel alone in Garrison. Present herself as a young widow, which she was, and not use the Rutherford name.

Georgina hurried past the darkened alcove beneath the base of the stairs used for storage and, for tonight's event, covered with a gold drape. A perfect spot for an assignation.

She was surprised she didn't hear a young lady's giggle from behind the velvet.

I was once such a reckless young lady.

The thought made her smile as she passed, until the feel of a hand, fingers sinking into her skin, took her elbow.

Damn.

Georgina rolled her eyes, praying for the patience she'd need to put off Woodstock. He must have spotted her and given chase. The least Ben could have done was trip him or engage him in conversation to stop his pursuit. Now she would need to refuse him in a very firm but polite way. Woodstock wasn't a bad sort. Under different circumstances, such as, if he didn't have fingers which were the stuff of nightmares, Georgina might have considered him.

Turning, she pasted a patient smile on her face and looked down at her arm, prepared for the sight of those obscenely long fingers, but instead saw only a broad gloved hand.

"I beg your pardon." She tilted up her chin, catching a hint of leather and sandalwood. "Please release me." The last word lodged in her throat.

Once, when visiting Grandmother's house, Georgina had taken it upon herself to climb a sprawling maple tree at the edge of the lawn. One of many poor decisions she'd made in her life. She'd slipped not even halfway up, her foot caught in her skirts, and fallen to the ground, knocking the wind out of her and breaking her arm. Georgina remembered looking up at the cloudless sky, unable to breathe and thinking she was dead.

It was exactly the same feeling. Except the sky before her was as dark as sapphires, with an unusual ring of indigo.

Barrington eyes.

Eyes identical to her child's but with no warmth.

"Hello, Georgina."

I*'ve had too much champagne.*

Georgina blinked, willing the image of Leo away, but he neither disappeared nor smiled. A prickling sensation washed over her skin as her heart hammered inside her chest.

"Leo," she said stupidly.

Leo was here.

At her mother's opera party. In Manhattan. Dressed in the same dark evening clothes as every other gentleman. As if he belonged here. She shut her eyes because blinking hadn't worked. Had she fallen and hit her head?

No. Impossible. The sounds of the guests drinking and laughing still reached her ears. She could hear her own breathing, startled and ragged.

Georgina's eyes fluttered open. He was still staring at her, furious and cold, like an unexpected winter storm.

"You haven't forgotten me, then." The words were icy and filled with such biting dislike, she shrank back. "Merely failed to impart certain important facts to me."

He knows. Of course, he did. Why else would he be here?

Leo stared at her with such loathing, such dismissal, Georgina trembled with fear, afraid of him for the first time since they'd met. She twisted, trying to wrench her arm from his grasp.

He tightened his hold. "Don't, Georgina. Let's not make a scene. Not at your mother's lovely party."

Her heart sobbed in relief at his presence even though he was hardly welcoming to her. No more guessing at how he would react if he knew about Daniel. Leo's manner made perfectly clear that Georgina had made the wrong choice in not telling him, especially after her conversation with Mr. Lind. After—

'Don't leave Georgina. Please.'

Taking a deep breath, or as much of one as she could in this gown, Georgina tried to compose herself. They were in a room full of people. This was not London. This was her home. Georgina straightened. Her chin tilted at a dangerous angle.

"Ah, now there's my girl," he purred.

God, how she'd missed the sound of him.

"Stubborn to a fault. Refusing to give in to anyone. Except me." His words rippled against her skin. "Do you remember the way you screamed my name when you climaxed?" he whispered into her ear. "I do. You destroyed a pillow on my settee. Tore the bloody tassel clean off."

"Are you sure it was me?" she snapped. "It could have been Lady Dunley. I'm sure she's spent some time on that horrid piece of furniture."

His fingers dug into her skin. "I'm not here to discuss Lady Dunley. Shall we dance?"

"I don't think so. I'm not really in the mood to be flung about in anger in front of most of Manhattan. You might lose your temper and toss me into the musicians." Her pulse beat madly in her throat.

"And I'm not in the mood for your witty banter. I wasn't asking, Georgina."

He flashed a charming smile. False. Slightly menacing. Pulling her close, he led her out to the middle of the floor. He held her stiffly in his arms, as if he couldn't bear to touch her. Still, Leo moved flawlessly between the other dancers. Their bodies in perfect sync together, as if they were still back on that stupid red settee in his office.

Secretly, she'd wanted him to be an awful dancer.

"Terrible acoustics." The roguish smile didn't waver, though his voice rumbled like cut stone. "I do hope the echo is confined to the atrium. Mrs. Rutherford has made such an effort on her opera house. Would be a shame if it were all for naught, wouldn't it?"

"You know I don't like it when you do this," she answered. Speaking of every mundane subject in the world instead of the one which was important to give his listener a false sense of security before he pounced on them. The tactic worked brilliantly if one were negotiating a stack of markers, for instance, but not when avoiding the obvious. "Please get to the point of your visit."

"I do *like* New York," he continued, the blue of his eyes flat. Hard. "I can see why you'd return. I walked down Broadway Street the other day taking in the sights. I confess I had a completely different perception of the size. I suppose that's something most women say." He wiggled his brows at his ridiculous innuendo, but his eyes maintained their chilliness.

Georgina had to look away. "Stop it." This was far more horrible than she'd anticipated, his blithe pretense of polite conversation.

"I've learned poker," he continued, ignoring her protest. "What an interesting game. I can see why you might like it so much. I imagine you're adept at poker because the main strategy seems to be . . . *bluffing.* You're rather good at bluffing. All that time in London after returning from the countryside. Flitting about throwing garden parties and taking tea with my stepmother and sisters." He swung her around hard. "Bluffing is not exactly a lie, I suppose, more an omission of the truth. A reluctance to inform others. Not even the irony of meeting my father and having him help you hide his grandchild shook your façade. Brava, Georgina."

"You aren't being fair," she hissed back at him as her skirts caught around his legs. "You made yourself perfectly clear, Leo. No children. No bastards. You didn't want me."

"Who says I want you now?" He smiled down at her.

Georgina looked down at his chest. The words hurt her more than she wished.

"Tell me, did it amuse you? Avoiding me as you did? Refusing to even allow me to speak to you? Taking tea with my sisters or playing cards with Tony, all the while knowing you'd given birth to my child?"

"How do you know he's yours?"

His eyes glittered like sapphires. Such beautiful eyes. So full of disgust for her.

"Others may assume you to be something of a lightskirt, but I know you are not, Georgina. I suspect the necklines and outrageous behavior," he said, "are merely punishment. First, for your parents—I suppose that's what got you into enough trouble to wed Masterson. A riverboat gambler, I've heard." He gave a careless shrug. "Your poor behavior continued because London didn't welcome you, and why should they, given your pedigree and waspish tongue? Lastly me, of course. I was never only your friend, Georgina. I always meant to have you. But I called you a shiny bauble and was treated to displays of you flaunting your breasts at Elysium for any man to admire them." He pulled her close against his chest. "But there were no other lovers."

Georgina pressed her lips together. When he laid things out in such a way, she sounded like a child throwing a tantrum. "Not in London, perhaps."

Leo's fingers dug into her waist at her taunt. "I might never have known I had a child."

"Whom you didn't want."

"If Marcus Barrington hadn't left me a deathbed confession. How he owed a debt to Masterson, of all people, and in trying to be a better man, had found a friendless widow he could help."

Georgina stumbled, her toe catching in her skirts. Leo let her nearly fall before he caught her. Marcus Barrington had been so kind to her. Helped her. And now he was dead, probably despising her for her deception as much as his son did.

"Oh, you didn't know? The Duke of Averell is dead. *Marcus.* Tony is now the duke and very much alive. That was the news the messenger from Cherry Hill brought to me the last time we saw each other, when I was trying"—his grip tightened, and she struggled—"to mend things between us."

"You asked me to be your mistress. Hardly mending, Leo, dooming me to the same sort of existence your mother had."

Leo's jaw hardened, but he kept the smile on his lips. "I did not, Georgina." He spun her again. "You have *no* idea what I meant to say because you *left*." He spat out the word as if it were poisoning him.

"I had to leave. I was going home to New York."

"Where you had conveniently sent my child."

"Yes. I didn't want Harold to know. He'd threatened me and—*you* would have sent me to some apothecary."

Leo swung her around again. There was nothing graceful in his movements now, only a simmering hostility. "You knew what you were to me. You *knew*. And you didn't tell me. You left."

"Yes." A decision she'd regretted the moment she was on the *Betty Sue*. "I made a decision."

"Decisions. Ones you took upon yourself to make for both of us. I know why you kept our child a secret from Harold and the rest of London. But not me." The rasp of his voice had gone raw. Broken.

"Leo—"

"I do not hold myself blameless. My own"—a deep ugly sound came from him—"*behavior* leaves much to be desired. But you meant to keep *this* from me for the entirety of my life."

Georgina didn't answer. Couldn't. She stared at Leo's chest. Counted the buttons on his very plain waistcoat. She'd hurt him, far worse than she could ever have imagined. How wrong she'd been about everything. Especially him. Looking out of the corner of her eye, Georgina saw Ben watching them. He didn't look surprised to see her dancing with Leo.

Because Ben knew Leo was in New York. She supposed their earlier conversation had been meant as a warning. Yet another man who couldn't bother to be direct.

"I thought it would be better if you didn't know," she finally said, wanting him to understand. "I thought I was doing you a kindness in not telling you."

His chin snapped back to her. "How *dare* you decide such a thing for me."

She couldn't get a deep breath, though she tried. Her corset was too tight, squeezing her heart with such force, Georgina thought she might well faint. What could she possibly say?

Once again, I am the architect of my own disaster.

She tried to pull away, but he held her firm, clearly unconcerned that the other dancers were casting curious looks in their direction. The blue of his eyes fell down between her breasts, searing her with one look. Leo wasn't prone to losing his temper. Or at least, he hadn't been.

He leaned in again, his nose brushing against her temple, inhaling deeply. "I am *so* very angry with you, Georgina."

Georgina looked down at her slippers, as if concerned the silk of her skirts had caught against his legs and she'd tear her hem. The pads of his fingers pressed painfully into her waist as regret coursed through her.

He will never forgive me.

When the dance ended, Leo bowed politely for the benefit of onlookers, his handsome features bland. Unfeeling. As if she were some elderly wallflower he'd been forced to dance with.

"Good evening, Lady Masterson."

He didn't once glance back as he strolled back into the crowd, leaving her battered and bruised. He was welcomed into a group of gentlemen at the other side of the hall, most of whom already seemed well acquainted with him. Georgina recognized Mr. Schuller of Merchant's Bank. She'd once been friends with his daughter.

Leo has been in New York far longer than I supposed.

There was little to set Leo apart from the other men in attendance tonight except for the precision with which he'd gutted her during their dance. Even his formal evening wear was perfect with no sign of the hideously garish waistcoats he so loved. Only his looks made him stand out. He was still so damned beautiful. Even if he hated her.

Georgina pulled her hands into her skirts so that no one would see her hands shaking. She knew she shouldn't have come tonight. Poor Mr. Woodstock had been the least of her worries.

LEO WATCHED GEORGINA GLIDE ACROSS THE ROOM, shoulders straight as she made her way back to her mother's side. She nodded to those around her. Smiled. Took another glass of champagne. Greeted two young ladies warmly. If Leo didn't know her so well, hadn't spent so many hours watching her, he would have assumed their conversation hadn't rattled her. But she had to struggle to hold her chin up, jerking it sharply whenever her manner slipped. And she was drinking far too much champagne.

Georgina, as a rule, didn't care overmuch for champagne.

He thought he'd feel vindicated after lashing out at her as he'd dreamt of doing since reading his father's letter. But he didn't. Hurting Georgina hadn't helped his mood at all; in fact, it had done nothing but make Leo realize how badly he'd behaved toward her from the day they'd met.

She's my person and always has been.

Easy to see now what he'd refused to acknowledge. A deathbed confession and a reexamination of your life often did that to a person. Left them seeing things in a different light.

Which brought Leo to his next point.

If Georgina thought for one bloody moment he was going to allow her to marry that oversized thug masquerading as a gentleman who was whispering in her ear, she was mistaken.

The gentleman in question cast a glance in Leo's direction, pulling Georgina closer. She nodded her head, placing a fingertip against her temple. A headache, he could almost hear her say. The gentleman placed a consoling hand on the small of Georgina's back, comforting her.

Leo gripped his glass so tightly, he nearly snapped the fragile stem.

Smiling and nodding automatically, he pretended to listen to Schuller and another gentleman, Klyburn, both of whom were discussing the price of cotton, which Leo found somewhat interesting. He *did* own a textile mill. And quite a bit of property in London along with a sheep farm. Then, of course, there was Beechwood Court.

His gut twisted.

Beechwood Court was for *her*.

On the eternity it had taken Leo to cross the Atlantic, a terrifying experience he was in no hurry to endure again, his feelings for Georgina had ebbed and flowed along with the waves that had pushed him closer to her and America. He'd had plenty of time to look hard at the truths of his life. Leo remembered with startling detail watching Tony cradle his dead mother at the bottom of the stairs at Cherry Hill. The screams of his own mother, Molly, at seeing her mistress at the bottom of the steps. How Molly had taken his hand and dragged him away, cursing both herself and Leo for being the instruments of the duchess's death.

In his heart, Leo blamed himself because she'd found out about him. Her husband's bastard. But it was Marcus Barrington's fault for making him a bastard. Maybe that's why, when Tony vowed that his father's legitimate line would end with him, Leo had vowed to end the illegitimate line as well. Solidarity with the older brother he adored.

Guilt was a wonderful motivator.

But Leo adored children. The only reason he'd ever gone to the Averell mansion in London was to see his half-sisters. He would bring them dolls. Ribbons. Hold serious discussions with Romy about dressmaking or study Theodosia's paintings pretending he had an eye for art. Olivia would have him drip honey on her toast while Phaedra pranced about, antagonizing the staff.

He'd been halfway to America, finally able to keep his meals from coming back up, when he'd allowed the pure joy of knowing he had a child to fill him. True, his child was a bastard, something he would have to remedy with money and a good solicitor, but so wanted.

As Marcus had wanted him.

Leo scratched his chest at the slight pain, regret over how he'd treated his father. Marcus had died a better man. Leo hoped he would too.

And yes, he had told Georgina he hadn't wanted a child and had sputtered something about an apothecary. But not *their* child. Not part of Georgina. His perfect person.

Leo set aside the champagne glass.

He glanced in her direction again. Everything inside Leo told him to go to her, but he didn't. It was time to leave Mrs. Rutherford's lovely party, as he had no desire to sit through an opera or endure any more of Miss Schuller's chattering.

Excusing himself, Leo walked through the crowd, beginning to make their way upstairs, stopping only to glance in Georgina's direction. He was unsurprised to find her gone, though her escort still lingered.

Miss Schuller caught sight of Leo and tried to waylay him as he made his way to the doors, but he ignored her. Once outside, Leo surveyed the line of carriages, wondering which one held Georgina. Anger still simmered beneath his skin, so it was probably for the best he hadn't caught up with her.

But he would. Eventually.

❦ 18 ❦

eorgina walked into the tall brick building on Pearl Street which housed Rutherford Shipping. It was a huge departure from the previous line of warehouses near the Battery that had once housed her father's business. The fire years ago had burned hundreds of tenements, warehouses, and even the Merchant Exchange, destroying nearly everything in its path made of wood. Wisely, upon rebuilding, brick or stone had been used.

Ordinarily, Georgina wouldn't have come down to Pearl Street. Seeking out her father wasn't something Georgina cared to do. There were only so many recriminations a daughter could take for her past mistakes. But Jacob Rutherford was still in Baltimore, so there wasn't any chance she'd see him today.

No, she was here to see Ben.

Her heels snapped sharply on the floor of Rutherford Shipping, several of her father's clerks looking up from their desks at her approach. Most stayed where they were and merely stared at her, so terrified of her father that they dared not speak to his daughter.

"Ma'am." A short, ginger-haired clerk came forward, his nose sniffing the air as if he'd caught her scent. He reminded her unfavorably of a terrier. "Is there something I may assist you with?" His eyes roved over her elegant walking dress of indigo wool.

"Good afternoon. I am Mrs. Masterson."

Two of the clerks immediately looked away and pretended to go back to their work, their eyes darting back to her every so often. One scurried off, probably to retrieve Ben.

Good.

The terrier cleared his throat. "Mr. Rutherford isn't in at present."

Georgina gave him one of her most disarming smiles. "I'm not here to see my father, Mr. . . . ?"

"Alfred," he stuttered, a blush reaching up his cheeks. Poor man was probably wondering why he'd bothered to leave his desk at all. "May I offer you some refreshment?"

"That won't be necessary, Alfred." Ben sauntered through the maze of clerks toward Georgina, eyeing her as if she were a dangerous animal. As well he might after he'd neglected to tell her that Leo Murphy was in New York. After the opera house opening, Georgina had been so shaken by her conversation with Leo, she'd been frozen by her mother's side for some time before her feet had led her out to Ben's carriage. She'd left without telling either he or her mother goodbye, her mind reeling from the fact that Leo had appeared in the middle of the opera party.

But he doesn't like ships. Or the ocean. Her confused mind kept sputtering as Ben's carriage deposited her at home. *How can he be here?*

Stella had taken one look at Georgina and ordered a bath and a bottle of bourbon.

Today, however, was a different matter. Before she visited with Daniel, Georgina meant to take her cousin to task for not warning her. He'd obviously known Leo was in New York but hadn't told her. Clearly, Ben hadn't considered Leo a threat to either her or Daniel. She supposed he wouldn't be. Once he wasn't so angry at her.

"I thought you could walk me to the ferry, Ben. I'm in the mood for your company." She leaned forward and took her cousin's arm. "Come now, don't be a coward," she said in a low voice so the army of clerks couldn't hear her.

"You're frightening. You realize that, don't you?" He turned to Alfred. "I'll be out for a short time. If Riley returns, please ask him to wait." Ben led Georgina out through the door and into the sunshine. She wrinkled her nose at the smell of the nearby docks.

"Have at it, George."

"You knew he was here," she said as Ben led her across the street, careful to keep her out of a small hole filled with filthy water. A group of children ran by, all dirty and bedraggled, their far-too-adult eyes first taking in Georgina, then Ben at her side.

"I did," he replied with no hint of apology. Ben stopped abruptly and gave the children a sharp look. "Go round the back of Rutherford's. Ask for Jimson if you wish a bit of bread and cheese." He tilted his head in Georgina's direction. "Don't ever bother this lady, or you'll answer to me. Understood?"

The children all exclaimed that no, they would never come near Georgina, before scattering in a small wave of stick-thin arms and legs toward the back of Rutherford Shipping. She wondered if her father knew Ben was feeding the guttersnipes along the wharves.

"Clever trick. I'm not sure warning them off me with only the promise of bread and cheese will work."

"You'd be surprised."

Georgina bit her lip. "I feel a bit betrayed, Ben. You knew he was here. Why in the world didn't you warn me?"

Ben sighed. "Last night didn't seem the right time; you were already in a snit over having to spend the evening with Cordelia."

"I wasn't in a snit." At least not about her mother. Her mind had been on the incident on the ferry. And Leo.

"You were. I tried to gently *advise* you that you should expect him to come after you at some point. But you weren't very receptive. I didn't know he would be at Cordelia's little party, drinking champagne with Miss Schuller dangling from his arm, George, or I would not have left your side. I certainly wouldn't have allowed him to engage you in what amounted to fisticuffs on the dance floor. Everyone in the room wondered at your relationship. Especially Cordelia."

"Well, she need not concern herself. Leo made his feelings toward me clear, which is to say, I am not the reason he is in New York. Or at least I'm not the only reason. Daniel is." She gave her cousin a sad smile.

"George." Ben placed his hand over hers.

"Leo and I have a rather complicated relationship. Fraught with misunderstanding and well-founded assumptions. I went to him only once after . . ." She waved her hand.

"You bedded him."

Georgina blushed. "Yes. We argued. We both said very horrible things to each other. Masterson died, and I found myself with child, something he was averse to. Or at least I assumed he was, based on a previous conversation. And I could hardly allow Harold to know about Daniel. Hiding his very existence seemed the best solution at the time."

"You should have sent for me sooner. You could have had Daniel here."

"I couldn't. Harold was already suspicious, and he knew I hadn't been back once since Father sent me away. Nor had any of my family visited. What I did was safer for Daniel. Harold doesn't know about him and never will."

"And Leo. What will you do about him? I don't sense his stay in New York will be short."

"Leo hates me. Just as I feared. He will want to see Daniel, but beyond that . . . I don't know. I'm not sure what I'm going to do, Ben."

Her cousin pulled her close as the East River glistened in the sun. "Murphy is angry. But he doesn't hate you. Far from it, I think. Look. There's the ferry."

❦

A SHORT TIME LATER, GEORGINA MADE HER WAY UP THE steps to Lilian's home, anxious to see her son. Hold him. Maybe whisper into his hair about Leo.

"Mrs. Masterson." Mrs. Gibbons, Daniel's nanny, greeted her at Lilian's front door. "We weren't expecting you."

Georgina smiled up at her. "I'm full of surprises, Mrs. Gibbons." She stepped through the doorway. "Goodness, but the weather has turned."

"Mrs. Harrison is napping, I'm afraid, and Mr. Harrison is in the city for the day. Master Daniel is asleep, but I was about to wake him. Unless you'd rather? I can have tea sent up."

"Thank you, Mrs. Gibbons. Tea would be most welcome."

William had found Mrs. Gibbons, citing the need for additional help with Daniel now that Lilian was with child. According to Lilian, Mrs. Gibbons, despite her youth, came with a stack of references from some of the finest families in Philadelphia. There was no mention of a Mr. Gibbons.

Georgina started up the stairs, passing the nanny. The aroma of lemons, clean linen, and some undefined spice met her nose, all coming from Mrs. Gibbons.

Her fingers ran along the banister as she made her way up the stairs. "What is that scent you wear, Mrs. Gibbons? I quite like it."

The nanny's lips pursed in annoyance before her features smoothed again. "A little something I put in my hair, ma'am. Keeps my curls from escaping my cap." She touched the bit of lace on her head from which a profusion of reddish curls could clearly be seen. "Unruly things." Mrs. Gibbons nodded politely before hurrying off in the direction of the kitchens.

Georgina couldn't place the scent, though it had to be a spice of some sort. She'd caught the aroma elsewhere. Perhaps coming from the kitchens. Cinnamon? Ginger?

A small cry sounded from the nursery, and she pushed all thoughts of spice out of her thoughts. Daniel was awake.

❧ 19 ❧

Georgina wandered about her lovely front parlor, picked up a book she'd been reading, and immediately set it back down. Pacing back and forth before the hearth, she finally stopped and went to the sideboard, pouring herself a glass of bourbon before proceeding to stare into the fire. The flames didn't hold any answers.

She took a sip of the bourbon.

There was no answer there either.

It had been several weeks since she'd seen Leo at The Rutherford. Georgina filled her time traveling to Brooklyn every other day to visit Daniel, Lilian assuring her that the staff had been alerted to watch for any strangers they noticed around the property or on the road. She'd dined with her mother because Father had gone on yet another business trip. Ben had accompanied her to the booksellers and come to dinner. But Leo hadn't appeared at her door, though he had leased a home not five blocks from Georgina.

Five measly blocks. He could walk to her house if he were so inclined.

Leo had been seen dining at Lorenzo's, a luxurious supper

THE WAGER OF A LADY

club near Washington Square, in the company of Mr. Schuller and one of the De Lanceys. Which made Ben curious. So Ben being Ben, he made discreet inquiries.

It seemed that Leo Murphy, wealthy Englishman, absent of his horrid waistcoats and not bothering to inform anyone of his familial connections, was busy strolling about Manhattan negotiating for various plots of land on which to build, of all things, a hotel. One that would cater to a European clientele. The constant flow of commerce between New York and England, already brisk, would only grow. Visitors to New York would want a taste of home during their visit. Schuller and his bank were partners.

A hotel that would take months if not years to build. Leo wasn't leaving New York anytime soon.

Other than his plans for the hotel, Leo spent his time, according to Ben's sources, in the company of other wellheeled gentlemen. He walked in the park. Visited various points of interest. And very firmly ignored Georgina's presence. Avoiding her as she'd once avoided him.

It hurt her more than she cared to admit.

The only other bit of news which gave Georgina any concern was that someone had broken the lock on her garden gate. The lock looked as if it had been picked. It could have been an accident. She had recently hired a new gardener she'd yet to question. Or possibly a workman mistaking her house for another had accidentally tried to gain entry.

Or it was simply a reminder that the incident on the ferry had not been an accident.

Would Leo harm her? Surely not. But he did want his child.

The thought upset her so much that while pacing before the fire, she stubbed her toe.

"You should be more careful." The low purr came from behind the curtains at the window.

Georgina backed up further, stumbled over an ottoman, and nearly fell to the floor, spilling the bourbon in her glass. Keeping her eye on the curtain as a graceful, masculine hand appeared, she sidled over to the table flanking her sofa. A large vase sat atop. Her hand hovered over the opening.

Leo emerged, pushing back the curtain with an angry flick of one hand, brutally handsome, looking as if he'd been entertaining patrons at Elysium instead of hiding in her front parlor. "Never realized how bloody clumsy you were, Georgina."

"How did you get in here?" Her hand started to dip into the vase.

"I've already taken out the little pistol you keep there, Georgina. Don't you realize that is the first place an assailant would look for a weapon? Clearly, it's hiding something. The bloody thing doesn't even match the décor of your parlor. Reminds me of one of my waistcoats."

Georgina looked at the vase. Really more of an urn. A gift from her mother. And Leo was correct. The swirling red and black pattern overlaid with gold didn't match her parlor.

"If I meant you harm, I would have already done so. I've watched you pace back and forth for at least a half-hour." His tone was nothing like the angry burn of the other night.

"Is that supposed to make me feel better? That you've been hiding in my parlor?"

The sun was just beginning to set over Leo's shoulder, gilding the windows facing her garden and Leo with soft, golden light.

"Did you break the garden gate? Try to force the lock?"

He raised a dark brow in offended disbelief. "Of course not. I *picked* your locks, Georgina. It's easy enough to do if you have the proper tools. Which I do."

"You picked my locks?"

"Yes, I've just said I did. The back door, specifically.

Whatever your cook is preparing for dinner smells marvelous."

He moved closer to her, his presence pressing the air of her parlor against her body. The sensation wasn't unpleasant. On the contrary, Georgina found her skin humming in a delicious way, though she felt as if she were being stalked by a large cat. One with blue eyes and endless conversation skills.

"Anyone could get in here. The rather nefarious gentleman standing across the street didn't even notice me. He isn't worth what you're paying him. Perhaps he needs spectacles, like my sister."

Ben had posted a man outside. He'd informed her last week. "Why doesn't it surprise me you know how to pick a lock?"

His eyes widened. "Owning a gambling hell doesn't immediately make one a criminal. I came by my skills honestly."

Leo sounded far too conversational for her liking. As if their horrible heated discussion at the opera party hadn't happened. Not a good sign.

"I learned how to pick locks when my mother and I left Cherry Hill." He shrugged his broad shoulders. "She chose one of the worst parts of London to drag me to. Not that it did any good. Marcus found us eventually. Just as I've found you. Though you've chosen far more luxurious accommodations. You've a lovely home. I was unsurprised to find you hadn't moved back in with your parents. You, being a merry widow and all."

"I so detest when you do this."

"Do what? I'm merely making conversation."

"Say what you've come here to say, Leo." Having him here, knowing how much he despised her, did nothing for her composure. She searched for her steel and found it non-existent. "He isn't here, if that's what you're hoping."

"Who?" He cocked his head at her.

"Our son." She plopped down on the ottoman.

A brief flash of wonder crossed his beautiful features.

He does want Daniel. Really and truly.

"Did you send my son," he emphasized the words, "away so you could have a night with your lover? Have I interrupted your plans for the evening?"

Georgina pressed her lips together.

"You'll introduce us, won't you? I assume your lover to be the man who escorted you to the opera the other night. I'm sure he's a perfect gentleman, except behind closed doors. Perhaps I can offer him some direction. I know exactly where to touch you."

A small quiver of heat ran down Georgina's spine.

"Does he bend you over just so," Leo made a crude gesture, "and fuck you over the arm of your sofa? Very enjoyable. The way your breasts bounce about when—"

"I want you to leave." Her fingers pushed into the ottoman. "Now. Before I scream the house down." She stood and pointed at the door. "And whether I have a lover or not isn't any of your affair, Leo. It never was." Georgina reached out, deliberately running her hand over the arm of her sofa, caressing the damask suggestively, goading him. "I do love this sofa. The cushions are excellent."

Something very much like jealousy flickered in the depths of his eyes. "Answer my question."

She jerked her chin in dismissal, waving at the parlor door. "Must I ask again? Leave."

"Going to call your lover to have me thrown out?"

The tension in the air of her lovely little parlor grew thick. The fingers of his beautiful, graceful hands stretched and curled against his thighs. Which drew attention to the bulge between his legs.

"I should." Georgina hastily looked away, her breath quickening. Leo had no idea what she'd been through. How hard it had been to continue to be outrageous Georgina while Lilian put an ocean between Harold and Daniel.

A sound came from him. Less a rumble and more of a growl. Like something savage trapped beneath his now annoyingly sedate and fashionable waistcoat was about to burst free. Leo stalked toward her, his larger body deliberately forcing Georgina back until her spine connected with the bookcase. Some large tome with an incredibly sharp edge poked into her back. Probably the book she'd bought with Ben. The Audubon illustrations of birds.

A soft ache started low in her belly, pulsing and stretching out across her body as Leo surrounded her. Sandalwood and warm male. The hint of a cheroot he'd probably smoked while waiting to pick her locks and break into her home.

"So, call for him, Georgina. Or anyone else. It won't matter." Heat radiated off his larger body, wrapping around her.

"I can't read your mind, Leo," she protested, her resolve weakening. "You never—"

"I did in a thousand ways. You weren't listening." His mouth swooped down hungrily, closing over hers, hard and uncompromising. *Punishing.* He took her wrists, pinning them easily above her head with one hand. "But you'll listen now, Georgina."

A soft moan left her. She didn't even bother to struggle. It didn't seem to matter how much he hated her. Or how wretched she felt for what had happened between them. One touch. One look from Leo and Georgina sparked to life. This was why she'd avoided him so studiously after Daniel's birth. She whimpered as he pushed his hips hard into hers.

"Obviously your lover," he hissed the word, "doesn't do a very good job satisfying you, Georgina." His breath fanned across her neck, tickling the edge of her ear. "Else you wouldn't be writhing against me."

"I'm not writhing." She should really call for help. Emily, the downstairs maid, would come. Stella was upstairs. Robert, her footman and driver, was in the kitchen.

Leo's tongue licked against her bottom lip. "You're mine. If your lover comes through that door, I'll shoot him with your pistol. Say it." A big hand worked at the bodice of her gown, cupping her breast, searching for her nipple through the layers hiding the sensitive peak. Gently, he teased and stroked until another moan left her. His hips tilted into hers, the hard length of his cock searing Georgina through her skirts. "Tell me who you belong to." He nipped against her mouth. "Say it."

Georgina had never been particularly obedient. A deficiency in her character.

"No." The word came out in a whimper as he stroked her nipple until the tiny point formed a sharp peak. He stroked the nipple through the light wool of her dress, the sensation of the fabric rippling across her breast more arousing than she'd thought possible.

"Say it," he growled.

"You've always been arrogant, Leo," she panted. "The most entitled bastard I've ever known. So bloody arrogant." The air paused in her lungs as his mouth nibbled at her breast through the wool.

"Entitled to you."

"But you're so angry." She flailed in his arms, which did nothing but push the ache between her thighs against him. "And you don't want me."

"I *am* furious." Leo ground his cock between her thighs, tugging angrily at her skirts. Grunting in frustration, he lifted her leg, placing her knee against his hip. Keeping her pinned against the bookcase, he ran his free hand up the silk of her stockings to the apex between her thighs, searching through the cotton. Brushing softly against the hair of her mound.

Georgina shivered. Trembled. "I won't say it."

His fingers trailed over her skin, warming her even as she struggled against the way he held her. The briefest brush along her damp flesh. Circling with maddening slowness.

She twisted, whether to get away or push herself more fully against his hand she wasn't sure.

"You often accuse me of being indirect," Leo murmured, watching her reaction to the movement of his fingers. "I agree." His fingers stilled for a moment before caressing her again with gentle purpose. "Consider this a pointed discussion about how things will commence forthwith so there are no further misunderstandings between us."

His mouth covered hers as his thumb pressed against the small bud hidden in her folds. Two fingers sank into her wetness, filling her, but not enough. Georgina's pleasure peaked sharply, pushed forward by the gentle pressure of his thumb. The sensation became unbearable, her muscles fluttering around his fingers, held hostage. Every nerve in her body was inflamed and aching for the release he had brought her to but now withheld.

Georgina pushed futilely against his hand, but Leo didn't move.

"I think," he murmured, holding her at the very edge of pleasure while she panted and thrashed softly against him, "there are some things we should discuss. Amanda, my stepmother—"

Damn him.

"I know who your blasted stepmother is, Leo. Get to the point. Please." He was very gently pinching her flesh between his fingers, driving her mad. Not allowing her any sort of fulfillment. "You're cruel."

"At times." His fingers slowly stroked a spot deep inside her. "Your lover must not be very well-endowed, Georgina." He shook his head as if he had an ounce of pity for her.

"Tight, as if you were still a maid." He held her on the edge once more, stopping the featherlight strokes. "Why didn't you come to me?" His lips grazed her cheek. "Do you loathe me so much?"

"No." A sob left her. Georgina panted as he pushed another finger inside her, stretching her, while his thumb moved a fraction of an inch. "Your intentions toward me were not made"—the air in her lungs froze as he hit a particularly sensitive spot—"clear."

He pushed down with his thumb and her muscles clutched his fingers like a vise.

"I've made mistakes." His voice was soft. "But I want no more assumptions made on my behalf, as to my feelings toward either you or our child. No more decisions without speaking to each other. Is that plain enough? Are my intentions clear *now*, Georgina?"

"I suppose. I mean—" She was hot all over, hanging on the very edge of the most blissful pleasure. Tortured. Aching. Because Leo felt the need to use this particular *instant* to teach her a lesson.

"You still haven't admitted you're mine. Say it."

"I am." Her voice grew pleading. "I'm yours. I have been since that first night when you wouldn't let me lose all my money at faro. Leo, please."

"It seems I've made my point." He pressed an open-mouthed kiss on her, his tongue sweeping between her lips to stroke and ravish. Still holding her wrists, he very carefully pushed her over the edge.

Georgina cried out, biting into the fabric of his coat, straining, trapped between him and the bookcase. The pleasure soaked through her veins, jerking her limbs, but Leo held her tightly against him. He milked every bit of bliss from her body, a long sigh leaving him.

Before the last of the tremors had left Georgina, his hand

withdrew, trailing along the length of one of her legs before coming out from under her skirts to pluck at the buttons of his trousers. He released her wrists, allowing her hands to fall to his shoulders.

"Mine, Georgina. To be absolutely clear. No matter my anger." His gaze was intent on hers. "It will fade in time."

"So will mine," she said as he thrust inside her. Georgina gasped, struggling to take him. He pushed into her hard and fast, pinning her to the bookcase.

Her fingers tore at him, sinking into his hair, wanting him closer. Needing for Leo to imprint himself against her skin. Pleasure pricked along her body like wildfire. The pads of his fingers sank into her hips with such force, she knew she'd be bruised.

Georgina wrapped her legs tightly around him.

Two books fell from the bookcase, hit Leo on the shoulder, then thudded on the rug. The landscape of the Hudson she so loved tilted wildly from its place on the wall.

"I crossed the ocean for you." He slammed into her. "I hate the fucking ocean. I was sick for days." Another thrust. "My heart broken even longer."

"I'm sorry." A tear rolled down her cheek as the world broke apart around them. It wasn't for Leo suffering onboard a ship, though that was terrible because she knew how much the water frightened him. But for everything else. Georgina urged him on with every filthy word she'd ever learned as her pleasure overtook her. It was like being in the midst of a violent storm, the winds and rain taking away her breath as her body could do no more than be buffeted by the gale.

"Georgie." Her name came roaring from him as he pounded into her once more, his big body shuddering against hers.

Georgina's body went limp with a small cry, but Leo caught her as they tumbled to the floor in a tangle of skirts and limbs. The only sound was the rough, uneven cadence of air around them as they both struggled to breathe.

She wrapped her arms around his neck, pressing her forehead against his chest with a sob.

Leo gently tucked a tendril of her hair behind her ear. "Shush. You never cry." He kissed away a tear.

"I was so frightened, Leo," she choked out as the tears flowed down her cheeks. "I—" Georgina clung to him, everything she'd gone through flooding to the surface. Her fingers curled into his coat. He had to understand she hadn't thought she had a choice. She hadn't known how much he cared for her, not until it was too late. "I'm sorry."

"Shh. I know." He pressed a kiss to her temple. "Don't cry, love."

A sharp knock sounded at the door. "Mrs. Masterson. Are you well? I thought I heard a noise."

It was Emily, her downstairs maid, who was probably terrified from the sounds coming from Georgina's parlor.

"I knocked over a lamp, Emily. Nothing more. I believe I'll go upstairs and lie down."

Silence for a moment. "Very good, ma'am."

What now? Would he leave her here in a sated pile on the floor while he adjusted his clothing and left? She couldn't force her fingers to leave his coat. There was so much— maybe too much—that needed to be resolved.

Carefully, he disentangled himself from her and stood. Adjusted his clothing.

Georgina stayed where she was, looking down at her rumpled dress. Her sprawled legs.

Leo took her hand and pulled her up before swinging her into his arms. He nuzzled the side of her neck as he carried her out of the room and in the direction of the stairs.

Georgina didn't protest; in fact, her heart sobbed and

reached for him. She clung to Leo until he muttered under his breath that she was cutting off his air.

Thankfully, Emily had fled the general area. No one else was about. Could the men Ben had hired to watch her home see Leo carrying her? The last thing she needed was her cousin bursting in with a pistol in his hand.

"Where?" Leo started up the staircase. He pressed a quick kiss to her cheek. "Your room, Georgie. Where is it?"

🦋 20 🦋

Georgina thought he would leave her.

Leo cursed himself a thousand times over for all the things he'd said and didn't mean. All flung at this brave girl he wanted with everything he was because he was a bloody idiot. How he'd railed at his brother for treating his wife with such little care and Leo had done the same to Georgina.

Never again. He pressed a kiss to her temple.

"I'm not leaving, Georgina. I will never leave you." He thought she would need to hear him say that quite a bit. She'd been disappointed by men in the past, Leo included. If he had to stay in New York indefinitely, he would. Tony could run Elysium in his absence perfectly well. Not as well as Leo could, of course, but that couldn't be helped. Tony was a duke. The *ton* would arrive to lose their purses at Elysium just to watch his brother prance about. And Leo liked New York. This was a good place for his son. For Georgina.

I don't want her hurt anymore.

Leo carried her toward the door she indicated, kicking it shut before laying her on the bed. He took in Georgina's bedroom as he returned to the door, locking it firmly behind him. There weren't any signs of anyone else in the room. Not his son. Nor Georgina's lover.

He tamped down the spurt of jealousy.

It was a pretty room. Feminine but not frilly, like Georgina. Tastefully decorated in shades of green and gold, much like her parlor. The furniture wasn't ornate but possessed clean, elegant lines.

"I wanted to come sooner, Georgina, but we were both angry."

She sat back on her knees, curls of gold springing from her head to tumble against one shoulder. So bloody beautiful, she made his heart ache.

"You, especially," she said. "It was a very hostile waltz."

"Yes."

"His name is Daniel," she said in a quiet voice. "Our son. He looks like you, Leo. I could never have passed him off as Masterson's even if I'd wanted to. He's with my sister, Lilian. In Brooklyn. Daniel is"—her face took on a glow of sorts—"wonderful. Learning to walk. He likes rocks quite a bit. You'll have to take a ferry to see him. I'm sorry about that."

Happiness bloomed across his chest. "He's safe? Well?"

Georgina nodded. "Everyone thinks he is the orphaned child of a distant relation of William's. Lilian's husband. Until I can claim him."

"We, Georgina." He stopped before the bed, took off his coat, and tossed it aside before unbuttoning his waistcoat. Leo suspected how she meant to do that. By marrying. He had an opinion on her remarriage but would keep that to himself for the time being.

"I won't let you take him from me, Leo." She tilted her chin.

My defiant American. "I wouldn't dare." He untied his cravat.

Georgina watched his movements with wide eyes.

"I told you, I'm not leaving, Georgina. I don't even care if your staff is indiscreet." He looked down at her. "I found our time apart to be . . . unbearable."

"Yes." She looked up at him. "I was always lonely in London. Separate from everyone else. Different. Strange." A smile tilted her lips. "I brought much of that on myself. But not with you, Leo." She pressed a hand to her heart. "I always felt as if you understood."

Because he had. *He did.* It was the same for him.

Leo tossed his waistcoat aside and sat on the edge of the bed to remove his boots.

"Harold sent someone to Beechwood Court to kill me."

His boot dropped to the floor with a thud. "What?"

"An assailant." She waved a hand. "He smelled of onions. I was terrified. All I could think of was that my grandmother would be so upset to know I didn't keep a pistol about. I hit him with a clock. I went to Elysium because it was the safest place for me until I could get onboard the *Betty Sue*."

Georgina had come to him in a manner of speaking, even if she didn't see it that way. His staff wouldn't have allowed anything to happen to her; they'd all been instructed to see to Georgina's comfort whenever she appeared. To watch over her.

"Since he hadn't succeeded in dispatching me that morning—"

The other boot dropped. "The same day you went to Lind? You knew how I felt, and yet you didn't tell me about Harold?"

Georgina looked down at her hands. "I'm not proud of it, Leo. But at the time, I thought I was doing what was best for everyone. I needed to leave. Daniel was here and I"—a tiny sob entered her words—"couldn't be away from him a moment longer. It wasn't easy to leave. But Harold sought me out at Elysium. I took a hack to the docks and got on the *Betty Sue*. Harold is mad but not stupid. He'd been telling people for weeks I was fragile and not in my right mind."

"Your behavior didn't help. That garden party—"

"A garden party isn't a sign of insanity."

"Tony told me you had your guests dress as woodland creatures. Carstairs went as a stag, for God's sake."

"The point I am trying to make is Harold meant to take me from Elysium. My only hope was to get away. I told Lind to send all the money in my account to Harold and say I'd gone to the Continent. I didn't want him to look for me."

Steps had been taken with Lind when Leo had set up the funds for Georgina to prevent Harold from ever touching the sum in her account. He'd never thought she'd try to pay Harold off. And Leo had called in Masterson's markers.

A slight bit of unease, as if he'd eaten a spoiled bit of meat, hit his stomach.

"Can you understand why I hid him? I didn't do it to hurt you, Leo. I need you to know I wouldn't have—"

Georgina's outward maturity often disguised the fact that she was still very young. Only twenty-two. She'd panicked. Had done what she thought she must to protect their child. And she hadn't trusted Leo to help her. And that was his fault.

"Your life would have been easier if you had given Daniel up," he said quietly.

She plucked at the coverlet. "I rarely do anything easy."

"So you plan to remarry? To that overdressed thug who escorts you about?"

She looked up at him in surprise, then a smile crossed her lips. "He isn't a thug. At least I don't think so."

"You aren't marrying him."

"I don't respond well to being dictated to, Leo. Ask my father." She held up a hand. "No, do not ask him. He'll bore you with details of all the ways I've embarrassed him, which, of course, inspired me to do much worse."

"I'm not dictating," he said calmly. "Merely stating fact. And I look forward to meeting Jacob Rutherford."

Her eyes, such a deep brown they appeared black, flickered to the exposed skin of his throat as he unbuttoned the top of his shirt. "Don't be ridiculous. You'll detest my father on sight. He'll immediately determine your worth to him and all the ways he can use you to suit his own ends." She tilted up her chin in the stubborn gesture he knew so well. "And Ben isn't my lover. He's my cousin. More like a brother, actually."

"*That's* Benjamin Cooke?" Rutherford's heir apparent. More cold-blooded, Leo had heard it bandied about, than Rutherford himself. His shirt came off next and Georgina's gaze lowered, cheeks pinking.

"Really, Georgie? You can blush after what I just did to you downstairs? I find the fact that you have a priggish streak to be highly erotic given the way your necklines dip."

"I'm not priggish." The color of her cheeks darkened further. "You are the only man I've been with."

There wasn't any doubt. She'd been so tight, she'd nearly strangled his cock.

"Well," she tapped her chin with a finger, "I suppose Masterson, if I must claim his fumbling and poking about. But I'd hardly call him my lover." She shivered in revulsion. "An altogether unpleasant experience."

"Let's not revisit it, then." He didn't even like to think of another man in her bed.

"A memory best put aside." She stiffened her shoulders, as she often did when about to make a point. "I'm sure that feeds your ego quite nicely. That I've had no other lover."

"I'm arrogant enough to tell you that it pleases me." Leo shucked off his trousers, standing naked by the bed, letting her drink her fill. Her eyes deepened in color, her breath catching softly as he moved across the bed toward her on all fours. She glanced between his legs, then back at his face.

"Everything still where it should be, Georgie?"

"Of course." She gave him a saucy look. "You proved all was in working order earlier."

Dear God, he'd missed her. All those nights at Elysium, when he'd taught her to gamble and lusted for her, Georgina had been threading their souls together. Quietly. Resolutely.

"I lied to you." He trailed one finger over the slope of her neck. Georgina possessed one of the most enticing necks in all the world, in his humble opinion. Smooth. The color of fine Belgian lace. And oh, so very sensitive.

She stiffened beneath his hand. "You did?"

"About the bourbon. There was never any mixed-up shipment to Elysium. I scoured London until I came upon a merchant who finally agreed to import it for me."

"Oh." Her back arched in his direction.

"I would save up everything odd or interesting"—he pressed his mouth to her skin and nibbled gently, feeling the pulse beating beneath his lips—"to share with you when you sought me out."

"I thought you merely a brilliant conversationalist. That you talk in circles intentionally because it forces your listener to lower their guard."

"Mmm." His lips continued down the slope of her throat. "Amazing you figured that out when scores of titled lords have not."

"I'm clever."

"Yes, you are."

Her palms slid over his naked shoulders, testing his skin with the scratch of her nails before moving to explore the lines of his ribs. Their lips caught, his mouth drinking in hers. He'd kissed dozens of women in his life, but none of them felt like Georgina. Not one of them had truly mattered to him except her.

"I couldn't be with anyone else, Georgie." Leo thought she should know that. "I tried, mind you, but none of them were you." He fell back against the bed as she trailed her hands over him.

A pleased smile crossed her lovely mouth. "You're very beautiful, Leo," she whispered before her tongue darted out to touch his nipple. "But you know that."

His cock twitched madly against her. "It only matters that you find me so."

He undressed her slowly, wanting to memorize each breathless sigh and gasp, the hum which started in her throat the more aroused she became. The beautiful lines of her voluptuous form, all softly rounded, fell into the palms of his hands. He pressed a kiss to each of the small, pale lines across her stomach, proof she'd carried his child.

Georgina's skin was warm. Her scent drifted into his nostrils. A garden in the first days of spring, when the dew still clung to the flowers. Not carefully cultivated roses. No, his Georgie was a bank of rolling wildflowers, thick with grass and fresh earth. Wild, like the endless forest he'd seen across the river.

When he finally settled between her thighs, she was panting and clawing at the skin of his back. Lovely sounds left her as she arched beneath his fingertips, opening every part of herself to him. His mouth found her breast, circling the nipple with his tongue, tasting her sweetness.

"You are worth every moment of that dreadful ocean crossing. I would sail the seas forever if you required it of me. Allow you to win every hand of vingt-un. Give up Elysium," he whispered. "I'll even stay in this bloody country for you."

A tear ran down one of her cheeks at his declaration. She tightened her legs around his hips, pulling him closer.

Leo prolonged the agony as long as he was able, inching into her slowly this time, mindful of how roughly he'd taken her earlier. For a man who was known for his conversation skills and charming manner, he'd never been able to adequately express with words what Georgina was to him.

He took her hand, pressed a kiss to her palm, and placed it across his heart. "You live here," he whispered. "No one else. Ever."

Georgina sighed, hips tilting up as she climaxed, her eyes never once leaving his.

🐿 21 🐿

"I'm starving. Aren't you the least bit hungry?" Leo's fingers toyed with the spray of golden curls falling over her shoulders. "You realize, Georgie, if I become weak with hunger, I won't be able to perform to your specifications. You might have to help me. Do a bit more of the work."

"I don't think you'd mind." Her fingers stretched over the taut muscles of his stomach, reaching down until her fingers circled the length of him. "Cock. Such a funny name."

"You find my *cock* amusing?"

"No. I take it very seriously." Her heart fluttered madly about as she took in the big, naked male sprawled across her very feminine bed, a sheet barely covering his hips. Leo's dark hair was messy, falling over his cheeks and ears in waves. A brush of dark hair covered his jaw. He was grinning at her, the tiny dimple in his cheek making an appearance. He was deliciously scruffy and wholly disreputable. And entirely hers.

Another flip of her heart.

"My cook makes an excellent roasted chicken. I suppose the least I can do for your valiant efforts is feed you."

"What about a bit of potato?" The blue eyes roamed over her. "Will you feed it to me?"

Georgina leaned forward so he could get a good look at her breasts, hidden by the sheet. "I will grant you a bit of potato." Her tone grew husky. "But you will have to do more to please me if you want a slice of bread or some butter."

"I crossed an ocean for you, Georgie." He tugged at the sheet. "I expect some butter. And possibly something more." His eyes focused on the nipple of her left breast before tweaking the bud between his fingers.

Leo *had* crossed an ocean for her, something that she knew terrified him. He'd given her Beechwood Court. A never-ending stream of funds. Made sure she had her favorite bourbon. All without telling her. When it came to emotions and his own heart, Leo had trouble being direct. He might never say the words, but Leo would show her, in dozens of ways, that he loved her.

"I love you." She leaned over, cupping his face with one hand. "And I know you love me in return."

He sucked in a lungful of air and looked away. "I do, Georgie." His voice broke. "You're my person."

Georgina had no idea what that meant, but she pressed a kiss to his lips anyway.

"I can still see you the night Masterson first brought you to Elysium. You wore a powder blue gown with an indecent neckline. The lace and beads around the edges made you sparkle and shine like the brightest of stars." He turned back to her. "Contrary to what you might think, Georgina, I do not spend an inordinate amount of time teaching women who enter Elysium how to gamble because I'd rather they lose." Taking her hand, he said, "Did I ever tell you about Tony's mother?"

Georgina was taken aback by the abrupt change of topic. "No. I know she died tragically."

"Fell to her death after discovering her husband's affair with her lady's maid. My mother. And the existence of a bastard son. Me. Her own son's playmate and best friend."

"It wasn't your fault, Leo. Surely you know that."

He shrugged. "I do. I blamed my father for a long time, wishing he hadn't claimed me. It guaranteed everyone knew of my origins. And even when they didn't, once finding out, I was tossed aside. Her name was Imogene, if you must know. I was fifteen and thought I loved her." He pulled her close. "Not anything like you, of course. She spoke with a lovely musical quality which didn't remind one of a goose."

She nipped at the skin of his shoulder. "Now you are surrounded by the honking of geese."

"After Imogene, I made sure everyone knew I was born on the wrong side of the blanket. I took great pains in becoming a bigger rogue than my father. Took the same vows as Tony to end the Barrington line, united as brothers in our hatred for a man we both blamed for ruining our lives with his own selfishness."

"But Marcus claimed you."

"And I hated him for it. I was forever torn in two between my father and my loyalty to Tony. A miserable existence, made worse by my own guilt and a girl who rejected me when I was fifteen."

"You've given this an enormous amount of thought," she whispered.

He shrugged. "I had quite a bit of time on my hands aboard that bloody ship when I wasn't puking into a bucket. Enough time to examine my faults, of which, thankfully, there are few." His hand glided over her stomach. "Didn't you promise to feed me chicken?"

"I did," she breathed as his fingers slid between her thighs.

"Wonderful. I'd like you to do so while naked."

22

"**W**illiam." Georgina looked up in surprise at her visitor. She put aside her book as her brother-in-law strolled into her parlor. She'd only just settled herself with a book before the fire, Leo having slipped out a short time ago through the kitchen door. He'd insisted on staying the night, rather indiscreetly. Greeting Emily cheerfully when she brought up dinner and causing Stella to nearly swoon when she came to the door. He'd only been wearing a sheet at the time.

I'll be helping Mrs. Masterson ready herself for bed.

Georgina had thrown a pillow at him.

Now Cook knew as well. Leo had promised to be discreet as he left her house. She didn't want another scandal. Not that she thought it would matter. Leo had made his intentions toward her very clear.

Abundantly. *Repeatedly.* The soreness between her thighs was a testament to such clarity of purpose. They would not be apart again. He'd promised.

Now William was here to spoil her newfound happiness.

"I hope you don't mind my dropping by like this,

239

Georgina." William shifted on his feet but made no move to sit. He brushed back a wave of sandy hair, glancing out the window.

Thank goodness Leo was no longer stomping about her garden.

"Jacob is back from Baltimore. I stopped by his office to drop off some contracts he'd asked me to review and thought I'd visit you."

Rutherford Shipping was far closer to the ferry than Georgina's house, meaning William had intentionally come to pay a call. Incredibly odd. His appearance immediately put her on edge.

"I hope Father's trip was productive."

William gave her a shrewd look, probably attempting to discern if Georgina knew about her father's Baltimore mistress. "By the amount of work"—an edge of bitterness entered the words—"he brought back for me, I would say your father's trip will reap great benefits for Rutherford Shipping. One of Baltimore's formerly successful merchants has filed for bankruptcy. Your father has offered to purchase the company for a number far below its estimated value."

"Yes, Father does adore a good bankruptcy." Jacob Rutherford was known for swooping in at exactly the right moment to assume the assets of a smaller company, probably one he'd helped put out of business, and making it his own. William's father, before his death, had once owned such a business. A supplier of stone and granite to the builders of the city.

William didn't answer, only walked farther into the room, circling around the sofa. He spent a few minutes admiring the odds and ends strewn across her parlor. Studied the spines of the tomes lining her bookcase and pretending great interest.

He couldn't possibly be enthralled with her collection of gothic novels.

"Well," Georgina finally said after the silence had

THE WAGER OF A LADY

stretched on for several minutes. "This is a lovely surprise, regardless of the reason." Why on earth was William here?

Her eyes slid toward the open door where Emily, the maid, waited. "Tea, if you please, Emily."

In the short time Georgina had lived here, William had not once visited. Nor had she thought William knew where she lived. He didn't like her, or her family, save Lilian. If he felt anything at all, it was resentment for the situation Georgina had put him in with Daniel. She'd meant to ask Ben what he'd said to force William to help her, but part of her didn't want to know.

"Is everything well with Lilian?" she asked. It was the only reason she could think of why William would drop in on her. Georgina had been plagued with nausea while carrying Daniel, but Lilian hadn't been ill at all. Only exhausted. She credited the tea Mrs. Gibbons often made her which settled her stomach. A blend the nanny had perfected while working for another family in Philadelphia.

William didn't reply immediately, only peered around the parlor, examining the painting of the Hudson River at sunset. The same painting which had nearly fallen to the floor after Leo had taken her up against the bookcase. Warmth heated her cheeks. She'd straightened the landscape only moments ago.

"Thomas Cole." He tapped a finger at the corner of the painting. "I hadn't thought you cared for art, Georgina. Must be a habit you picked up while in London. I'm sure you had many fine paintings in your home with Masterson."

"My husband didn't care overmuch for art." In truth, Masterson had sold off most of his art collection before Georgina had ever set foot in London. "Besides, you know how much I love the Hudson." She waved in Emily who had appeared with the tea tray. "Thank you, Emily." She waited until the maid left before pouring William a steaming cup.

"Sugar?"

"No, thank you."

She handed William his tea, which he took and immediately set on the table without taking a sip. His hands stretched over his knees as he regarded her, barely concealed dislike flickering in his pale eyes.

"*Is* Lilian well?" she inquired again. "I find myself growing concerned."

"I'm worried, Georgina. This current situation is causing her undue stress. Lilian has a delicate constitution, unlike yourself. She isn't used to duplicity."

Georgina sipped her tea. And unlike Leo, William had no trouble expressing himself.

"Surely you are not oblivious to the upset you've caused. She is much too kind to tell you so herself, but things are rapidly becoming unmanageable."

This discussion was about Daniel. Apparently, whatever Ben had used to coerce William into helping her was no longer enough incentive.

"How odd. Lilian seemed perfectly fine not two days ago. Nanny Gibbons barely allows her to lift a finger. She is not being overtaxed, William. Nor do I think she finds Daniel to be a burden."

"How selfish you are to put your interests above your sister's welfare. Not surprising, I suppose."

Georgina really disliked William. There was such a churlish, bitter person hiding beneath his finely tailored clothes. She wondered that Lilian didn't see it. "My sister is of great importance to me, William. I would do nothing to cause her harm. Lilian *offered* to care for Daniel until I could do so myself."

"Lilian is a kind woman. A saint. She would never turn you away because she loves you. But you've put her in an untenable situation which threatens her health." He gave her a sympathetic smile, one that showed all his teeth. "I realize your choices are limited. The mistake you made, bringing that child into the world, must weigh on you. I am not without understanding for your circumstances. We are family, after all, which is why I went to great lengths to help you."

"Daniel is not a mistake."

A puff of frustration left him, making him look like a petulant child. "I don't mean the designation harshly. But now that you've returned to New York, surely you know your chances for remarriage will diminish if a future husband knows of the child."

It unnerved her, the way William refused to say Daniel's name.

"I worry the child will become a burden to you in your pursuit of a suitable husband." He reached over and lightly patted her hand. "I don't judge you for your misstep, Georgina. You are not the first woman to find herself in such a state."

"So I've been told."

A slight frown crossed his lips. "Lilian and I shouldn't be forced to raise the child for you, especially not when we are expecting our own. And I don't want you to have any difficulty making a splendid match."

"I'm sure I'll manage."

"But you don't have to, Georgina. That's why I've called on you today. I can relieve you of this burden so that you may go on with your life and be happy. No harm done. Your reputation, such as it is, will stay intact. Your parents need never know. I've taken it upon myself to make some discreet inquiries to place the child with a loving family."

"His name is *Daniel*." She forced herself to set her teacup down rather than throwing it at William's head. "And he's hardly a burden. It isn't as if you see to his care yourself."

His nostrils flared. "I had to engage a nanny."

"Whom I compensate you for." Georgina pressed her fingertips into the cushions of the sofa to keep from launching herself at William. "A rather large sum which more than covers her salary."

"No amount of money," he flung back at her, "is worth Lilian's well-being." He shook his head. "I didn't come here to fight with you, Georgina. Nor was it my intent to insult you. I truly believe placing the child with a loving family is the right thing to do for us all. My only concern is for Lilian. And you, of course," he hastened to add. "It was merely a suggestion."

Georgina glared at her brother-in-law, trying to seek out his true motive. Certainly, it wasn't out of concern for her. But William *did* love Lilian.

"I appreciate your concern, however unnecessary it is."

She and Leo had already decided to take the ferry to Brooklyn tomorrow, a decision reached right after she awoke to the sight of his dark head notched between her thighs.

A hum ran through her despite having William sitting in her parlor. She pushed thoughts of the previous evening out of her mind.

"I understand. Perhaps once you consider my suggestion, and you are less overwrought, you'll feel differently."

Overwrought?

"Perhaps."

She couldn't wait until tomorrow. Leo was out for most of the day looking at yet another plot of land, so she would go herself. The horrible twisting in Georgia's stomach told her that Daniel must be fetched today. *Now.* The very second William left her parlor. Lilian couldn't possibly know what William suggested. She loved Daniel. Her sister would never allow him to be sent away.

"I apologize for upsetting you." William stood, hands smoothing down an unseen wrinkle in his coat. "I truly do have your best interests at heart, Georgina." Pulling out his pocket watch, he said, "I've another appointment which I fear I'm late for. Please think about what I've said."

Daniel would be brought here. Her staff would be discreet. Loyal. Stella had helped raise her younger siblings. Or maybe Mrs. Gibbons would return with her.

"Good day, William."

The front door hadn't even shut behind William before Georgina was yelling for Stella to take a note to Ben.

23

Leo whistled to himself as he strolled down Broadway Street in the direction of the half-completed building at the corner. The lot was huge, more than enough space for what Leo had in mind. Schuller knew the owner of this piece of property. A gentleman who had fallen upon difficult times and needed the money the sale of the land would bring.

One man's misfortune was Leo's gain.

He did miss London and his family. But Leo had meant his words to Georgina. If she wished to stay here, so would Leo. In either case, building a business empire in New York made sense. He would start with a hotel.

The Barrington, as he'd decided to name his new venture, would be a sought-after destination. He envisioned the exclusive supper club he meant to put on the main floor, as well as the private area for gentlemen to enjoy their cigars and brandy. The lobby would be elegant, expensive but understated. Refined but welcoming. Perhaps he should ask Cordelia Rutherford her opinion.

Roots here, in this city, were important not only for

Georgina and Daniel, but for Leo. The sting of being the Duke of Averell's bastard wasn't quite as sharp here. Leo had allowed his birth to dictate his life for so long, it would be a relief to become someone else. A better man.

This morning, Georgina had agreed to take him to see Daniel tomorrow.

Joy, the sort he'd never expected to feel, struck him full in the chest. He had never thought to have a child. Nor Georgina.

He closed his eyes and said a silent, grateful prayer for the soul of Marcus Barrington.

Leo would find a way to bend the truth of Daniel's parentage. He possessed a great deal of money and connections. He refused to allow his son to bear a moment of the taint Leo had worn his entire life.

"Ah, Mr. Murphy." Schuller stood on the street before the enormous lot with the half-built building. Bricks and bits of wood were strewn in disarray. A pile of discarded blankets sat in one corner along with the remnants of a burned-out fire. "What do you think?"

Leo thought The Barrington would take up the entire block. A big, grand building. Not of brick or the brownstone he'd seen, but fine cut stone. Gray, he thought. There was a quarry that supplied stone for construction, which he wanted to visit, but it meant a boat ride up the Hudson.

Just the thought of all that water beneath him made Leo queasy. If he could get to the quarry without losing most of his breakfast, Leo would count himself lucky.

"I like the location," Leo replied to Schuller.

"It's a desirable one. I have a strong feeling Broadway Street will become important, stretching as it does nearly the length of Manhattan." Schuller pierced him with a shrewd look. "I wouldn't agree to partner with you if it wasn't."

Schuller had nearly as much to lose as Leo if the hotel didn't become profitable.

Leo meant to leverage his connections in London to ensure the success of The Barrington here. It would take some time. New York was still recovering from a spate of disasters. But Leo could be patient. And the odds of success were in his favor. "My thoughts exactly, Schuller."

They walked around the lot for a bit, speaking of companies best suited to the construction versus what the cost would be. How soon the hotel could be started. How much of the existing building would need to be removed. Other than Elysium, The Barrington would be the first time Leo had created an idea from the ground up. The project would be vastly time-consuming. Expensive. But in the end, he thought The Barrington would be worth the trouble. He couldn't wait to see Tony's face when he told his brother he was naming a hotel after the family.

After settling some of the more urgent matters between them, Schuller and Leo parted, promising to speak the following day. The owner of the property would receive their offer today, and Schuller assured him it would be accepted. Construction could begin in the spring.

Lighting a cheroot, Leo walked back to the house he had rented, but his mind stayed on the hotel. The entire top floor of the Barrington would be a series of large apartments where he and Georgina would live with Daniel, plus an entire guest suite large enough to accommodate the Barringtons should they ever descend on Manhattan.

Phaedra would love New York.

The door of the home he'd leased swung open as he jogged up the steps to reveal his housekeeper, Mrs. Flick, ready to greet him. She was a lovely woman. Irish, of course, as many of the servants in New York were, with a comforting roundness about her small body. She made the most delicious apple pie he'd ever eaten.

"Waiting for me, were you, Mrs. Flick?"

The older woman blushed several shades of pink. She'd taken to mothering him, always appearing in his study with a plate of lemon cookies or a tray loaded with food if he missed breakfast. Her fussing reminded Leo oddly enough of his stepmother, Amanda, though the two women looked nothing alike.

"There are several letters for you, Mr. Murphy." She handed him the small stack. "Will you be dining at home tonight?"

"Unfortunately, Mrs. Flick, I will not. Business, I'm afraid." He meant to dine with Georgina, perhaps entice her to walk around the park down the street from her house. He wanted to hear her laughter and have her tell him more about Daniel. Then he meant to take her to bed.

He leafed through the stack of letters, seeing Mrs. Flick's dejection at the knowledge Leo wouldn't be dining at home. She nodded and headed in the direction of the kitchens to inform the rest of his small staff. The solicitor he'd engaged since coming to New York had helped secure this house which came with Mrs. Flick, the cook, a maid, and a groom. More than enough staff for only Leo. Most of the neatly addressed letters were invitations to dine at the home of potential business associates. Schuller had been instrumental in helping him make connections and would make a splendid business partner.

His fingers halted on a note with his name scratched across it in a feminine hand.

"Mrs. Flick." He paused halfway up the stairs.

The sound of her footsteps sounded as she came back to the foyer. "Yes, Mr. Murphy? A change of plans, perhaps?" A hopeful look was firmly placed on her pleasant features.

"No, unfortunately not. When did this arrive?" The note dangled between his fingers as he held it up. Something pressed against his heart. Foreboding. His next thought, oddly enough, was of Harold. Who would never have received any of Georgina's money.

The foreboding turned to fear.

"Two hours ago or so, I believe," Mrs. Flick said as Leo opened the note. "A boy came to the door. I gave him a coin and sent him on his way." Her face grew concerned. "Has something happened, sir? A problem with that hotel you're wanting to build?"

"Not at all, Mrs. Flick." He tore open the note, scanning the few lines Georgina had written as the prickling sensation across his chest increased. "Merely a business appointment which slipped my mind. Mrs. Flick, can you ask Jamie to bring my carriage around? I need to go to the ferry." Even the word made Leo's stomach roil.

"The ferry, sir?"

"Yes. The one that will"—he looked at Georgina's handwriting—"take me to Brooklyn. Brooklyn Heights."

"Brooklyn Heights? Why that's very nearly in the country. You've a meeting all the way out there?"

"Buying property, Mrs. Flick. I like the countryside. Where is the ferry?"

"Jamie knows the way. I'll fetch him immediately." She looked dubious at Leo going across the river this late in the day to look at property in Brooklyn, but she waddled off just the same to find the groom and have the carriage brought around.

Horseback *would* be faster, but Leo didn't want to take the chance of getting lost which might delay taking the ferry. The urgency to find Georgina forced Leo up the stairs two at a time. Reaching his rooms, Leo went straight to the bed, pulling a pistol out from beneath the mattress. A habit from living for years above a gambling hell. This wasn't Elysium, but Leo still thought it prudent to be armed. It certainly couldn't hurt.

Anxiety crawled across Leo's chest as he ran down the stairs to his carriage.

Leo, I've gone to fetch Daniel and bring him home. I'll be back soon, and we'll all have dinner together. A picnic in the parlor.

He and Georgina had already decided to visit Daniel tomorrow. Something had prompted her to go to Brooklyn today, and not to visit.

I called in Masterson's markers. The dread increased. He should never have left her this morning.

"Jamie," he greeted his driver. "I need to get to the ferry. The one to Brooklyn."

"You've time, Mr. Murphy. Last one doesn't leave until six."

He would be on the ferry well before then. "Good. I need to make a stop first, then straight to the ferry." Giving Jamie Georgina's address, Leo climbed inside the carriage, his fingers closing around the solid weight of his pistol.

The last time Leo had this horrible, prickling sensation had been years ago when the unhappy Earl of Manfield had tried to stick him with a knife. Manfield had lost heavily at hazard and accused the house of cheating him. Leo had pivoted at exactly the right time and the knife glanced off his ribs instead of plunging into his heart..

Needless to say, the Earl of Manfield's membership had been revoked.

He leaned out the carriage window. "Hurry, Jamie."

❧ 24 ❧

Georgina hurried off the ferry, hailing a hack to take her to Lilian's. Cold seeped into her bones and she pulled her cloak tighter. The chill icing her skin had nothing to do with the weather though the clouds above her looked ominous.

Snow is coming.

The panic over Daniel threatened to swallow her. After William's visit, she'd immediately sent for a messenger and Stella. Dashing off a note for Leo and a much more urgent one for her cousin, she'd gone straight to the ferry. The entire trip across the East River, she'd stood at the rail, willing the ferry to reach the shore faster.

Climbing into the hack, Georgina wrinkled her nose at the smell of garlic leftover from the last occupant. She gave the driver instructions to Lilian's home. "Hurry, please. It is a matter of some urgency."

She fell back against the seat as the hack started forward, cursing William for his abhorrent suggestion earlier today. Did he expect Georgina to calmly sip her tea and agree to give her son away to a set of strangers, no matter how loving? Because flitting about in society was more important to her?

Lilian won't allow anything to happen to Daniel.

Georgina always knew William would eventually start to grouse about keeping her child no matter what Ben had promised for her brother-in-law's help. But she'd thought she'd have more time. No matter. She would retrieve her son and return to the city. Leo was coming tonight for dinner. Daniel would be frightened at leaving Lilian, but it couldn't be helped. Georgina didn't trust William not to do something stupid.

The hack turned, heading down through the trees in the direction of Lilian's home, narrowly missing two deer who dashed from the woods and across the road.

Her note to Leo had been brief. She hadn't known when he'd return home and didn't want to worry him. The note she'd sent to Ben, hand-delivered by Stella, had been much more urgent.

Fingers clenching in her lap, Georgina watched as the first bits of snow fluttered past the window of the hack. Her sister's home was remote, at the very end of a long road. The property had once belonged to William's father and once William and Lilian had wed, her brother-in-law had constructed an immense home for his new bride. Their closest neighbors were nearly a mile away if one cut through the woods and a clearing containing a large pond.

Please let him be all right. And Lilian.

Georgina hoped she was overreacting. She could feel foolish later, she assured herself, once Daniel was ensconced in her parlor, playing with the wooden horse she'd bought for him. She and Leo would be on the floor next to their son.

Her heart felt as if it might burst from her chest.

When the hack finally arrived, Georgina leapt from the carriage, stopping in her tracks when William came out the front door to greet her. He crossed his arms over his chest, watching her approach the house. He was still wearing his suit from earlier today and looked as if he'd only arrived himself.

"Georgina, what are you doing here?"

"I might ask you the same." He'd lied to her. Deliberately.

"I live here," he replied calmly. "Lilian is indisposed." He spun his hand. "You'll have to return tomorrow."

"I'm not here to see Lilian. I've come for Daniel." She started up the steps. "After considering our conversation earlier, I think it best he come home with me. I don't want him to burden you and Lilian any longer."

William's stance didn't change; his eyes moved over her with a curl of his lip. "Is that really what you think is best, Georgina? Because I don't think it is. You are overwrought." A chuckle left him. "I'm not even sure you're fit to raise a child."

A chill passed over her, like a cold finger trailing up her spine.

The door opened behind William. Lilian appeared, drawn and pale. Purple smudges lingered beneath her eyes. She looked at Georgina in confusion, then back to her husband.

"Georgina, what are you doing here? I thought you were coming tomorrow."

"A change of plans, Lil. I thought I'd take Daniel with me back to the city tonight. I've something to show him." She smiled brightly.

"But—what will people think?" Her sister absently rubbed the small mound of her stomach.

"I'm not concerned in the least. I've worked everything out."

"But it's started to snow. You can't possibly mean for him to be out in this weather. Come inside, Georgina. We'll have hot chocolate. I've developed a craving for it. You can stay the night."

"Get back in the house, Lilian," William snapped. "You're not well. Go back to bed."

Georgina agreed. Lilian did look ill. Two days ago, her sister had been pale, but nothing like this wraith-like creature. "You can come with us, Lilian," she smiled. "We'll go shopping tomorrow. Buy some things for the baby."

"I don't think so. Lilian's place is here," William said, moving to stand in front of Lilian.

"William." Lilian touched his arm. "Whatever is the matter with you?"

He jerked his arm from her fingers.

"Please inform Mrs. Gibbons to pack Daniel's things and bring him downstairs," Georgina said. "Then I'll be on my way. And have him brought down as well." She took in her sister's appearance. "Why don't you get your cloak? Come with me," Georgina pleaded. Lilian looked so fragile standing next to the door frame.

"No, I—"

"Lilian isn't going anywhere." William cut off her sister, his eyes flitting out to the road before coming back to Georgina.

He's waiting for someone.

William walked down the steps and past her to the driver of the hack. He had a low conversation with the hack driver, who climbed back into his seat and shot Georgina a dubious look before snapping the reins and driving off.

"No," Georgina yelled out as the hack disappeared down the drive.

"I'll send you back to the ferry in our carriage. Much more comfortable than a hired hack and warmer. For Daniel's sake." He shot a look at Lilian, who was still standing at the door. She wobbled slightly, clinging to the frame, as if about to faint.

"Then call for the carriage."

William only smiled at her.

Georgina's unease unfurled. He made no move to call for a servant to bring his carriage around. In fact, it didn't look like any servants were about. Snow landed on his shoulders and in his hair as he stared at Georgina.

"William, what is happening?" Lilian's fingers were stark white against the door frame.

"Mrs. Gibbons!" William nudged Lilian aside as he yelled up the stairs. "Bring the child down, please." His eyes went to the road again.

The nanny appeared, a small bundle in her arms. The breeze lifted a strand of Daniel's dark hair, visible above the blankets he was swaddled in. He was asleep. Thankfully. A rush of relief filled Georgina.

"Give him to me this instant." Daniel was dressed for traveling. But William had only *just* called upstairs. Fear stole her breath. "Whom are you expecting, William? My God, you *didn't*." But it was clear he had. He'd already found another home for Daniel and was prepared to give her child to perfect strangers. "Give him to me." Georgina's voice echoed in the late afternoon air as she strode toward the porch. "How dare you, William."

Lilian slid further down the door, pain tightening her lips. "William, what have you done?"

Mrs. Gibbons stepped around Lilian, nudging past her as William had, as if Lilian were no more than a piece of furniture or a troublesome dog. She walked in Georgina's direction as Georgina held out her arms. The smell of clean linen, lemons, and spice filled the air as the nanny passed her.

Now she remembered why the scent was so familiar.

Hands shoving her over the railing. The water of the East River directly below her.

Georgina, terrified at her sudden realization, reached for Daniel. "You. It was you on the ferry."

The nanny gave her a mild look. "Would have been kinder had you gone into the water, don't you think?"

Georgina reached for Mrs. Gibbons, but William's arm shot out, shoving Georgina hard until she fell against the steps. A cry of pain left her as her knee made contact with the wood.

The nanny came to stand next to William, nearly as tall as he.

"Troublesome little bugger, isn't he, Anna?" William peered down at Daniel. "Is he bundled up warmly? I'd hate for him to catch a chill. Ah." Her brother-in-law looked up. "Finally."

A carriage came up the drive, coming to a stop before the porch. The driver on top gave Georgina a curious look but didn't get down from his seat.

Where were Lilian's servants? She had at least two strapping young lads who worked in the stables. And a gardener.

"You shouldn't have come here," William said to her. "Now things will only be more difficult. I tried to help you, Georgina. Tried to talk some sense into you."

Georgina struggled to her feet.

Mrs. Gibbons looked over at William, lifting her chin for a kiss as they waited for the carriage's occupant to step out.

William pressed his lips to hers.

"William," Lilian nearly screamed from the doorway, her eyes wild as she took in her husband and the nanny.

A voice emanated from the depths of the carriage as the snow began to swirl faster.

"Ah, there he is, the little cherub." The accent was upper crust. Snide. One Georgina hadn't heard since she'd fled

London. A leg stepped out, the rest of his lean, angular form unfolding itself as his feet landed on the gravel of the drive.

No. No. No. No.

Georgina ignored the pain shooting down her leg. She leapt past William, determined to snatch Daniel from the arms of her treacherous nanny before Harold could even touch her child. Curling her fingers, thumb outside her fist, as Ben had taught her when they were children, she punched smug Mrs. Gibbons right in her nose. Grabbing Daniel, she squeezed him close, only stopping when she heard a pistol cock.

Daniel let out a disgruntled wail, objecting to her treatment.

Georgina's heart raced. Terrified. *Oh, God. Harold.* The old terror poured over her skin. *What had William done? How had he brought Harold here?*

William glared at Georgina. "You bitch." He rushed over to the nanny, who sat sobbing on the ground, weeping hysterically while Harold, pistol in hand, watched with amusement.

"She broke my nose." Blood poured from between the nanny's fingers. "I should have drowned you," Mrs. Gibbons screeched at Georgina.

"Yes, you should have." Harold smiled. "Would have made things that much tidier."

William lifted Mrs. Gibbons to her feet, placing an arm around her and handing her a handkerchief.

Lilian, tears running down her pale face, collapsed against the front door. "William." She reached out with one hand.

"You should never have brought Daniel here, Lilian." William made no move to go to her. "*Never.* But one word from your harlot of a sister and you're running off to England. Cooke forced me to take him. Your cousin threatened to—" He stopped, his chest rising and falling as he turned on Georgina. "If you had only agreed today, you would never have known. You could have gone on with your life."

"Georgina has never been very good at direction, have you?" Harold drawled, still holding the pistol. "Impressive punch. Quite the little fighter." He looked up at the confused driver of his carriage. "A family matter, my dear man. Stay put. You'll be paid double."

"My cousin knows I'm here," Georgina spat, rocking Daniel as he started to wail. She looked toward her poor sister, shaking in the cold air, half lying against the door in a state of shock.

"Ah yes. Mr. Cooke," Harold answered. "William went to great lengths to ensure he wouldn't be able to join us. There was an accident on the docks earlier. A most tragic one. I expect your cousin is floating in the East River at the moment. Am I not right, William?"

William didn't look up at Harold, giving Georgina hope that Ben remained unharmed. Her brother-in-law was clearly a vile human being, but he was also a coward.

"All of this could have been avoided if Anna had just followed instructions."

"Someone came upon us," Mrs. Gibbons said through the blood running down her face. "I would have been caught."

Georgina stared in horror at Mrs. Gibbons. The woman who had been caring for Daniel had tried to kill her.

Lilian was panting, her knuckles white as she clutched the doorframe, pulling herself just inside the house. "William, you are my husband. I'm begging you to stop—" her words trailed off. "I forgive you."

"I don't need your forgiveness. I *never* wanted to marry you, Lilian," he snarled. "You're beautiful but incredibly dull. Hell, Georgina's more exciting than you. But your father had me backed into a corner. I had nothing but a bankrupt company, trying to finish law school. I don't want to be Jacob

Rutherford's pet politician for the rest of my life. Masterson has offered me a tidy sum for your nephew."

A cry left Lilian. "No, William. Our child—"

"Let your father raise it. He's the one who wants a dynasty."

Georgina stared in shock at her brother-in-law. "My father—"

"Will not be able to touch me." He turned from her back to Lilian. "Anna and I are going to England. Masterson has offered me entrée into London society."

A laugh came from Georgina as she watched William's chest puff at his proclamation. "Is that what Harold promised you? Money and influence?" She laughed harder. "*His* influence? I always knew you to be weak, William, but I assumed you were intelligent. Harold doesn't have any wealth. His uncle's markers are all over London, aren't they, Harold? I saw the stack myself at Elysium."

"You never did know when to shut up. Give me the child." He pointed the gun at her.

"He isn't the heir." She held Daniel tighter. "He isn't anyone to you."

"Do you think I'm an utter fool, Georgina? As much as I don't care to have a cuckoo in the nest, your child's birth is fortuitous, as it turns out. Clarissa is a clever thing, though unfortunately, it appears, barren. This little bastard I will claim to be my uncle's, a child his unfit mother fled to America with and whom I had to rescue. You'll be dead, so hardly in a position to disagree."

"Your markers—"

"Are no longer important. You like to gamble, so you'll appreciate the fact that I hold the trump card, so to speak. The child is Leo Murphy's. He will doubtless be happy to destroy my markers in return for his child's safety. His child, whom Clarissa and I will be raising as the next earl. He might even pay me a stipend to ensure the child is well cared for. What do *you* think, Georgina?" He nodded, his black pebble eyes gleaming at her. "It turns out your child will be useful after all. I think we'll live at Beechwood Court, and Lind will be forced to give me the money he holds for you. That sweet child is *your* heir, is he not?"

"No." She tightened her hold on Daniel who was looking at her with wide, sleepy eyes. "You're mad, Harold."

"Madly clever, Clarissa says. She's the one who figured everything out after Wentworth came to dine. Then you led me on a merry chase, and now here we are. Did you really think I wouldn't find you?" Harold took a step in her direction.

"He won't take you," Georgina whispered to her son. "I won't let him." Would Leo even know where to look for her? And Ben? Surely if he'd gotten her note, he'd be here by now.

"You lied to me," William hissed, stopping Harold from advancing on Georgina.

"I never lied," Harold snarled. "I told you I was wealthy, and I am. Or at least I will be once she's gone." His eyes bored into Georgina. "God, I detest you, Georgina. You refuse to give me everything that is mine. You greedy chit." Spittle formed at his lips as the walking stick he carried in his other hand came crashing down against the ground. Snow swirled about their heads, the tiny flakes landing on Harold's nose. It helped distract from the madness in his eyes.

"My lord?" The driver had come down from his box.

"William, are you really going to be a party to this?" Georgina said as calmly as she could to her brother-in-law. "He's *lied* to you. He'll kill me and Lilian. He'll probably kill you and Mrs. Gibbons." She turned to the driver. "And you."

"No, I won't," Harold said to the driver. "I need you to drive the carriage."

"Do you really want to be complicit in the murder of the

daughters of Jacob Rutherford?" Georgina said to the driver. "You know who my father is. And Benjamin Cooke is my cousin."

The driver took a step back, holding up his hands.

Harold roared in rage. "Shut up, Georgina. *Just shut up.*"

"If you think you can hide in London, William, allow me to dissuade you from the notion. Harold has neglected to inform you that Leo Murphy, *the father of my child*, is *also* the brother of the Duke of Averell. And they are very close. The duke is a powerful, wealthy man, with equally powerful friends."

Harold snarled, the pistol wavering. "Give me the child."

"You lied to me." William, bless him, came forward, his fists clenched, and Harold turned in his direction.

"Lilian," Georgina hissed under her breath. "Run inside. Lock the doors." A red bloom had appeared on her sister's skirts between her legs. Blood. "Where are the servants?"

"William gave them the day off," Lilian whispered as her eyes closed and she pulled herself inside. Tears ran down her cheeks. "Run, Georgina. Save him."

"I won't leave you."

"You have to." Lilian's voice could barely be heard. "Go to the Griests." Her sister managed to shut the door.

Georgina glanced in the direction of her sister's nearest neighbors. The trees, even devoid of most of their leaves, were so thick, she wasn't sure she'd find her way.

"I always said you Americans were idiots." Harold took in William who was standing before him. "Fine. I never had any intention of paying you or helping you in England. Imagine. Me. An earl. Escorting about a solicitor and his mistress." He shook his head. "Clarissa would never allow it. I'm surprised you haven't figured that out by now."

Harold raised the pistol and calmly fired, hitting Anna

square in the chest. "That's for not pushing Georgina into the river when you were supposed to."

The nanny dropped to the ground.

A cry escaped William. "Anna!"

Harold smiled, took aim, and shot William. A look of surprise crossed her brother-in-law's handsome face as he fell.

Georgina looked away from the bodies of William and Anna, trying not to scream, her gaze fixed on the trees. She didn't want to leave Lilian, but what choice did she have? Harold was insane. He'd shoot her too.

"Now where do you think you're going, my good man?" Harold turned his pistol to the driver who was attempting a retreat. "I suppose I can drive myself."

Georgina took her opportunity while Harold's attention was fixed elsewhere. Clutching Daniel to her chest, she ran.

Leo stood on the deck of the ferry, careful to keep his gaze from the churning dark water rushing past him. At least there was the wind outside. It was worse below decks. Too warm. The smell of so many bodies together far more foul than the crush at one of London's largest balls.

He took deep breaths, something he'd been told would help, but the hasty meal he'd had earlier today still threatened to spill over his boots. *Christ*, he hated rivers. Oceans. Ponds. The slightest bump of the water and his stomach would pitch. The gathering unease in his mid-section was like a spill of grease upon a napkin. It kept spreading.

He'd never in his life felt such fear.

Leo had stopped at Georgina's house on the way to the ferry, praying the prickling sensation against his skin was wrong and she'd already returned with Daniel, hoping the two of them would be sitting calmly in her lovely parlor wondering why he was so upset.

But Georgina wasn't home. Her housemaid, Emily, stammering and refusing to meet his eyes, not unexpected after she'd caught sight of far more of Leo than she should have last night, assured him that Mrs. Masterson had left for the ferry some time ago.

"She sent me with a note for Mr. Cooke." Stella, Georgina's lady's maid stood at the top of the stairs and had come rushing down. "Right after a visit from Mr. Harrison."

William Harrison. Her brother-in-law.

"She was unsettled after his visit," Stella said. "I thought perhaps he'd come about Mrs. Harrison, but Mrs. Masterson assured that was not the case. She was worried, though," Stella confided.

Stella had given him directions to Lilian's house, explaining what he would need to do once the ferry docked in Brooklyn. Leo knew Georgina wouldn't have sent for her cousin unless something was wrong, though Stella couldn't tell him anything more. She'd been unable to find Mr. Cooke as he'd been gone on an appointment, so she'd left the message with one of his clerks.

The ferry rolled, and Leo nearly lost his footing. He'd tried to light a cheroot earlier but had thrown it out immediately after lighting it. The smell hadn't helped the nausea making its way up his throat.

"George did say you aren't good on the water. I believe that was her reasoning as to why you wouldn't chase her to New York. I'm not sure how you'll manage to get up the Hudson to inspect the stone for your fancy hotel."

Leo didn't want to move his head too quickly, because it would worsen the feeling in his stomach, but he got a good look at the man next to him. It would be poor manners to cast up his accounts on the boots of Benjamin Cooke, though it could only improve his appearance. Georgina's cousin looked as if he'd been in a fight. There was a bruise on one cheek, and his coat was torn.

A mongrel. Even knowing who he was to Georgina, Leo's

opinion hadn't shifted.

"Benjamin Cooke."

"Leo Murphy."

The two sized each other up for a moment before Cooke said, "Don't ruin my boots."

"Bugger off." But Leo was relieved to see him all the same. It meant Cooke had received Georgina's message. "You look like hell."

"Hmm. George told me you were charming. Frankly, I don't see it."

"Is that what you call her?"

"Since we were children. It suits her."

"Well, stop it." Leo's worry made him curt. "You received Georgina's note."

"I did. I would have been on an earlier ferry but was delayed by an inept footpad who tried to beat me senseless. He was supposed to stab me and then throw me in the river, but he didn't quite get to that. And before you ask, I know because the idiot told me. Harrison hired him."

"Lilian's husband?"

Cooke nodded. "He went to George today to convince her to allow him to place Daniel with a family. Give him away. As if she would ever do such a thing."

Bile rose up in Leo's throat, and it wasn't from the ferry, though the pitching waves were certainly not helping. "No, she would not."

"I've always found Harrison to be weak. He's a coward. Couldn't even do the job himself."

"Yet you placed my son in his care. I'm beginning to understand why someone would want to toss you into the river."

"*Because* William has always been afraid of me. The situation was only meant to be temporary. I knew you'd eventually cross the big terrifying ocean to fetch George."

Amazing, since Leo hadn't been entirely sure after his father's death that he would.

"I wasn't the least surprised when you showed up in New York. I didn't expect you at Cordelia's opera party. She was horrified by your impassioned dance with George. But once she finds out you're the bastard of a duke, she might take to her bed for a week."

Leo merely grunted in response.

"And because William is a coward, I don't think he would have decided to have me killed on his own. He's a worm. I tried to talk Jacob out of allowing Lilian to marry him, but I was overruled. As I was when he sent George off to Masterson, though there was little else I could do in that situation, except toward the end." A flash of something vicious crossed his face. "I assume she told you why she was banished."

Well, that answered Leo's question as to how the gambler had met his end. "She did." Last night as she fed him bits of chicken between kisses.

"The thing is, William is an aspiring politician. And he has a gambling problem. He can be bought."

"You think Harold is behind this." Leo thought so too.

"I do. He's stayed hidden, using someone else, William, I assume, to do his dirty work."

Leo looked out across the river. "I called in his markers. It's an enormous sum. And he had no access to the money I'd left for Georgina nor Beechwood Court, which he thinks he has a right to." He had driven Harold, desperate and mad, right to Georgina's door. Perhaps he was the one who should be flung in the river. "Her garden gate was jimmied. She thought I did it. The men you had posted around her house are worthless."

"No, they do a fine job. They let you in, didn't they?" Cooke said. "Why do you think you weren't stopped? I didn't know about the gate, though. It must have happened before I posted a guard." He frowned. "She didn't tell me."

"Well, she didn't tell me about Harold either before she left London."

"You should know, Murphy. I'm Daniel's legal guardian. Not William Harrison, though he thinks he is. Or Lilian. I made sure to have the paperwork done before Daniel even left England, then again here." Cooke turned to him. "Quite frankly, George was so distressed over Daniel and you, I'm not sure she was completely aware of what she was signing. I do feel bad about that."

Leo mused over the information. "You were in England. You brought him back."

"I did. Lilian came with me. I also may have taken a trip to London and visited Elysium."

Against his better judgment, Leo was starting to like Benjamin Cooke.

"Thank you," Leo said quietly. "For taking care of them when I could not. I am in your debt."

The taller man next to him nodded. "Just stop being a horse's ass. She loves you."

Leo said nothing, just looked out over the East River as the shore drew closer. If anything happened to Georgina or Daniel, the son he had yet to meet, Leo would be a broken man for the rest of his life. He wanted nothing more than to hold them both, protect them, forever.

"There was an incident on the ferry a few weeks ago," Cooke said quietly. "George doesn't think I know about it, but I do. And last month while we were walking down the street together after the theater, a wagon suddenly came barreling out of a side alley, nearly running us both over."

Jesus. It was Harold. "How far from the ferry dock to Lilian's house?"

"At least half an hour."

Georgina held Daniel tightly to her chest as she ran through the woods, cursing her skirts and cloak which seemed to catch on every bit of bramble. If she could get to Lilian's neighbors, whose house was somewhere beyond the pond now coming into view, she and Daniel would be safe.

Lilian crawling inside the house, her skirts full of blood.

"Oh, God. Please let her be alive." She didn't think William was any longer. Certainly, Nanny Gibbons was dead. A small cry left Georgina at the remembered sight of the nanny's eyes, staring up at the sky.

William, you fool.

Daniel started to cry, protesting Georgina's rough treatment as she fled through the trees and rapidly falling snow. His face reddened and scrunched up as he let out a particularly loud wail.

Georgina pulled him close to her chest as he started to wiggle. "Shhh. Please, sweetheart. Don't cry."

She'd been worried for so long that Harold would hurt Daniel, but now he needed her son for all his horrible schemes. He wouldn't hesitate to kill her, just as he hadn't paused in the least in shooting William and Mrs. Gibbons. Or that poor driver.

Lilian.

Georgina hadn't heard another shot from Harold's pistol, which she hoped meant he'd left Lilian alone. She paused long enough to catch her breath and listen for any sounds of pursuit. The woods around her were quiet. Nothing moved as the snow floated down around her.

Snowflakes covered Daniel's cheeks, and she brushed them away. The Griest family lived just through the next clearing. They were German and didn't speak much English, but they would help her. The pond was right in front of her.

She started around the perimeter, stepping near the withering cattails and grass before heading back into the safety of the trees. Careful to move as quietly as possible, she rocked Daniel against her chest, trying to keep him warm. Ben would come. Leo would come.

He'll have to cross the river. Georgina had planned to make Leo a special tea, one her cook said would help soothe his stomach for the ferry. She had planned to hold him close to her, as she did Daniel, kiss him senseless until he stopped thinking about the water.

As she moved, Georgina concentrated on taking small, careful steps, not wanting to slide on the wet leaves beneath her feet. She despised her own foolishness at not telling Leo about Harold sooner. She hadn't thought Harold would come here. How had he found William?

A sob caught in her throat. And Lilian. Her poor sister—

A branch snapped to her right.

❦

THE WAGER OF A LADY

Bᴇɴ ᴀɴᴅ Lᴇᴏ ᴅɪsᴍᴏᴜɴᴛᴇᴅ ꜰʀᴏᴍ ᴛʜᴇɪʀ ʜᴏʀsᴇs ᴀꜰᴛᴇʀ flying down the road in the direction of Lilian's house. Mile after mile, the houses had become further apart, the stretches of forest longer. Eventually, Cooke turned his horse up a short drive with a large, brick home sitting majestically against the woods beyond. The snow was coming down faster now, wetting his cheeks and nearly covering the two people lying in front of the house. A man and a woman. A carriage sat off to one side, the horses stomping and shaking their manes.

Leo's heart jumped into his throat at the sight of the woman, but it wasn't Georgina. The woman's auburn hair spilled across the snow, the small cap on her head askew.

"Nanny Gibbons," Cooke said. "And William. I suspected she and William were involved with each other. I wanted to confront him but worried what the news would do to Lilian. She was far too young and pretty to be a nanny. She must have been helping him."

Leo looked inside the carriage, but it was empty. He walked around the side, speaking in a soothing voice to the horses until he saw a dark form in the snow. "I found the driver." The man was dead as well. Red splattered the snow around his body.

"It couldn't have been that long ago," Ben said, kneeling next to the two bodies. Steam came from the pool of blood forming around the man who Leo assumed was William Harrison. "They're still warm."

"Where are the servants?" Leo asked. The house and grounds were eerily quiet as he and Cooke made their way toward the porch. Suddenly, Cooke broke into a run, leaping up the steps. The front door was slightly ajar, a small bit of green fluttering in the doorway.

"Lilian." Cooke's voice broke.

At first, Leo's heart nearly stopped at the sight of the woman lying at the base of the stairs, a pool of blood stretching out across the floor. It reminded him so strongly of what had happened to Tony's mother, he had to shut his eyes.

"Where are you hurt, Lilian?" Cooke bent over her, his face stricken. "It's Ben. Where are you shot?"

"She hasn't been shot," Leo said quietly, nodding to all the blood on the floor. "She's lost the child and needs a doctor. Now."

Lilian stirred in Cooke's arms. She was beautiful, a slender, more delicate version of Georgina. "The woods," Lilian croaked. "Georgina took Daniel." A sob left her. "I told her to run. He—he shot William and Mrs. Gibbons. I tried to lock the door, Ben. I tried." She clutched Ben's arm. "I told her to go to the Griests."

"Lil," Ben said gently. "Where is he? The man who shot William."

"I don't know. He came up the steps and looked at me. I stayed very still when he nudged me with his foot. Then he mumbled that I was nearly dead anyway and didn't . . ." A cry left her. "He didn't want to waste a shot on me. Then he went after her. I—must have fainted. I yelled for help, but then I remembered no one could hear me. William gave all the servants the day off." A tear escaped one eye. "He told me he wanted us to be completely alone because he had a surprise for me." A trembling hand went to her mid-section. "The baby. He's gone."

"I've got you, Lil." Ben held her. "I'm here."

"What direction Cooke?" Leo snarled. "Point. You have to find her a doctor and stop the bleeding."

"You don't know the area," he snapped back. "You'll get lost."

"She'll die if you don't get her to a doctor. Point."

"I'll take the carriage. Leave you the horses. Against my better judgement." Cooke raised his arm. "Through the trees and across a small clearing. There's a pond. You won't be able to miss it. The Griests have a farm just on the other side. "I assume you're armed."

Leo jerked his head. "Of course. I run a gambling hell." He touched Lilian's hand.

Her eyes focused on him for only a moment. "Ah. Leo Murphy." Her voice was weak. "Don't let him hurt Georgina or Daniel."

"I won't." He turned and jogged down the steps before he took off running, looking at the ground for any sign of either Georgina or Harold. He'd hunted a bit from time to time. Didn't enjoy it. But still, he could follow tracks, especially in the snow. A bit of blue fabric fluttered on a branch, and he plucked at it with his fingers.

Georgina.

There were two sets of footsteps in the fresh snow. A woman's. And a man's.

He ran as quietly as he could, straining his ears for any sound, but the thick trees surrounding him stayed silent. Rounding the right side of the pond, Leo finally spotted her. A bundle was clutched to her chest as she moved slowly around the thick grass at the edges of the water. She was using the grass for cover.

"Georgina."

She turned, hearing his voice, and stepped back from the still water of the pond. Ice was forming around the edges. He looked away. The very sight of the pond filled Leo with a sort of mindless, irrational terror. And now was not the time to relive a bloody fishing trip.

Leo put his pistol back in his pocket. "Thank God. Georgina." He was nearly at her side, his arms outstretched, when her face collapsed into rabid fear.

"I thought you'd show up eventually, Murphy." The cocking of a pistol met his ears. "Thank you for flushing her out."

Leo didn't think. He couldn't. He ran forcefully at Georgina, hearing her gasp of surprise before he pushed her out of the way. The move would send him into the pond, but it was the only way to shield Georgina and Daniel.

A searing pain shot across his right side as Leo fell into the water.

Georgina rolled away, falling against a pile of downed branches and limbs.

A splash sounded as the cold invaded his legs and back. A scream bubbled up his throat at the smell of mud and decaying vegetation. Filthy water rippled over his chest.

The pond at Cherry Hill. The one the duchess sometimes took Tony to on sunny days. Leo hadn't liked fishing. Putting a hook in a defenseless worm felt wrong to him. But Tony liked to fish and wanted to show Leo. He'd slipped into the water. The algae on the top of the pond had been thick. So thick he couldn't see. Where was Tony? He thrashed about, but he was wrapped up in the fishing line. The worm was still attached, wiggling against his cheek. Tony was screaming his name. The dirty water was in his mouth, choking him. The algae invaded his nostrils. He couldn't breathe—

Leo forced himself to turn his head, terrified to be in the water.

Please let me die on land. Not in this pond. Not in the dark water.

Where was Georgina? Had the pistol shot gone through him only to hit her? A painful rasp left him as he struggled to catch his breath. He touched his side and grabbed at the strands of grass to keep from floating completely into the pond, his fingers coating the dying cattails with blood.

Harold, leering at him like some insane jester, stood at the edge of the pond, the pistol still in his hand. "I suppose my plans will have to be revised yet again. Well, no matter. That is no longer of any importance. Only the child matters."

Leo rather hoped Harold would just shoot himself accidentally in the head with the way he was carelessly handling the pistol.

"My brother," Leo croaked. It hurt to breathe. The water was so cold. Filthy, as it had been that day. He swallowed down his panic, not wanting Harold to notice. "Will ensure you are stripped of everything you own, Masterson. He'll ruin you in London." Leo coughed, seeing a shadow moving behind Masterson.

Georgina.

No. She needs to run. Get away from Harold.

"I suppose it goes without saying that your membership to Elysium is revoked."

Harold gave a bitter laugh. "Never cared for your club anyway. Always holding that bloody membership over everyone's head. I'll gamble elsewhere."

"My brother is a duke, not a bloody idiot, Harold. He'll know you had something to do with my demise."

"No, he won't." But Harold's bravado faltered. "The duke will never know what became of you. I'll leave your body here to be picked clean by the animals in this savage place. Or even better, you'll sink. It will be ages before anyone finds you. I'll have Georgina's money. Beechwood Court, which she's renovated for me. And of course, your child."

Harold really was mad. Completely.

Leo blinked, trying to clear his vision. The area around the pond seemed to be deserted. No one but him and the very insane Lord Masterson. How ironic that Leo had studiously avoided water and anything that floated upon it since that day with his brother, only to drown in a pond after being shot by Harold. Foul-tasting water slipped into his mouth, and he spat it out.

The algae slipped down his throat, wobbly, like aspic. He hated aspic. Tony was screaming at him to wake up.

If he could just keep Harold here a while longer, Georgina

would have a chance to make it to Lilian's neighbors. Find help. Ben would keep her and Daniel safe. Cooke would probably have Harold murdered in some dark alley, which suited Leo just fine. He would be sad to miss it.

"I don't think you are in possession of all the facts, Harold. I wouldn't get attached to Beechwood Court." He coughed again, spitting out a mouthful of stagnant water. "I own it, not Georgina. Didn't she mention that to you?"

Harold's face reddened. His eyes bulged.

"The money in her account was put there by me as well. There was nothing left of her dowry, you pompous prick. Your uncle saw to that. The only reason you have anything at all is because I didn't call in your uncle's markers until recently. I've already written to my brother, *the duke,* who will see you are impoverished."

"You're wrong." Harold danced back and forth on his feet. "I'll have your son, Murphy. I'll make myself his guardian. Claim he's my uncle's spawn. No one will deny me, especially with you and Georgina both dead. Your brother will give me whatever I ask. My markers. A stipend to keep that brat alive. I'll have everything."

"My brother will have you disposed of if Benjamin Cooke doesn't get to you first. I doubt you'll leave New York alive." At Harold's look of surprise, Leo laughed, though it hurt dreadfully, and it forced water up around his nostrils. Why couldn't he have bled to death in the snow? That was honorable. Instead, he'd sink into the muck, just as he almost had when he was ten.

"Good luck, Masterson. Oh . . ." Another cough wracked his body. "I forgot to mention you can't be declared Daniel's guardian. Benjamin Cooke already is. He has papers. Duly witnessed in both England and New York."

Harold made a sound like a wounded animal before he fell strangely, eerily silent. "You won't be around, at any rate. One less bastard gambling hell owner in the world. I wonder if you'll drown or bleed to death first."

"Neither." Georgina's voice came from behind Harold, a thick branch clenched in both hands. She swung with all her might at his head. "You mad, vile prick."

Harold's skull made a horrible sound as the branch made contact, then he fell to the snow face down, groaning, trying to reach for the pistol where it had landed just beyond his outstretched fingers.

Georgina swung twice more with such viciousness, had Leo not been dying, he would have been aroused.

That's my girl.

Then the dark water took him.

27

*D*amn it hurt to move.

But he wasn't in the dirty, cold water anymore. He was dry. Warm. Pain throbbed over the right side of his body. There was a thick pad of cotton over his ribs. The pad itched. He tried to pull at it with his fingers.

"Don't, Leo. Stay still." Cool fingers smoothed back the hair from his forehead and pressed a kiss to his temple.

He managed to get one eye open, though it was a struggle. *Georgie.*

Worry etched her lovely features as her face hovered above him. He forced his other eye open.

I thought I died in the pond.

Georgina brandishing a thick piece of wood at Harold. The sickening sounds as she'd hit him over and over until she was sobbing. The splash of the water as she'd struggled to drag him from the pond.

He glanced behind her. Pale yellow walls with wood paneling along the bottom. A wide window with a view of the woods and a delicately upholstered seat beneath it. There was a blanket there and a pillow.

"Where am I?" It hurt to talk; his voice was rough, as if he hadn't spoken for some time. "Am I dead?"

She stroked his cheek. It felt so good, he didn't want her to stop. The deep brown of her eyes filled with tears. "No." Her fingers on him trembled. "You are in one of Lilian's guest rooms."

"Daniel." He tried to move again. "Daniel." He repeated the name of the son he had yet to meet.

"He's fine." Tears fell from her eyes, landing on the blanket covering him. "But you must stay still. Your stitches could pull free." She started to rise from the bed, but she was halted by his fingers wrapping around her wrist. "Stay, Georgie. You keep running away from me." The pain radiated across his chest.

"I'm only going to get you some water. Aren't you thirsty?" She pointed to a pitcher. "I'm not leaving."

He grunted, watching her with greedy eyes as she moved across the room to a pitcher of water and poured him a glass. Her hips swayed gently beneath her skirts, tempting Leo even though he felt weighed down as if by heavy stones. It hurt to move even a little.

"You're my person," he rasped as she tilted a glass of water to his lips, and he drank. "*My* person." She didn't understand. It was much more profound than just loving her. She needed to listen.

"I know, Leo." She pulled back. "You're my person as well. Now close your eyes and rest."

"Stay." He fumbled about for her hand and felt her cool fingers lace with his.

"I will." She kissed him. "Now sleep."

Wʜᴇɴ Lᴇᴏ ɴᴇxᴛ ᴀᴡᴏᴋᴇ, ɪᴛ ᴡᴀs ᴛᴏ sᴇᴇ ᴀ ᴘᴀɪʀ ᴏꜰ ᴇʏᴇs nearly identical to his own staring back at him. A small hand grabbed at his chin, pulling at the beard lining his jaw before sharply sliding away.

A sound escaped him as a small heel made contact with a rather sensitive appendage.

"Daniel." Georgina carried a wet cloth back to the bed. "If you want to sit with him, you must stay still. He's hurt."

Daniel tilted his chin at a stubborn angle, very much like Georgina, before returning his attention to Leo.

"Hello, Daniel."

His son's eyes widened at the deep sound of Leo's voice. Daniel leaned forward again, fingers tangled in Leo's beard, tugging at the course strands. Apparently, Daniel found him to be incredibly fascinating.

I've never been so happy in my whole bloody life.

Georgina walked toward the bed, placing the cloth in her hand on a chair, and reached for Daniel.

Leo put up a hand, horrified to see his arm trembling. "No. Leave him. Please."

She pressed her lips together. "I don't want him to hurt your side. Dr. Olsen said to watch tearing your stitches."

"Stop fussing, Georgie," he said more harshly than he intended before catching her hand. This side of Georgina was one she'd kept well-hidden. A woman who worried over him. Nursing him. Caring for him. Leo actually liked her fussing over him far more than he should.

She's magnificent. And mine.

"Fuss? I merely don't want to have to explain to Welles how I let you perish in the woods of Brooklyn." She paused and nodded. "*Averell.* I keep forgetting. I don't know if I can get accustomed to calling him that. But you. Jumping in front of Masterson as if you weren't going to get shot." She sucked in her breath. "You nearly drowned in that damned pond. *Water*, Leo. That you are afraid of."

"I'm well aware the pond was filled with water."

Another sharp intake of breath. "This isn't Elysium where you have Peckham and Smith at your side. Or where you can trot about like a king."

"I do not trot." His thumb stroked along her hand.

A ragged sob crawled up her throat, and she looked away. "I didn't think I'd be able to get you out of the water, Leo. You got stuck in the mud. Weeds. You were bleeding—"

"Shh." Leo pulled her hand to his lips.

Tears ran down her cheeks. "You kept begging me not to leave you to die in the dark water. You thought I was Welles. Averell. Damn it. I'm sorry. I just—sometimes I dream that I couldn't get you out of the water. I—"

"My brave girl." He pressed a kiss to her palm. "But you did save me. And Daniel."

She nodded and wiped at her tears. "I did. I really did."

Daniel made a trilling sound in the back of his throat, his gaze darting between Georgina and Leo, blue eyes wide. He reached out with one hand and patted Georgina's arm. "Ma. Ma."

"Mama is fine, my love." She ran a hand through his curls.

"I assume Harold is gone?" Leo ran a shaky hand down Daniel's body, feeling the fragility of his son. An image flashed before him of Georgina, a fierce, cold look on her face as she brought down the branch on Harold's skull.

"Yes." Her voice was soft. "I split his skull. I hit him more than once to ensure he would never harm my family again." Georgina held his gaze. "You probably didn't notice because you were in the pond. I—suffice it to say, it was quite gruesome. But I'm not sorry. Ben found us after I pulled you from the pond." Her eyes shuttered closed, still in that clearing and far away from him for a moment. "He handled everything."

Leo was assured Harold was gone. Cooke never would have allowed him to live. "Good, my love. He left you no other choice, Georgie. He would have killed me. You. Daniel."

She nodded. "I know."

"How is Lilian?" The vision of her lying at the bottom of the stairs, her dress soaked with blood, haunted Leo. Reminding him of the death of Tony's mother and everything that came after.

"She's a widow, of course. I suppose that is the kindest thing I could say. If William weren't already dead, he soon would be. My father was beside himself. He never thinks anyone under his thumb will defy him. You'd think he would have learned with me. She lost the child. Which Ben and I agree is for the best, given the circumstances. Mother was here for a few days, sneaking peeks at you and fluttering nonsensically over Lilian. Eventually, she became so annoying, Ben took her to the ferry."

Leo tugged her closer. "Come lay next to me, Georgie. Put Daniel on my stomach. He can't do much damage there."

When she'd settled against his good side, Leo stroked her hair, feeling her, warm and soft against him. Daniel pressed his head to Leo's chest, giggling when Leo's stomach grumbled.

"You smell like spring," he whispered into her hair.

"I told you, it isn't spring, or any other damned season, Leo. It's soap."

"I want to marry you. As soon as I am able to leave this bed. You might even be with child again. I took no precautions at all. Not that it seemed to make any difference the first time. The point is, you are obviously very fertile and—"

"What a terrible proposal. Possibly the worst one imaginable." Her palm covered his heart. "I'm not even sure I should accept. You put no thought into it at all."

"Agreed. I've been stuck in this bloody bed with no time to prepare." He pressed a kiss to the top of her head and felt the weight of his eyelids pushing him toward sleep. Daniel had settled on his chest, his breathing even and deep.

"But my answer is still yes."

"Good," he whispered before drifting off.

❦

"MAY I GET OUT OF BED NOW?"

"Dr. Olsen has expressly forbidden you moving about unless it is to see to your needs."

Her one concession to Leo's humiliation, after he'd found out it had been Georgina who saw to every aspect of his care. He'd assumed a faceless male servant had rendered aid while Leo was unconscious. Or as unappealing as it was, Cooke. But not so much as a nurse had been brought in.

No. Only Georgina, Lilian had assured him.

Lilian had taken to visiting him in the afternoons, keeping him company so that Georgina could rest. She read to him in her lovely, lilting voice, which, Leo informed her, didn't sound at all like a wounded goose. Lilian was so pale and fragile after all that had happened. Leo imagined her a wisp or a fine piece of lace that had somehow taken human form. He worried for her.

Leo pushed himself up against the headboard. "I tell you I'm fine, Georgina. I need to walk about."

"Yes, you mentioned you didn't need help last week right after you pranced over to the washbasin and collapsed on the floor."

"Pranced. Trotted. What am I? A bloody horse at Tattersalls?" He caught a glimpse of her hips through the simple muslin gown she wore. Her hair was pulled back into a thick braid flung over one shoulder. Tiny sprigs of gold curled about her temples and ears. If he didn't know better, he'd think her a complete innocent. Fresh and dewy.

Like bloody spring. It was *not* the soap.

"A week ago," he grumbled. Horribly embarrassing. He'd fainted. Like a virgin on her wedding night. "But as you can see, Georgie, I'm feeling much better." He stroked the twitching bulge beneath the sheet.

"Absolutely not." She puffed at a stray curl that had fallen across one eye. "You'll tear your stitches."

"Lock the fucking door, Georgina."

A bit of pink darkened her cheeks at his language. She shot a glance at his cock, growing larger by the moment, on her way to the door. But she obeyed, throwing the lock, and stood to regard him with her hands on her hips. "You are not to move. I will do everything." She walked to the washbasin and dipped a clean cloth into the water.

"Well, that takes all the fun out of it."

"You could use a bath anyway."

"I'm not a helpless child." His cock twitched again.

She pressed a long, luscious kiss to his lips. "I will be very angry," she whispered against his mouth, "if your stitches open. You almost died."

"But I didn't."

Slowly, she pulled the sheet down across his hips, tugging when the cotton caught on him. Taking the cloth, she moved it over his skin. She took a great deal of time making sure his nipples were clean before moving lower.

His stomach muscles jumped.

Careful to stay away from the bandage on his right side, Georgina ran the cloth over his ribs and across his hip. Gently cupping his balls, she pretended first to examine then clean him in a very suggestive way with the cloth.

A groan left him. "What are you doing?"

"I'm seeing to your needs, Leo." She lay down next to him, dropping the cloth on his stomach.

"You've forgotten to clean the most important part." His voice had grown uneven.

Her hand gently moved over his cock, fingertips exploring his length. Her thumb rubbed over the tip.

"*Jesus.*" Leo thought he might explode, and she'd barely touched him. He'd never be able to bathe again without thinking of this moment.

Her fingers curled around his cock, rubbing up and down his length with slow, even strokes, punctuated with a gentle squeeze. "Like this?"

"Yes." The word came out in a moan. When she cupped his balls again, fondling them in her hand, Leo's head fell back on the pillow.

"No moving," she reminded him, pressing an open-mouthed kiss to his stomach while stroking him.

"I promise, Georgie. Not a muscle."

To Leo's shame, he lasted approximately as long as a boy of fourteen. She muffled the sound of his release with a kiss, while her clever hands caressed him. As he lay there panting, Georgina took the cloth from his stomach and cleaned him off.

Leo grabbed her hand to keep her from leaving. "That might be the best bath I've had in some time."

Georgina giggled. A lovely, musical sound. One he wanted to hear for the rest of his days.

She pulled the quilt over them both, molding herself to his side. A winter storm had started outside, bits of ice and snow hitting the window. The fire hissed as moisture dripped down the chimney. His fingers found her braid and loosened her hair so the mass of golden curls would spread across his chest.

"I love you, Georgie," he whispered to her. "I love you."

EPILOGUE

"**M**ama!"

The sound of her son's footsteps rang against the deck of the ship as he made his way over to Georgina's place at the rail. The sun glinted off his dark head of curls, the blue of his eyes like that of the ocean before her. She could see land in the distance. England. Damn it. She had so been hoping she would never have to return. But a wager was a wager.

"What is it, my love?"

"Papa is green again." Daniel made a horrible face.

A shadow loomed over her son. "No. Not green, Daniel. A much lighter shade." Leo's arm slipped around her waist.

Pale. Washed out. Not green. She would have compared the color to milk which had spoiled.

"Did you have some tea?" Her fingers brushed along his jaw. He'd kept the beard because she liked it.

"I did. Which is why I'm out here with you instead of below." He reached to pull Daniel closer to him with one hand. "I'll be very glad to get off this ship, though the crossing has been much quicker than my first." He kissed her cheek. "Thank you for compromising."

She and Leo had indeed been married the same week he'd finally walked out of Lilian's guest room and made his way down the stairs with little assistance. Her parents had objected to Leo until they'd caught sight of Daniel and discovered that Leo, bastard or not, was the son and brother of a duke.

The news earned Georgina not only a smile but an actual embrace from her father.

The Barrington was nearly finished. The remainder of the details, which were minor, would be overseen by Schuller while Leo and his family spent a long-overdue holiday in London. The hotel was nothing short of spectacular. There was already a waiting list for membership to the exclusive gentleman's club housed within the hotel. A chef had been hired for the restaurant. They would be back in time for the grand opening, hopefully with actual Barringtons in tow.

She and Leo had played poker to determine how much time they would spend in New York and London, respectively. Georgina had won several hands but lost at the end. A year in New York, followed by six months in London. They'd adjust as time went on, but for now, Georgina thought it the best solution. Leo missed his family, and he had a variety of business enterprises which required his attention, including Elysium.

Georgina had married a very wealthy, ambitious man.

Leo's hand flattened over the small mound of Georgina's stomach. He touched the tiny bump frequently. Sometimes speaking directly to her mid-section rather than Georgina. She found it all vastly amusing. As did Daniel.

"We'll stay for a time at the Averell mansion. Tony will insist. But we should find a house of our own." Leo nuzzled against her neck. "I'll sell Beechwood Court."

Georgina nodded. She no longer wanted the estate. Not after what had happened there. The memories of Harold had faded, but she doubted they would ever be gone completely. Clarissa was still Lady Masterson but would need to remarry. The estate was bankrupt and would revert back to the Crown without an heir.

Much like William had been bankrupt.

How Harold made the acquaintance of William and the nanny, Mrs. Gibbons, remained a mystery. Ben suspected Harold had made inquiries about her which had eventually led him to William. Her brother-in-law had probably been impressed with Harold's title and the opportunity to get out from beneath her father's thumb.

Lilian's entire marriage had been a sham. Jacob Rutherford had purchased the company William's father had once owned and then made his new son-in-law into an indentured servant of sorts. No wonder he'd wanted to escape New York, though it didn't excuse what he'd done to Lilian. Her sister was still a shell of who she'd once been. She'd moved back in with Georgina's parents, though she refused to speak to their father.

Georgina worried for Lilian. But Ben had promised to coax her into coming to London with him in a few months.

"What are you thinking, Georgina?"

"That I wish I'd won that last hand of poker."

He hugged her to him. "We've faced far worse than London, Georgie. Of course, the true test will be dinner with all the Barringtons."

❦

THANK YOU FOR READING **THE WAGER OF A LADY**. Georgina and Leo's relationship has been hinted at in the first three books of **The Beautiful Barringtons** and their love story is one of my favorites.

If you want more Barringtons, the prequel novella to the series, **The Study of a Rake** is free to download. Marcus Barrington meets a young lady reading the Iliad beneath a tree and decides to become a better man. **CLICK HERE TO GET A FREE COPY OF THE STUDY OF A RAKE.**

But if you haven't yet read The Theory of Earls...

"Chemise. Stockings. Piano." Those three words, uttered by the beautifully rakish Lord Welles, leave Margaret Lainscott speechless. His improper request, that she play the piano for him in her...*underthings* is as shocking as it is titillating. Welles is one of London's most committed bachelors, known for his notorious dealings with women and his part ownership of one of London's pleasure clubs. Welles is *certain* Miss Lainscott will not entertain his improper request despite the attraction burning between them.

A young lady such as Miss Lainscott would *never* ruin herself willingly, would she? **START READING THE THEORY OF EARLS NOW.**

Wait...have you read **THE WICKEDS?**

Alexandra Dunforth didn't plan on creating a scandal. She's just trying to avoid the marriage her uncle has arranged. But one chance meeting with the infamous Marquess of Cambourne and suddenly Alexandra finds herself kissed, nearly set on fire and she's gained the attention of the biggest rake in London. **CLICK HERE TO READ WICKED'S SCANDAL.**

If you love reading my books spread the word! Write a review. Tell a friend. Join **Historically Hot with Kathleen Ayers** and be the first to see my cover reveals, announcements on new books, fabulous contests and more!

COMING SOON

Next in *The Beautiful Barringtons*

Recipe for a Rogue (Summer 2022)
The Making of a Gentleman (Fall 2022)

V ISIT WWW.KATHLEENAYERS.COM FOR A COMPLETE LIST OF my books.

AUTHOR NOTES

I've always found the history of New York City to be fascinating, especially the creation of the upper class elites. There is a fabulous book, *In Pursuit of Privilege: A History of New York City's Upper Class* by Clifton Hood that served as a basis for my research.

I spent quite a lot of time on my vacation reading about the history of gambling among the upper classes in England (which resulted in a lot of curious stares around the pool), but most of my research didn't make it into **The Wager of a Lady.** Any gentleman wishing to game properly read something of *Hoyle's Complete Games* (first published in 1742). Mathematical probability and how it relates to gambling has been around for a long time. One of the first books on the subject, *The Doctrine of Changes* by Abraham De Moivre explains probability and how it applies to games like hazard or faro.

Vingt-un or vingt-et-un (the terms are used interchangeably) is one of the oldest card games and is now a staple in every casino...Twenty-one.

Poker (originally Poque and Georgina's favorite card game) was brought to America by French colonists where the name was anglicized sometime after the Louisiana Purchase. Poker became popular around 1834, spreading to the rest of the country by riverboats sailing the nation's waterways. I thought it would be a nice touch for Georgina to have learned the game (and her love of bourbon) from a disreputable gambler. The game of poker didn't make its way (at least officially) to England until 1871 when Queen Victoria overheard the U.S. minister discussing how to play. There are quite a few articles on the subject, but this one is short and to the point. https://www.history.com/news/where-did-poker-originate.

Bourbon or bourbon whiskey is a uniquely American spirit. Popular since the mid 1750's in the U.S. the name comes from Bourbon County in Kentucky (the county itself named for French royalty). Calling the spirit bourbon didn't become popular until the 1840's but for clarity's sake I used "bourbon" throughout the story. If you want to learn more check out this article https://www.thespruceeats.com/bourbon-history-timeline-760176.

The Rutherford opera house is fabrication, though there were several opera houses (all presenting operas in Italian) competing in New York during the time period, the most notable being the Palermo. Jacob Astor did build his own (Astor Place) in the mid 1840's.

Brooklyn was considered the countryside in Georgina's time and Brooklyn Heights (first called Brooklyn Village) was one of the first "commuter" suburbs. The area became populated with well to do merchants, lawyers, bankers, physicians, and other prominent New Yorkers. Fulton started a ferry service to Brooklyn around 1814.

New York City did suffer from multiple catastrophes in the early part of the 19th century. **The Great Fire of 1835** which destroyed 17 city blocks was devastating to a city that was just beginning to rise in prominence. The fire was followed by a collapse of financial institutions and insurance companies, which further devastated New York. Another great, quick read on what happened can be found here https://www.history.com/news/great-fire-new-york-1835.

Finally, while many of you are probably familiar with The Four Hundred, the Gilded Age term used to describe New York City's elite, fewer probably know the term ***upper tens*** **or** ***upper ten.*** Nathanial Parker Willis (who wrote of New York's society) used the word in an article he published in 1844 to describe the city's wealthiest citizens. The article was a few years before Georgina's story, but I still think the concept fits.

And lastly, this is a work of fiction. I may sometimes bend historical facts now and again for the sake of the story.

Printed in Great Britain
by Amazon